Two Women - Two Lives

by

Joy Burnett

ISBN: 978-1-914933-51-6

Best Wishes
Joy Burnett

Copyright 2023
All rights reserved. No part of this publication may be reproduced, stored in a retrieval system or transmitted in any form or by any means, electronic, mechanical, photocopy, recording or otherwise, without prior written consent of the copyright owner. Nor can it be circulated in any form of binding or cover other than that in which it is published and without similar condition including this condition being imposed on a subsequent purchaser.

The right of Joy Burnett to be identified as the author of this work has been asserted in accordance with the Copyright Designs and Patents Act 1988.

A copy of this book is deposited with the British Library

Published By: -

i2i
PUBLISHING

i2i Publishing.Manchester.
www.i2ipublishing.co.uk

3

Prologue

KATE - THURSDAY 18th NOVEMBER 2012

It was a cold day, the sort where I wish I'd remembered my gloves. As I crossed the street, I thought I would stop for a warming cup of coffee before I headed back home to finish the packing. I cut through the park where the autumn leaves were creating a golden carpet along the footpath. They cascaded all around me and I knew it wouldn't be long before the trees would be completely bare, and winter would take hold. I was dreading the winter.

I glanced at the babies in their buggies, wrapped up against the November chill, the toddlers in fluffy boots kicking at the piles of leaves and muddy puddles.

My boots echoed on the footpath as I watched them - lonely I walked, and my heart pounded. I felt tears welling at the backs of my eyes. It was over a year since... it seemed like yesterday.

I'd locked up my grief like some wild scary beast; it was time to let go, to get on with my life, to identify that grief for what it was. I am on my own — at times, I feel that there is no escape from the sense of helplessness, the sense of guilt that has scarred me from inside. There is no escape, so I must bury the memories so deep that they are completely submerged in the past.

I knew it would always be with me, but I also knew I must learn to tame it. Nevertheless, my heart still felt crushed in my chest and my breath was still shallow and forced. There was an empty space in my body, a hole so large that it felt like part of me had disappeared or disintegrated. There were days when I could no longer function and my life swam around in my head like a persistent fly, trying to find somewhere to land. I'd sobbed time after time into this void, but now I had made a decision — a decision to try to gather myself back together.

My sorrow subsided and my anger at myself diminished. My addled brain, though still incoherent at times, was starting to release; yet again, it was time to move on.

So many things had been wrong but there I was, on that damp Thursday afternoon, about to take another road: I felt different and relieved.

5

What I didn't know, was that this day would be a turning point in my troubled life.

CHAPTER 1

KATE 2007 — Bristol

I've made a lot of mistakes, I know that now — but in all truthfulness, I think that I have done pretty well all things considered.

On reflection, I probably shouldn't have gone out with Jackson in the first place. That's where it all started, that was when I changed my resolve. I was determined to be independent and self-sufficient, something that I had spent all my adult life perfecting. By now I should probably be manager of the bank instead of hiding, instead of living with such important secrets.

It had all started simply enough one coffee break. Everyone else had gone back to work, and Jackson and I were preparing the rotas for the following week.

"I'll take you somewhere out of town so no one will know us." Jackson assured me with a cheeky wink. "It won't make a jot of difference. I shall still call you Miss Channon at work and boss you around."

As I didn't know anyone in Bristol, I thought that least it could do was to get me out of the tiny, claustrophobic flat that I'd rented for six months. It was better than making a meal for one and watching TV soaps, so I eventually accepted.

I'd met Jackson in January, on my first day at work at the bank in Bristol, having been promoted to deputy manager from the Basingstoke branch.

It was a big and exciting move for me. As soon as I arrived on that frosty January day, I knew that this could be a new beginning. I loved the city from the moment I arrived, and my new job was exciting and challenging. It was time to settle down.

Jackson was the accounts manager and took responsibility for my induction, even though the manager, Howard Kendrikson, was the senior and it should have been his responsibility. Mr Kendrikson had been in the same bank all his life. He was ponderous and old-fashioned according to Jackson, who had taken on many of the duties for the management of the bank.

I'd been so lucky to get the job. At twenty-eight, I was considered to be very young to be for a managerial role, but

9

I'd worked hard and had elbowed my way into a well-paid and sustainable position. My employers viewed me as a useful asset. They knew that I was good at my job, hard-working and reliable and happy to move anywhere; I'm sure they saw me as an ambitious spinster. In other words, from their point of view I was a dedicated employee who knew her role, was never late, had no family issues (as I didn't have one) and did not get involved in overly friendly relationships with other members of staff — at least, not usually. But that was about to change!

I was attracted to Jackson Ingram immediately. He was smart, smoothly cultivated, tall, lean, dark haired and handsome. He had a slight Irish brogue and always looked immaculate.

When he asked me out, I had at first declined, but I have to admit that I was flattered, and he *had* been insistent.

We went to a lovely little Italian restaurant on the outskirts of the city, and he was considerate and charming. He did little things that I noticed immediately: he opened doors, pulled back the chair in the restaurant and took ages to explain all the dishes he had tried there.

10

"If you like spicy, you'll like the prawn dish with chilli, otherwise the lasagne is excellent."

"Have you been here often, then?" I asked.

"No, not lately. Used to live around the corner before I moved over the other side of town. Ate here all the time. I don't often come now, too many calories in most of it!" He gave me one of his charming smiles and continued. "Definitely don't eat pasta or pizzas any more now that I'm training."

He showed me a little disc shaped thing he carried everywhere that actually calculated calories, and he spent a few minutes deciding what he wanted to eat. He ordered a steak and salad, no dressing, and fizzy water.

I had no such qualms. I loved Italian food, and I was hungry. "Would you mind if I ordered the tetrazzini?" I asked.

He gave me a cheeky grin and nodded toward my cleavage. "If you are not worried about gaining weight, go ahead, but don't spoil that gorgeous little body for the sake of a few calories."

Mmm, I was happy with my trim figure, so I ordered the chicken tetrazzini and the house wine.

11

Jackson was a well-practised flirt and good company. Our conversation was easy and light-hearted, and I liked all the attention I was getting

"Have I told you how gorgeous you are?" he grinned as I enjoyed my plate of delicious, garlicky pasta. "You're the best-looking girl in Bristol and bloody smart too to get the job you've got."

I wasn't used to being complimented and I could feel my face begin to redden. I took another large slurp of wine, "Thanks," I said and added, "I've worked hard for it, you know."

Jackson reached over the table and took my hand. Looking me in the eye, he said sincerely, "I admire anyone who sets themselves a goal and doesn't let anything get in their way. Especially women. Most of them get married, have babies and disappear into the woodwork. You've never married then, had children?"

"No, I like my independence. It took me a long time to realise that I don't need anybody to keep me and that I can make all my own choices," I told hm confidently as I reached for my third glass of wine. "People often assume that since I'm single, with no maternal feelings, I am lonely—but I'm really not. Perhaps I am just too selfish."

His wide grin showed his approval. That was all I intended to tell him. I wasn't going to tell him what a struggle my life had been, how my heart had been broken when—without any explanation—my beloved baby brother Alex had been adopted. He'd disappeared from my life forever when he was four years old.

Taking a deep breath, I turned the conversation around to him: "What about you then? Have you never married?"

"No, I was engaged for a while, but no thanks, don't want kids or pets. I want to travel and see the world. Not alone, I didn't necessarily mean that, but I don't want the old mortgage, school runs and dog walking kind of life. I've got plans."

I was intrigued, "Oh, anything in particular?"

"Yep, I'm going to try the London marathon in April and then I am seriously considering a big one in Chicago next year. I go to the gym most days and have started to run every day."

13

"Mmm... Well, the best of luck with that." Personally, I couldn't see the point in running unless it was for a bus!

All evening I managed to steer the conversation away from myself. I never wanted to talk about my life, because I thought there was little worth talking about. Nor was there anything that I really wanted to tell anyone. As far as I was concerned, the less people knew about my past, the better. Growing up in care and foster homes had toughened me and made me wary of trusting people. I'd been messed up for a long time, but I'd learned that if I looked after myself and worked hard, I could eventually become smart and independent. It hadn't been easy, but I covered it up well, and I was finally feeling happy enough with myself to settle somewhere and make a new life. I never wanted to be reliant on anyone, ever!

Even so, that evening a little voice in my head told me: *This is what I need. Here is a strong man who will look after me.*

I have to admit that I was secretly delighted. I loved his gorgeous good-looks, his quirky sense of humour and his ability to make me laugh—hence I ignored his vanity and his self-obsession with his needs and his body.

14

Throughout the evening Jackson sipped his water while I drank the house wine, which was dry and fruity. By the time we left I was light-headed enough to allow him to kiss me, regardless of my obviously garlicky breath! It was a long time since I had been kissed and it was delicious, mysterious and so much more erotic than I had expected. Mm... lovely!

As time passed, we got into a dating routine and it didn't take long for the staff at work to get to know that 'Mister Sexy Ingram' as he was known, was seeing Miss Channon. Most of the time he didn't work directly with me, so we had little contact.

Several of the girls in the bank had a crush on him and I often heard the admiring remarks they made. He did flirt outrageously with all of them, but he was a hard-working and efficient manager, so although he winked at me occasionally, we never brought our relationship into the open at work.

At first, Jackson cared for me, and made me feel important. He insisted that, outside of work, we went everywhere together. He wanted to show me off, and I liked Jackson's uninhibited sociability. He could walk into a crowd and stick his hand out to a stranger and say, "Hi, I'm Jackson and this is Kate — my boss and my girlfriend." He always referred to me as 'his boss' with a wink, although of course that wasn't strictly true as our roles were completely different. He made silly jokes about keeping the 'boss' happy with his friends, and I think he was proud of the fact that he was dating someone with a decent salary and a job title.

Jackson got into the habit of taking me back to my tiny flat and he usually came in for a nightcap. Although there was only a single bed, there was a huge lumpy couch that we made good use of, but he always went home afterwards. I never went to his flat on the other side of town, and I was quite content with the way things were. At the beginning, sex with Jackson was fumbling, vaguely textbook and polite. Nonetheless, it was enjoyable, insistent and energetic — although it excluded any real feelings of connection or love. The sex always seemed to be based entirely on his lusty needs, and although he was talented and careful, I somehow never really felt included — only physically satisfied. I hadn't really minded. I had never found myself able to get really close to anyone; I hadn't had a sexual relationship since Pete Blakeley at university. Other than that, I'd only had an occasional one-night stand when I lived in Basingstoke. That was my choice of course, because I didn't feel settled then, nor ready for any sort of long-term commitment.

It wasn't until about a month later that Jackson first noticed my scarred left arm. I laughingly gave a brief outline of a bad time in my teenage years, but I guess he wasn't really that interested. All he said was, "Good for you to have done so well. I'm off to do my run. See you later."

I wasn't proud of the fact that I had been a 'cutter'. I had been in my early teens — I was living in a squat in Reading, shop lifting occasionally to eat, working part-time in a sauce-bottling factory and trying to study for a Maths A level. I was getting nowhere, and I constantly felt ill. I was in a permanent state of simmering rage. Anything would set me off: falling over, dropping something, hearing a rude remark or going a day without food would send me into a screaming paddy. In my exquisitely learned self-hatred and hopelessness I had slashed at my wrist in a vain attempt to stop the boring misery of my life. One time, I had bled a great deal and a social worker called Harriet from a church charity, Churches in Reading Drop-in Centre (CIRDIC), had been called. She had taken me to A&E, and then given me a proper meal—the first that I'd had in days. It was the lovely, plump, smiley, little Harriet who cared and listened. She arranged for me to move into their hostel, and it was there that I managed to continue my studying. It was a rough and noisy place, but I had access to a computer, and took my first A level exam at the local college. I passed with the lowest marks possible, so I decided that I had to work and study much harder to improve my chances of getting a decent job.

I was a feisty and difficult girl, crying and cursing and stamping my anger in frustration—but I was ambitious. I learnt to use my anger as a power to achieve and survive. It sounds trite, I know, but it worked for me. I quit cursing and turned my energy into determination; I had a genuine passion for learning in spite my chaotic lifestyle. Reading and studying became my salvation.

I enrolled in evening classes to get a qualification in business studies, and I needed to do a practical work experience module. I hounded local stores, estate agents, banks and accountants until—with Harriet's help—I finally got an unpaid part-time job for six months. It was with an accountancy in Woodley run by an unpleasant guy named Joshua Regent. He used me as an odd-jobber, a runner and a tea maker, but I learned a great deal while I was there and he eventually gave me a good assessment that helped my marks in the final exam. With Harriet's help I eventually took my A level in economics and a BTEC professional diploma equivalent to an A level in business studies. I got brilliant pass marks, and I was happy to exist on my job-seekers allowance for a while before getting a part time job in a shoe shop.

By the time I was eighteen I had been on my own for nearly four years (having run away from my foster parents a few weeks before my fifteenth birthday). I was a scraggy and unruly mess—I guessed that was one of the reasons I had never been adopted. Nevertheless, I was gutsy and determined: with the help of Harriet and the church I was clothed and fed, before opening a bank account and applying to Reading University to try for a degree in finance and economics.

19

The last time I 'cut' myself, I ended up in the Royal Berkshire hospital; I was with Pete Blakely, and at the time I thought it would be a long-term partnership. We'd had a sexy and loving relationship throughout the course of uni and I thought that he was the 'one'. He dumped me a week after our final exams.

"Kate, I am going back to my family in Southampton, and I am afraid you just wouldn't fit in. Sorry babe, but it's been great. Have a good life." That was all he said, but I knew! It was my shabby and mismatched clothes, my accent, my temper and my ability to drink myself into a stupor when life took a bad turn for me.

Six months later I was still struggling, convinced that I was indeed unlovable. In the confines of my lonely bedsit, I swallowed as many paracetamols as I could—forcing them down, pill after pill—and awaited death; instead, I spent the following day with searing and gut-wrenching pain, vomiting bile and half-digested pills all over my bed and carpet. My stomach burned with pain, yet I realised that I didn't want to die—I hadn't even lived yet! I went back to my studying with renewed determination.

20

It was so long ago that it seemed like another life. Yet fate took my side for a while—not only did I gain a degree in finance and economics, but also my first banking job in Newbury.

I set about reinventing myself. I took elocution lessons, had my unruly curls styled, upgraded my wardrobe, did some extra training and got promoted to the Watford branch of the bank, where I stayed for six months. Boy was I lucky: against all the odds, I got another promotion and returned to Reading where I stayed for nearly three years. It suited me and my confidence grew.

I had become self-sufficient and independent with the help of a lovely counsellor—Graham Belling—who Harriet had found for me. I stopped all forms of self-abuse and learned to like myself; I created my own little world of protection, wherein I stayed alone and worked hard. I lived in one room, with a shared bath and toilet, and I had no social life whatsoever. I saved every penny that I earned. It was what I preferred, as I found any sort of deep relationship impossible.

In the summer I sat in the local parks reading and sunbathing; in the winter I read as many books as I could. I was touched, intrigued and enchanted by the lives and loves of the characters — stepping into their world gave me all the excitement I needed; in fact, I only went out to go to work or to buy essentials.

After three years I went to Basingstoke, before I was promoted again and sent to Bristol. That all seemed like someone else's life — by the time I got there, I finally felt fulfilled and happy. I had a healthy bank account, and I was enjoying life and my job. At weekends I often accompanied Jackson to the gym or the track where he was perfecting his running skills. Afterwards we would meet his sporty friends in the local pub and, for the first month or so, I feigned interest.

"Not today Jackson," I told him one Saturday morning, two months later, when he wanted me to go and watch him running. "I'm off to look at a property. I've never had a home of my own, so I think it's time that I stayed in one place and settled down. I love Bristol. I've saved enough for a good deposit, but I will need you to help me get a mortgage."

He smiled and did seem inordinately pleased; he grabbed me into a sexy hug.

"Well, good for you, Katie babe. With your salary it should be easy enough. I'll help of course and I love the idea. Perhaps you will let me stay over occasionally?"

Later that month I put an offer in for a little house which was just a fifteen-minute bus ride outside of town, and I was looking forward to doing it up and settling down. I'd been running away for far too long; there were so many things in the past that still haunted me, but it was time to stop. The sound counselling which Graham had given me in Basingstoke helped me to realise that the time had come—I had to identify what I really wanted in life and leave the past behind.

CHAPTER 2

ELENA - Ukraine 2007/8

I was tired and desolate with frustration. I'd spent yet another day heaving boxes of produce on to the old wooden cart and pulling it down the hill to the Ruzhyn village market. I had helped harvest most of it too, a job I'd been doing since I was a twelve-year-old. I was strong and fit for my fifteen years, but I also knew that I couldn't earn enough to keep us in this miserable place for much longer.

As I scrubbed the ingrained dirt from my hands and arms in the cracked old sink in our shabby outhouse, I heard Margo start to cough and gasp for breath. I quickly found her inhaler and massaged her back until the coughing slowed and her breath returned to almost normal. She was so ill for most of the time now—her chest condition, primary ciliary dyskinesia, meant she couldn't go to school or work. My beautiful little sister was nearly two years younger than me. Even though she always looked pale and fragile, her round face and curves endowed her with a soft, cherubic beauty; contrastingly, I could easily be taken for a boy: I was thin, tall and angular with long legs and a muscular body.

"I've got to do something, Margo. There is no way we can go on living like this," I said as I tied my long blonde hair into a tidy bun.

I picked up a blanket and wrapped it around her, holding her close. It broke my heart to see her so ill. I needed to get a job somehow so that I could earn enough to get her some professional help. I *had* tried of course, but with no transport and no money there seemed little hope. I no longer went to school, and I had no qualifications; regardless, I believed that I was smart, resourceful and determined enough to do more than dig and cart vegetables about.

Thank heaven that we had got through the worst of the winter. Now that each day was getting a little warmer, we could get Margo out into the fresh air — winter was always difficult for her.

I often stared at the older women of the village, at their shrivelled, sour expressions which were wrought through poverty and hardship, and resolved that I would get us away, make a new life somewhere else and earn enough money to provide a better life for myself and my sister. All the young people were leaving the villages to work in the towns and cities, but I felt I couldn't leave Margo.

Sometimes, our brothers Jurgen and Walter, would help me, but they were often away. They worked intermittently on the fishing boats of the Ikopot river, and in summer they ferried tourists along the water to see the Starokostiantynic Castle. Even so, between us we earned barely enough to keep ourselves. I got occasional cleaning or baby-sitting jobs in one of the big houses or farms nearby, but nevertheless we all lived hand to mouth, sometimes going hungry and cold. Ever since the Ukraine became independent and moved into a market economy we have been struggling. Jobs are almost impossible to obtain, and food is short because practically everything is exported.

Our mother had been dead for five years and our father was so drunk that most of the time we hardly saw him. Many nights he didn't come home at all but stayed at the sawmill where he worked which was several miles away. He contributed little to the hovel in which we lived and was a bad tempered and bitter man. Both his parents, the Shevchenka's, had been killed during the repression of dissidents in 1972. Many of his friends had died and our father had never recovered from the pain of those times.

It was a month later when our mother's brother, Uncle Gregor came to visit from Vinnytsia. He was a good man, and we were pleased to see him. The last time he had visited I had begged him to try to find me a proper job.

This time, Uncle Gregor arrived with a smile on his face. He told me, "There is a good job for you in a café near where I live, close to the main road that goes to Letychiv and the Aquapark Mayak. It belongs to a friend of mine, and he is looking for someone who is hard working, healthy and pretty. I told him about my lovely niece who is honest, strong and reliable." Uncle Gregor grinned and lifted his tufty eyebrows. "Now don't let me down, Elena, I have given you a great reference and Nikki will appreciate you if you work hard."

"Of course, I won't let you down, Uncle." I said, apprehension and excitement coursing through my body.

He glanced around the cold, leaky shack that was our home and shook his head. "It pains me to see you so destitute, Elena. Your mother would be horrified by the way you live now. I feel bad about how little I have done for you. I had intended to help you more when your mother died but I've had some hard times myself."

He took a dusty card from his top pocket and handed it to me. "Take the bus into Vinnytsia tomorrow and tell Nikki that I sent you. Here is the address. I can't take you myself as I am on the way to Lviv to make a delivery."

"Don't worry. As long as I can get back occasionally to see that Margo is safe. Thank you so much, Uncle Gregor." I planted a kiss on his whiskery cheek. I could barely contain my excitement.

"Good. Things are a little better for my family now I that have a job, and I will try to help you. I know Walter and Jurgan will take care of Margo. I will come here to see her as often as I possibly can. I'll also have a word with your father." He grinned knowing how difficult that could be. "Now what can we rustle up for our tea?"

Uncle Gregor left early the next morning, but he gave me the bus fare and promised to help when he could. Margo was upset that I was going, but the opportunity of a job meant that perhaps we could soon find a room in the town and get her some proper treatment.

I put on the only respectable clothes I had: a black miniskirt, slightly frayed down one seam with an over-washed white blouse. I pulled on a denim jacket and thought myself quite presentable. I walked to the bus station the next day, clutching the name and address of the café, which Uncle Gregor had assured me was in a respectable area on the outskirts of Vinnytsia. It was a nice sunny day and, even though I was a little apprehensive about leaving Margo, I was happy that life was changing for us at last. I clutched a small bag of belongings and sat back to enjoy the long bus journey that took me through many villages and towns on the way to Vinnytsia.

Nikki, the new owner of the café, was a tall and balding man of fortyish; he was an ex-chef from one of the large hotels that had recently closed. I knew he liked me straight away, but as he explained the long hours I would be expected to work, he said "I will pay you according to how the business goes. It is new, so it will vary, but you can live above the café. There is a spare room upstairs so it means you will be here all the time. The other room is let to an apprentice plumber who also works long hours and is rarely here. There is a toilet and washbasin downstairs but there is no bathroom. Will that suit you?"

Oh yes, it did suit me. "I don't mind," I assured him. "I am strong and used to hard work. I need this job to look after my sister. I'll not let you down, I promise."

I was excited, and the little room above the café was so much better than I had expected. It was warm and the bed was comfortable; in the cupboard there were quilts for both summer and winter — there was even a spare pillow. I took my small bag of belongings and put them carefully away, before starting work in the café immediately. Nikki was pleased with my standard of work, and we got on well.

I settled into the routines very quickly, and I learned fast.

Life in the city gave me an insight into how much I was missing, living in a poor village with little to no income; I watched girls of my own age with their new I-pads and mobile phones, their pretty clothes and manicured nails. They came for coffee and doughnuts in their breaks from the offices and shops, often with men or boys who paid for them. In between dashing from the kitchens to the café's main hall and pavement tables, I watched them flirting and showing off.

Over the next few weeks business increased as Nikki broadened his menu to include more homemade dishes like borscht, holubtsi, chicken Kyiv and the beautiful stuffed pancakes, nalesnikis. The more hours I worked, the more I got paid; I soon managed to improve my wardrobe with neat ballerina-type shoes, black jeans and a variety of sweaters and tee-shirts bought from the city market. I ate well too, and soon my gaunt features softened — I knew I looked better than I had ever done.

Whenever possible, I took the bus home with varenyky — parcels stuffed with mushroom and cabbage — and holubtsi for Margo and the boys.

Sometimes our father was there, as grumpy as ever — but I knew he was pleased that I was earning money for the family.

"He has mended the roof." Margo told me with a smile. "I think Uncle Gregor gave him a good talking to, as he hasn't been drunk at all. He stays here when Jurgen and Walter are away on the boats. He has looked after me," she reassured me when I lifted my eyebrows in disbelief.

Nevertheless, I returned to Vinnytsia with the reassurance that Margo was being taken care of.

It was a hard-working life, and I had little time to myself throughout the summer months as the popularity of the café grew. I had my sixteenth birthday on October 2nd and Nikki made me a cake; it was the first time I'd ever had a birthday celebration and, even though I worked all day, it felt special.

Business slowed as winter took hold, and the outdoor seating on the pavement was no longer used.

Uncle Gregor called in occasionally, to check on me and to make sure that I was doing well and getting paid. The café was open for the celebrations over Christmas, and I earned extra money. I was delighted with my new life, and even though a recession loomed, I could only see things improving in the new year of 2008.

I went to visit my ailing grandmother who lived with Uncle Gregor and his family in a tall grey block of flats in Vinnytsia. My mother's father, Gregori, had died very young and I never knew him, so Baba Beatrice lived with her son, my uncle Gregor. She had no idea who I was, but I was happy to see her as I had lovely memories of her visits from when I was a small child. She had been a seamstress and, when we were young, she made pretty dresses for Margo and me, whilst the boys were fitted with smart dungarees.

Soon I got to know a few of the customers by name and made a few new friends. Anca was one of them. She worked in the refrigeration company across the road and often stopped at the café for coffees and buns when she came in to get her boss his lunch. Anca was twenty years old, rounded and pretty with glossy brown hair and chocolate fudge-coloured eyes. She was full of ambition and told me that she intended to get another qualification that would get her a job in Germany. I found her funny and exciting.

"Three, no, four times what I am earning now, Elena, less hours and a proper social life: films, dancing and lovely shopping. I am studying German in my spare time, and I hope to get there by next year."

"How did you find out about it?" I asked. "I never see ads for jobs anywhere."

"It's who you know," Anca winked and tapped the side of her nose. "Got to know the right people. I'll introduce you next time my friend comes. He knows what's going on everywhere. Often tells me about jobs, mainly abroad, Holland, France, USA, Britain and Germany of course, that's where the money is. Sod all around here anymore, is there? Our economy is in such poor condition in comparison to the western countries. It makes sense to go where the jobs and money are."

I sighed, I would love to leave, travel and see a bit of the world, especially when Anca told me how much money they could earn in the exclusive clubs and bars. Apparently, they are always looking for bar staff, dancers and even hairdressers and beauticians who could earn four times that which they made in the Ukraine.

"I can't really go anywhere while my sister is so ill," I told her. "Perhaps I should encourage one of my brothers to go and try his luck. They could get a job in the bars or clubs, I'm sure. That might be the answer." I decided that I would have a word with them on my next trip home.

"Most of the jobs I hear about are for women, but I will ask Boris, my boyfriend," Anca replied, with a giggle and a flick of her glossy hair.

34

By the spring of 2008 I had been in Vinnytsia over a year and although I had managed to help Margo in practical ways, I still hadn't managed to save enough money to get her the medical help she needed. Nevertheless, she was now warm and well fed because I had paid for repairs to the house and sent her money for fuel and food. She still needed regular antibiotics and nebulisers. Perhaps this coming year I could get her some physiotherapy treatment too.

Spring was blooming and the weather was improving, so Nikki wanted the outdoor seating on the pavement area to be set up again. The sun was glorious and bright the day that I met Anca's boyfriend, Boris Valosa. He was with his brother Sasha, and they came to sit and have coffee in the spring sunshine. Boris was definitely the elder, probably in his middle thirties, while Sasha looked a few years younger. They were both good looking, expensively dressed and wearing modern fedoras.

"Elena, this is Boris, who is arranging my passport and visa to go to work in Germany." Anca turned to her boyfriend with a flirty smile. "Perhaps you can find Elena a job too and we could go together." Boris donned his hat and sat down eyeing me appreciatively. His hair was thick and greying at the sides in contrast to Sasha, who had black, shiny hair. Sasha too was watching me, and I found myself blushing at his stare.

"No, no," I protested, "I can't go away from here. Margo, my sister, is ill and I can't leave her, I have to stay here and look after her."

"All the more reason you should look for a job abroad. You can earn enough to send money home whilst having good life yourself," said Sasha the good-looking younger man. "That's what most people do when they work abroad. I know of several good jobs in Europe. You could even send for your sister to join you."

"She is not well enough to travel. I couldn't leave her... I'll get your coffee now." I skipped off into the main café to collect their orders.

After that, the brothers came almost every day, sometimes in the evenings too. Anca and Boris were arranging her passport and visa applications, so I would often join them when I had finished serving.

"I thought I needed a work visa," I heard Anca ask Boris. "Isn't that the first step to getting a job?"

"Well, yes, that is necessary but if you go in on a visitor's visa, it's easier. Once you are in the country and have applied for a job it is just a matter of time before you get a work visa. Not a problem at all." Boris was stroking her leg. "And I'll be there to help you."

Anca was excited and I guess her enthusiasm rubbed off on me.

"Come with us," she said. "I can teach you German on the way. You only need to know the basics at first. Boris will be there to help us. First, we go to Odessa, and then we get on a boat to Constanta where we will meet up with Boris's Aunty. She will be with us all the way from Bucharest to Berlin. Apparently, it is easier to go to Romania first." With a flirty look she turned to Boris. "Why is that Boris?"

"The visitor visas are easy from there. It is difficult from here, too much red tape. Trust me, I have arranged it many times." Boris answered with a smile. "It will be easier when we are in the European Union."

Anca grabbed my hand in her enthusiasm, "There, you see, Elena. Come with me. It is a long distance, but it will be an adventure."

"Why not fly there?" I asked. "It would only take a few hours and you are talking about a journey that takes days,"

Boris replied immediately, "Not only is it a lot cheaper travelling across country, but we have business along the way, and places to stay, so it will be like a vacation for you girls."

"Is it safe to do that?"

"Of course, and we will all be together. Aunty Veronyka is coming with us so she will chaperone you girls. Believe me, it is fairly simple."

"I'd rather go to England and learn to speak English." I said, "I think it's a much nicer language than German." I was still sure that I could not leave Margo while she was so unwell even though I was tempted when I listened to my friend.

"No," I said firmly, "I cannot leave my sister and I'll not be persuaded that I need to go abroad to help her. I will find a way here."

What did happen though, was that I fell in love with the handsome Sasha Valosa.

CHAPTER 3

KATE

I was so excited when I told Jackson of my plans; soon my offer for the house was accepted, my mortgage was arranged, and I had a date to move in. Over the next few weeks, during my lunchtimes and any other spare time I could find, I did something that I had never really done before: I shopped. I found charity shops and bought cushions, rugs, lamps, cutlery, a couple of saucepans and some pretty crockery, a coffee percolator, a mop and proper cleaning materials; I bought things that I had never needed to own previously. Sometimes Jackson would come with me, and together we scoured the shops for things I could afford or trailed through the internet for bargains. We chose a new bed — a double of course, a milk chocolate-coloured couch, a carved coffee table, a fridge and a wrought iron garden seat before he dashed off to run his allotted miles. He wanted me to join him afterwards with his mates and their partners in the local pub, but I declined. I wanted to be interested in what he did, and I really did try, but I had little in common with any of his friends. All the other girlfriends were equally physically impressive in their spandex outfits and body tight trackies. They were all tall, lean and fit, whereas I was small and curvy; my naturally curly blonde locks would never be tame enough to screw into one of those tight little buns which they all sported.

It was a sunny Saturday in 2007 when I moved into 7, Harlow Crescent, a pre-war brick-built semi in a quiet, leafy street. It had a pass-through lounge and diner that looked out through French windows onto a long garden that wasn't overlooked. Trees, large shrubs and a flower border were established, and although it was a little neglected, I could see that with a few pots and an ornamental seat, it would be perfect.

In fact, I thought that everything was perfect for me: a bus going into town stopped right outside the house and there was a park across the road with a large duck pond and a playground. There was also a good corner shop a block away.

Everything I owned came with me, and my new furniture was delivered on the same day. The two bedrooms were old fashioned and quaint, both came with fitted wardrobes, and one still housed an old iron fireplace. I could already envisage how I would decorate it. I was ecstatic as I made up the bed in the second bedroom with my new floral bedding and hung the deep blue curtains that I'd found in a charity shop. I planned to move into the bigger room after I'd painted it. My first real home! I was so happy.

I began to feel safe and settled for the first time in my life. I had never really felt safe anywhere, always knowing the places I'd lived at were temporary, some of them even dangerous. I felt inordinately proud of myself. This was mine, my very own house!

Engrossed in emptying my essential food items into the fridge, I didn't hear the knocking on the front door. It made me jump, I wasn't used to having visitors and the only person I knew who was aware of my new address was Jackson. I knew he was at the gym and would come over that evening. I put down my cheese and bread and went to open the front door.

In front of me stood a tall, slim woman with a huge sunny smile.

"Mollie Burton—number five—we are attached." She waved a slim hand toward the house next door and then thrust it toward me: I took it and we shook hands formally. She was dressed in jeans and a yellow tee-shirt. Her mop of curly grey hair was tied up in a multi-coloured scarf. I guessed she was probably old enough to be my mother, but she had a lively, infectious energy and I liked her immediately. In her other hand she waved a bunch of pink roses. "Welcome to Harlow Crescent." She indicated towards the flowers. "From my garden. About the only thing I grow there now. I think it's a bit smaller than yours... the garden that is, but my house is bigger as we have an extension over the garage. It makes a big difference; you should do the same with this one. Oh sorry...I do talk too much. Here you are and welcome." She pushed the roses in my direction. "I intended to cook you something nice, but I am not really good in the kitchen. Bill's the cook... my husband. Anyway, it will be nice to have someone young living here. Old Mrs Porter wasn't very nice, you know. She used to throw her rubbish over the fence into my roses."

I laughed. "Oh dear, I won't do that, I promise. I'm Kate Channon, pleased to meet you, Mollie." Taking the roses from her outstretched hand I said, "How lovely. Do you want to come in? I'm afraid I only have coffee and sugar but no milk yet."

"Great, I'm not bothered about milk. Have you got a vase for those?" she stepped into the hall and peered into my lounge which was still piled with boxes.

"As it happens, I do. Found it in the 'Help the Aged' shop. Those roses will look lovely in it. Let me find it while you put the kettle on. It's in one of these boxes but I'm not sure which one."

Mollie made the coffee while I scrunched around in the boxes until I found my bargain. It was glossy and white with two fuchsia stripes around the rim. Perfect!

Two cups of black coffee later, and with my vase of roses adorning the coffee table, Mollie left, insisting that I call on her if I needed *anything.*

I really enjoyed her company, and I was pleased with myself, as ordinarily I would not have invited anyone I didn't know into my private space. But Mollie was great, and I came to rely on her much more than I expected.

Although I enjoyed the relationship with Jackson, it didn't really impose on my plans for the house until two months later in September, when he asked me if he could move in with me.

"The lease on my flat is coming to an end soon, and I already spend a great deal of my time here, so perhaps I could stay with you for a while." Seeing my hesitation, he grinned his knee-buckling smile and continued, "I could help with the mortgage and of course I wouldn't interfere with your plans. I don't own a great deal, so I won't take up much room."

He grabbed me, and without giving me a chance to answer, kissed me firmly, pressing his strong body against mine and squeezing my buttocks. "What do you think, darling?" Leaning back and looking into my eyes he said, "In fact I think we should get married. You are the best thing that ever happened to me, and I adore you."

I flushed with surprise and pleasure. "Are you serious? Is this a proposal?"

"Of course, it is, lovely Kate. Why not?"

The life that I had previously led had not included any thoughts of marriage. There had been times when my only thoughts revolved around improving my chances of survival in a world that had not been kind to me.

He was grinning from ear to ear. "I think we're well suited. Both of us are independent and motivated, we are perfect for each other," he said confidently.

I raised my eyebrows and thought, '*I have just bought my own house. Is this what I want? Is this what he wants?*'

But he had pre-empted my thoughts and said gently, "Don't worry, whatever happens the house will still be all yours. I know how much you wanted it. I won't make any claim on it and eventually I might get a property that we can let. It will help our finances. What do you think?"

We had known each other for less than six months. I was flattered and overjoyed. Although I'd never let anyone get close to me, perhaps I thought I was ready. It was nice to feel so wanted, so much the focus of this gorgeous man's attention. I think, even then I knew, that I was deluding myself into believing that it was real. I wanted to. After all I didn't really understand love or commitment, but I thought I should give it a try.

"I'll get you a ring as soon as I get my finances sorted. I'm a bit short at the moment. Perhaps next month..." Jackson pulled a pouty face, "If we wait, we can choose it together."

Was I worried about not having a ring? I'm not sure, but I convinced myself that it didn't matter and that he was being sincere. We would get one when he was ready.

I said "Okay."

It was decided!

With very little noticeable difference to my life, he moved in — even then, I didn't feel in any way threatened. It was October 2nd — my twenty-ninth birthday — when he arrived with a bouquet, a couple of suitcases, two large boxes and some sports equipment; he told me that everything else had come with the flat he'd rented. Incidentally, I had never seen that flat! I didn't own a car, so Jackson always picked me up — if not, I would meet him at the track, the gym or the pub. It always seemed more convenient. After all, they were closer to where I was living.

I continued with my plans for the house, redecorating the main bedroom into which we both moved — he was right about not taking up much space. He owned very little, his smart suits and shirts hung in the wardrobe in the spare room. He had one drawer for his socks and underwear, another for his jeans and sweats, and a box full of sports gear. He had a few books, CDs and an old record collection, which he didn't unpack. He carted the boxes into the storage at the back of the carport, where they stayed until he left.

The day he arrived he pinned a list on the fridge door telling me what he was going to eat each day; he shopped for his own food, and never expected me to cook for him. A calendar told me which days he would be training. It was all so easy!

I found out later from one of his sporty friends that his previous long-term girlfriend, Samantha, had dumped him and gone off to work abroad. She had returned early and wanted her share of the flat that they had owned together, she had taken all of the furniture too. He hadn't told me anything about that either. The fact was, there were quite a few things that he hadn't told me.

We arranged a date for our wedding, November 25th, at the local registry office; there was to be no family, of which I had none anyway, and Jackson's lot were all in

Ireland and apparently couldn't afford to come. So only Bill and Mollie, as well as a few friends from the bank and the sports club attended.

I thought to invite Harriet from Reading, but decided not to, as she was part of my past. I bought myself a flowing white and lilac dress, a faux fur wrap and a bunch of white roses to carry. I really thought I was happy, I had everything anyone could possibly want: a great job, a good salary, a lift to work every day, my own home and garden and regular sex with a man who professed to adore me. It seemed like the perfect relationship.

I soon found out that there were also conditions, lots of conditions. Most of which were never openly discussed, but generally agreed upon, because they didn't really interfere with my life at all: his food, his training, his nights out with his mates, his plans to travel (I would only be included if it was a place I wanted to go, such as a trip to Ireland at Christmas to see his family). Most of all though, he didn't want any children or pets that might interfere with our lives.

Mollie and Bill took me to the registry office, and as they were the nearest I had to a family, Bill walked me in as if he was my Dad. The day was sunny and cold, and although I was nervous about the ceremony, I really had no qualms about marrying Jackson. Why didn't I? I suppose I had become complacent and overly comfortable — I genuinely believed that this was how it was supposed to be. Howard Kendrikson arranged a little reception in a local hotel, and although we didn't have a formal meal, the champagne and canapés were delicious. Bill had made us a splendid cake, which he decorated with unidentifiable lilac flowers — it was fabulous.

Jackson and I settled into our extraordinarily separate lives, meeting briefly in the morning and in the bedroom at night to have sex, often with little conversation. The mornings were orderly and while I ate my cereal and toast, Jackson prepared his fruit and yoghurt and his protein packed lunch for the day. We mainly interacted during our journey to work when Jackson would inform me of his schedule for the evening, and what he was aiming for next.

On December 23rd we flew to Dublin. Christmas away was to be our 'honeymoon'. I wore my pretty turquoise zirconia engagement ring for the first time — my present from Jackson! I had found it myself in a second-hand jewellery shop the week before our trip.

I loved Dublin, the shops were fabulous, and I bought loads of gifts for Jackson and his family. The Christmas decorations that lit up the city made it magical. We sang carols with a group of revellers, before returning to the hotel for a lovely, extravagant, romantic meal. I'd bought a new red dress and made an extra effort to tame my curly locks. I felt on top of the world: Jackson was duly admiring, telling me I looked exquisite. I ordered lobster thermidor with a thick creamy sauce and a chocolate pudding. Jackson ate his usual meat and vegetables, with no dessert — he did buy a bottle of champagne, however. He sniffed at the bill, but I was so happy.

The following morning, we hired a car and drove to a beautiful rural village called Dromahair in County Leitrim to stay with Jackson's sister Brigitte and her husband Colm for Christmas. They lived in a tiny stone house near the river, and it was charming. Just two streets away, Joe — Jackson's younger brother — lived with his wife Anna, their two teenage girls and a four-year-old boy.

51

It wasn't long before I saw another side of my new husband. I thought that Jackson was masterful and strong, but I soon realised that he was also mean and controlling. He decided everything that we did — bullying his sister and her husband into driving us around — and bought the minimum amount of food and gifts for his family.

Brigitte and Colm had a smelly rescued cat called Fluff (who left hairs everywhere), and a baby girl — Kelly; like most one-year-olds, she was noisy and endlessly attention seeking. I thought she was delightful, but Jackson avoided both her and the cat as much as he could, showing his distaste whenever they got too close to him. I ignored his derisive comments about the house, the poor internet reception, Brigitte's 'post-pregnancy belly' and 'rugrats'. He found the whole family's frugal way of life 'pitiful'.

"Jackson, please don't be so sniffy. We are lucky to be in the position we're in. They've made different choices to ours and they seem content enough," I said as we climbed into the narrow bed in their small spare room. But Jackson was not easy to convince.

"Colm could have done better if he'd tried harder. He had a wealthier family than ours. Who would want to live like this?" He waved his hand dramatically at the tiny room. "I've worked hard to get where I am, and I am only here because of my Mum. She gave up a great deal to help me with my education. She would have done the same for my brother, Joe, but he couldn't be bothered."

"You could help out a bit more. Buy the food for Christmas day and get some decent presents." I said carefully.

He glared at me and said in an angry whisper, "You know I want to go travelling Kate, and that's expensive, so I have to be a bit careful with my money. Next year there's a marathon in Florida that I want to attend. I need to save as much as I can. That's the reason I don't want any ties, no screaming kids or needy pets. No bloody thank you."

I still thought Jackson could be a bit more generous with his family, who had made us both very welcome even though it was obvious that they struggled. Our salaries at the bank were princely in comparison to their incomes.

Jackson insisted that we all went to his mother's tiny cottage in Sligo to have our Christmas day together. When his brother Joe suggested that it was unfair on their mother to have seven adults and four children all squashed together in the old-fashioned kitchen, Jackson laughed. He said, "Give it up Joe, we are only here once a year. Mum is the best cook, and she can manage. She will love us all being together."

"She'll need some help then." Joe muttered.

"Of course, Kate will help." He turned to me with a smile. "Won't you, Kate?"

"We all will." I told him, with a warning look that he ignored completely.

On Christmas morning we all arrived at Nancy Ingram's house laden with gifts and food. She was indeed overjoyed to have us all there together, and Jackson looked smug and annoyingly superior: I found him embarrassing. He behaved as if he were doing them all a favour being there; I found the whole experience a bit wearing, but I kept smiling and tried to help as much as I could.

In the past I had always avoided being with people at Christmas, usually spending it with a turkey ready-meal and a bottle of gin or vodka to get through the holiday. Never in my life had I been involved in a family Christmas, not even with my last foster parents, the Lamberts, as their religious beliefs — whatever they were — did not include celebrating Christmas.

I loved watching the children opening their presents, and the genuine affection that they had for each other was heart-warming and a little overwhelming.

Even though the house was small, and it was a bit of a struggle, Brigitte, Anna, her girls and I divided the preparation between us, while Nancy played with the two younger children. She'd got up early and prepared the huge turkey that was slowly cooking in her old range.

Colm and Joe went to the pub to keep out of the way and — predictably — Jackson went for a run.

"Are you and Jackson going to have a family?" asked Anna as we were preparing the gravy and sauces.

"No. I don't think Jackson wants the responsibility of a family and I've never imagined that I would ever want a child." I replied carefully.

"Why ever not? I love being a mum," said Anna as she whipped the white sauce for the cauliflower cheese.

"Don't you worry about them? Being responsible for them?" I asked.

"Of course, everyone worries about their kids, but we do the best we can to take care of them while they are young—but they are only borrowed, you know," said Anna. "We have to teach and guide them to grow into individuals who have to make their own decisions and learn about life in their own way, sometimes that means making mistakes."

Anna's thirteen-year-old daughter laughed as she collected the plates to set the table.

"Hope you say that when I decide to have a tattoo or join a commune, Mum."

"You'll not be joining any commune, my girl," said Anna with a smile. "Nor any tattoos. Over my dead body, so."

"Love you, Mum," said the girl as she winked at me and disappeared into the sitting room. My insides melted as I watched the interplay of affection between mother and daughter. It was something that I had never known. Memories of my own childhood came flooding back, putting me in touch with the dark bruise that hides inside of me.

Anna was watching me and must have noticed my almost tearful reaction. "So now Kate, you may just change your mind."

"That sort of love is different, isn't it?"

"The way we love our children is different to any other sort of love. It is more demanding, for sure, but it is absolute. I wouldn't change it for all the shamrocks in Ireland."

No more was said about our decision not to procreate, and the dinner was excellent. Nancy fell asleep with sheer exhaustion after we had eaten, so after we had cleared up, we all went for a walk through the beautiful, frosty lanes to give Nancy a bit of peace and quiet—all of us except Jackson of course, who took off to do another run. For the rest of the day and evening he was bossy and self-centred: in the end, I was glad to leave. The following day we drove back to Dublin and flew home.

In the 2008 New Year, Jackson's training for the marathons became more intense and everything else (including me) fell far down his list of priorities. I didn't really mind at all. I guess at the beginning of this regime I found his childlike enthusiasm endearing; he was light-hearted and funny about his need to go to the gym for two hours every evening and run an increasing number of miles each week. I did get used to it, and often found the time on my own a relief from the endless talk about body mass index, enhanced training schedules and muscle strength. The fitter he got, the more obsessed by his own body shape he became. When he was at home he did stretches and press-ups, watched and talked about sport while I read my books, redecorated the house and planned the garden. In my own small way, I was content. Jackson didn't interfere with my choices of colours or décor, and after a few mistakes, I was pleased with the results.

I was working long hours — I still kept my own bank account — and I went out when I wanted and made my own decisions. As long as I did nothing to get in the way of Jackson's schedules and eating habits, which became stricter as the next marathon loomed, all was peaceful.

By April 2008 he was ready for the London marathon. I was aware that I was spending a great deal of time on my own. That was nothing new, but with a good degree behind me and with my brilliant, well-paid job, I felt I needed something else to occupy me. With all the studying I had done in my earlier life I'd had little time to read or have a hobby, so I bought myself a camera, a Canon Digital, with an optical zoom. I had absolutely no idea how to use it, so I joined a photography class. I also joined a local book club and I set about reading Nikki French's latest book. I found that reading took me into another world and exposed me to emotions and situations that I had never dreamed of — I was content.

My job, the photography projects and the reading filled all my time and needs, and I could never imagine that my life could narrow into crisis ever again.

Jackson's training became more and more intense, and his body was becoming hard and sinewy. Cuddling him was like clutching a tree trunk. Yet still, the fitter he got the less interested he became in me. We rarely had any sort of disagreement and I never questioned any of the structure of our life together. I don't think he noticed very much about me; as time passed, even if I bought something new or changed my hair, I don't think he even registered the fact that anything had changed. Nor did I take much interest in what he was doing. Looking back, I think it rather distasteful the way we hid behind our own sterile mediocrity.

I took photographs, had driving lessons, read copious amounts of books and learned to cook nutritious meals for one. I went to the cinema on my own and allowed myself to indulge in the pleasure of my comfortable life. I enjoyed the endless, meaningless tasks in my new home: the cleaning, dusting, tidying, cooking and most of all the gardening—which was a surprise to me, as I had never so much as plucked a weed before. Mollie gave me tips about planting and mowing the tiny lawn, and as time went by, I learned to sit quietly, listening to the birds and insects with my book and a glass of wine. I had pushed my sordid, unhappy childhood into the distant past, and I met lots of new people; however, cultivating friends had never been my forte. Although I now considered myself perfectly sociable and happy to spend time with others, the thing I was not terribly good at were the kind of honest self-revelations or shared intimacies which are the backbone of lasting female relationships. I made a few friends at the book club and settled into the easy lifestyle that I had created for myself.

Jackson paid a lot of the household bills but never bought anything for the house or contributed to the mortgage as he had promised — it was like having a lodger with benefits! I must be honest with myself; I became more and more complacent. People saw us as the perfect couple, and we played our parts well.

The year flew by, and to my delight I passed my driving test on the first attempt!

CHAPTER 4

ELENA – 2008/9

Over the next year Sasha came and went, sometimes staying for a few weeks before setting off for business elsewhere. He told me about property deals that he was involved in – deals that took him to Budapest, Brussels, Amsterdam and London. His worldliness and wealth contrasted my sheltered, poor upbringing, and he treated me so well. When he was in town, he always came to see me – sometimes he drove me back to my village with food and gifts for my family in his big, new Toyota Tsusha car. One day Sasha asked Nikki if I could have an afternoon off, so he took me to a fashion shop in the middle of town and bought me some expensive toiletries and cosmetics, a pretty dress, a handbag and shoes to match.

"I can't believe how wonderful you are to me, Sasha," I said every time I saw him.

"It is because I am falling in love with you and I want you to have nice things," he told me as he wrapped his arms around me. How could I resist? I was young and naïve; my heart bounced with excitement every time I was with him. We went to the fair in Gorky Park, where we laughingly rode the big wheel and ate popcorn. I had never had such a wonderful time or been treated with so much attention. Every moment I had off from work, he would take me out somewhere special, to markets, museums and art galleries.

He was so knowledgeable about everything—he lovingly told me about how he had educated himself as he travelled and how he had worked in different places around the world. I had so much to learn about everything, so I allowed myself to be his willing pupil. That was our relationship from the start. He was the leader, and he made the decisions for both of us. I was his willing, heart-fluttering student, happily compliant. I trusted him and would follow wherever he thought best for me.

Sasha and Boris had a business interest in the refrigeration company where Anca worked and had rented a flat in town for the summer. Sasha would take me there, eventually making gentle love to me. He taught me to please him, and I was an easy student.

"You are too good to be lost in this god-forsaken place. With your looks you could do anything you want," he told me. Even though my looks had improved with the good food and lovely cosmetics Sasha had bought me, I knew that I was still a gawky teenager, and he was a sophisticated older man. He never told me exactly how old he was, but I guessed him to be in his early thirties — I didn't care, I was in love!

It wasn't long before Sasha started to tell me again about jobs abroad which he claimed I could get — but I was still unsure, so I would laugh gaily and say, "No, not yet but I will think about it."

Toward the end of the summer, he told me that he would be leaving soon to go travelling again. I was mortified that he could go and leave me. "When will you come back Sasha?" I asked, as we lay naked together.

"Who knows? I have to earn a living, Elena. It might not be until next year, and I'm not sure whether I will come back to Vinnytsia at all."

"How can you leave me?" I asked tearfully.

I had enjoyed the attention of my new 'boyfriend' (that's how I now thought of him); I couldn't bear the thought of not seeing him again, and eventually began to consider what it would be like to go with him to another country. Sasha was from Burlacha Balka—a village close to the ferry port Illichivsk—and he suggested that he could take me there for a visit, but I would have to return on my own or follow him to London. I had a choice.

"I don't want to leave you, my beautiful Elena, but I have businesses in Odessa that needs attention and I have to go to England soon. I will stay there for a year or so. Why don't you come with me, and I will find you a perfect job there?"

Knowing that Sasha would be leaving very soon, I talked to Margo and asked what she thought about me going to another country to earn money to buy treatment for her.

"Only you can know, Elena. If you think it is for the best for you, you must try it. Your life has improved already, and the opportunity is waiting for you. I don't want to stop you from having a good life because I'm sick. I know you'll come back, but in the meantime our brothers will care for me."

In October, on my seventeenth birthday, Sasha bought me a travel case. With a smile, he told me that, "It's for when you decide to get away from here and travel and make your fortune. By the way," he added, "I am leaving at the end of next month."

"So soon, Sasha?" I was devastated.

"Yes, my darling. Come with me. I can soon arrange it."

Winter was fast approaching. My friend, Anca had left in the summer, and I really missed her. I'd only had a postcard from her telling me that they had arrived in Berlin, but nothing more.

"They will be enjoying themselves. I haven't heard from Boris either," Sasha told me.

I couldn't bear the thought of Sasha leaving too, so I thought it time to make a decision. At our next meeting I told him gaily, "I think I should like to go to London with you, Sasha."

"We will make the arrangements then," he replied with a satisfied smile. Little did I know how dramatically my life would change!

Once the decision was made to go with Sasha, I started to learn English, a language I found relatively easy. I was a smart girl and applied myself to most things with a natural enthusiasm. Sasha was pleased and often encouraged me. My ability to learn impressed him.

"You will do well, my angel. You are so clever," he said as he gently caressed my cheek.

Less than a month later I had my new passport, and it was time to leave. I had told Nikki, but I hadn't informed Uncle Gregor yet; I was sure that he wouldn't approve – he did not. He tried hard to dissuade me from going but by then I had made up my mind.

"What do you know of the world? There are many dangers for a young girl," insisted Uncle Gregor. "I have heard stories of girls disappearing and never coming home."

"Sasha will take care of me," I answered confidently. "He's promised to get me a mobile phone. I'll contact you regularly, I promise. I want you to keep an eye out for Margo."

"I am not happy, Elena, you are still only young," he told me. "You will come back soon, eh?"

"Of course, Uncle," I told him, "As soon as I can."

We were due to leave at the end of November and Sasha had assured me that we would be in London in time for Christmas and the New year. I was beginning to feel excited, and although I was worried about leaving Margo, I had convinced myself that it was for the best. With a good job, and plenty of money, I was sure that it wouldn't be long before it was possible for Margo to join me somehow. In the meantime, our brothers had both found better jobs, and promised to take care of our little sister.

We stayed overnight at Sasha's beautiful apartment in Bulacha Balks, and I was so happy and excited at the prospect of being with him full-time. He had a very modern phone that beeped almost continually, and he spent a great deal of his time 'wheeling and dealing' as he called it, often speaking in German or English. Although much of his business seemed to be done over the phone, he informed me that he still had to travel to meetings, and that his time with me would be limited. I assured him that I knew and understood, and that I too would have a job to go to.

The following day we headed for the ferryboat at Illichivsk port that would take us to Constanta in Romania.

The weather was icy cold, but I had a new puffer coat and good fur lined boots. My woolly hat and scarf were also new — Sasha had bought them for the trip. He was so undeniably thoughtful! I felt my life was going to be such an adventure; with Sasha by my side, what could go wrong?

As we got out of the taxi that had brought us to the port, Sasha's phone beeped. "Yes…yes later," he said and clicked it shut. Turning to me with a smile, he took my hand. "Nothing important."

"Tell me again, where are we going?" I asked eagerly as we made our way through the crowds of people heading for the boats and ferries.

"When we get to Constanta, we will travel by bus to Bucharest, where we will stay until we can continue by boat along the Danube to Budapest. From there we go to Berlin, perhaps by train, where we will stay a while before eventually taking a journey by road to London." Sasha had made it all sound like a long-stay holiday.

His phone beeped yet again. This time he walked away from me to take the call.

I sat and waited on a low wall with my small case of belongings clutched to my side, watching with fascination as people all around rushed toward the different ferryboats, yachts and trawlers.

Sasha returned with a worried expression. "So sorry, my darling but plans have to be changed." He took my arm, and as we walked toward the docking area, he explained: "I don't know how to tell you this, but I can't come with you today. Something has come up that I have to attend to."

Before I had a chance to digest exactly what Sasha was telling me, he said, "Come with me now and meet my relatives, they will take care of you for me."

I stopped and turned to him, "No Sasha, I can't go without you."

"Of course, you can," he replied somewhat irritably, "you're not a child."

Two people had walked toward us, so Sasha turned away from my protests. "This is Uri, my cousin, and Aunty Veronyka, who will accompany you to Bucharest."

Infront of me stood a tall, well-built thirty-something-year-old man with a receding hairline and a scratty ponytail; a kindly looking older lady of about fifty-five or sixty, with drooping eyelids and a row of discoloured teeth was by his side. They both smiled a welcome, but I was immediately uneasy—I turned to Sasha and said, "I want to wait and go with you."

"Sorry, can't do, my darling. But don't worry yourself. I will meet you in Bucharest tomorrow. It's all much easier from there anyway."

"What is?" I asked.

"Mainly because getting the visa's from here is sometimes a problem—but don't you fret, Elena, all will be sorted. Once all of your papers are in order we can go on our journey, so that you can get to the job that I have lined up for you in London. It's a nice club where you can live as well as work—it's a great opportunity. There will be other girls going with you, so you will have some company." Sasha looked into my eyes, and I believed that he was sincere.

Nevertheless, a sliver of doubt passed through my mind. "No Sasha, I want to go with you," I said again.

"Come here, sweetheart." He pulled me towards him and wrapped his arms around me. "It's impossible at the moment. That's why my relatives will take care of you. Aunty Veronyka will make sure you get there safely."

"You told me that you would take me yourself," I pleaded.

"I am so sorry, Elena. I know I promised, but I have to make another really important business trip. I will catch up with you." He kissed me passionately. "I can't tell you how much I want to be with you. Very soon, I will be by your side again, I promise. We will have a wonderful time together in London."

"We will take good care of her, Sasha." Aunty Veronyka said as she took hold of my arm. "Come Elena, we must hurry to get the boat now."

Sasha had already started to walk away as she said, "Blow Sasha a kiss. You will see him again shortly. We must hurry now and meet the other girls."

I was so disappointed, but I knew that Sasha was a busy man, and we would be together again very soon. I sobbed softly as we waved goodbye. Aunty Veronyka moved me towards what looked like a tourist ferryboat and said, "Don't you worry. Come on now, the sooner we get going, the sooner you will see him again."

Altogether there were six girls and I soon discovered that I was one of the youngest. Aunty Veronyka kept an eye on us all. Galyna and Oksana were sisters from Moldova who were going to London with me. Both were very young, sixteen and seventeen, blonde and very pretty. Natali was nineteen — she was also from Moldova — and Lilia and Yeva were eighteen and came from Ukraine. They told me they were only going as far as Budapest.

As we settled into the scruffy trawler that was to take us to Constanta, I chatted happily to the other girls, still convincing myself that all would be resolved when Sasha arrived in Bucharest. I sat with Lilia and Yeva whilst the three girls from Moldova sat together, talking and giggling amongst themselves — they were obviously all friends.

"I thought we were all going to England?" I asked Aunty Veronyka as she collected our passports to show at customs when we arrived in Constanta.

"No, no, only three of you, the others will probably stay in Germany."

I was confused. "Probably? They said they were going to work in Budapest."

"It's not decided yet, perhaps they will stay in Budapest — we are not sure."

"Why not, surely they have jobs to go to?"

"Yes… yes, I expect so. All in good time."

"Why are you taking our passports?"

"We still need more documentation, and we know how to do it." She held out her hand, but I hesitated and tucked my passport firmly into my pocket.

"Don't be stupid. Would you rather get on with it by yourselves? It is not easy, and we know the right people to see." She waited.

"What does that mean?" I asked naively.

"You ask too many questions, Elena." Aunty Veronyka said, pushing her face close to mine. I handed her my passport.

CHAPTER 5

ELENA

From the boat in Constanta, we took a small private bus to the outskirts of Bucharest. By then, we were all hungry and shivering with the cold.

"We stop here for a while and our friends will come and collect us." Uri told us as he led us along a wide street full of tall buildings and fancy shops. He took us to a large warm café and indicated to a booth at the back, nodding to Aunty to get us seated. "Sit down, girls and I will get us refreshments. Aunty will explain."

We sat silently in a corner of the café, entranced and slightly overwhelmed, not only by the décor and size, but more by the bustle of people rushing about collecting plates of food or trays or steaming cups of frothy coffee.

Uri returned with a tray of drinks, ham and cheese filled Panini's and plăcintă cu mere — a flaky pastry stuffed with apples, nuts and spices.

"See how I spoil you?" he grinned and pushed the food around the table. "Has Aunty explained about what we have to do here? About the visas?"

"No, she hasn't. What is the problem?" Natali, the eldest girl asked.

"Well, we have visitor visas for Romania, but we will have to get others as we travel. It will take a little time, so when we get to Budapest we will probably stay there for a while."

"But we have jobs there?" said Natali.

"Ah, yes, my dear, you do," said Aunty with a smile, "You three do have jobs to go to," she indicated Natali, Yeva and Lilia, "But you have only visitor visas at the moment, and you need work visas so we will apply for them there. That's why we still need your passports. There are borders to cross before we get to Budapest."

"Will we have time to go site seeing?" asked Lilia.

"Of course," was Aunty Veronyka's quick reply.

I was getting more and more confused, because I had asked about their work permits for Budapest and Aunty had inferred that they — the three girls — were going to Berlin.

It was only when we were about to leave the café that the friendliness and geniality of our chaperones changed. Aunty Veronyka split us into two groups and I became concerned. Uri none too kindly informed Natali, Lilia and Yeva that they were to go with him to stay elsewhere, and that they would be taking a different route to Berlin.

"We are not going to Berlin we are going to Budapest to work in a club. Look, I have a contract." Lilia waved a document at Uri.

"You three are heading to Berlin but not until next month because we need to get your paperwork sorted," Uri told the girls as he pushed them towards the waiting car. "We are not going to Berlin. We have visitor's visa for Budapest—I will show you." She pulled another document from her bag and pushed it in front of him. "This is it."

Uri smiled, "Yes, okay, don't worry. We'll check them out when we get to your accommodation. We will sort it out. Let's get going. Get in the car now."

Still protesting, Lilia, Natali and Yeva got into the hired car that had just pulled up next to them. All of us had assumed that we would stay together until we got to

Budapest. They waved as the car pulled away. I was never to see them again.

Aunty Veronyka stayed with me and the sisters Galyna and Oksana.

"We have a taxi coming for us," she informed us after a quick telephone call. It arrived within minutes and we travelled into the city. We passed bustling shoppers and tall buildings, the like of which we had never seen before; it was a huge and beautiful place. We drove by quaint winding streets, frescoed churches, the Palace of the Parliament with its multitude of arched windows, the hotels, cinemas and great billboards advertising a concert by somebody called 'Rieu'.

"What is that?" asked Oksana.

"André Rieu. Comes here often, very popular! We have a lot of interesting things happen in Bucharest," Aunty informed us. "We had a film festival here earlier this year too."

We eventually left the centre of the city and were dropped off outside a sordid backstreet building where we were met by a hulk of a man called Max. He could have been Uri's twin brother, only without the ponytail. His pumped-up biceps were encased in a dark shiny suit, his gelled hair black and spiked. Aunty Veronyka obviously knew him, and as he scowled a greeting to us, he guided us toward a door beside a noisy nightclub. I was beginning to be seriously frightened and I knew now that this whole trip was a dangerous joke.

"What are we doing here?" I asked, alarm sparking through my spine. "This is not a good place to stay." We were all equally distressed and terrified of what was really happening to us. Nothing was going as we had expected.

The noise that emanated from the club dispelled any fanciful thought that we might have had about the city. Motorbikes blocked the pavement and their owners lounged against graffiti covered walls; music pulsed from inside the club. A crudely painted sign above the door proclaimed the club was called 'Bonbons'.

The sisters giggled nervously and started to back away from the entrance but the big gorilla, Max stood in their way. As we mounted the stairs, Aunty Veronyka said, "Don't worry, girlies. We only stay here until everything is ready in Budapest. Then we take a boat up the Danube. It will be fun."

Galyna, the younger of the sisters, began to cry as we were taken up a flight of stairs to a group of ugly rooms.

"This is a terrible place, Aunty," said Oksana who was holding her sobbing sister, "Why are the windows barred? It's like a prison."

"For your own safety," Aunty Veronyka told us as she showed us into a room and locked the door firmly behind her. "This is a dangerous town for young girls on their own." She no longer sounded like the kindly aunty who had met us all at the Illichivsk ferry port.

"Where is Sasha?" I asked, "he promised to be here."

"So, he did," said Aunty with an ironic smile. "Perhaps he got delayed. No worries — we will leave for Budapest in two days, and you will be expected to do a little work there."

"What do you mean? Why would I need to be working in Budapest? Sasha is to take me to London. I am not leaving here without him." I found myself shivering, panicking at the thought of being tricked.

"We shall see. He's a busy man. Perhaps he will meet us in Budapest. When we get there, we will be staying for a while to get everyone's papers in order. It takes some time, and you will need to earn some money to pay for your travel. You will all be set to work," Aunty Veronyka widened her eyes and smiled. "And you will learn to enjoy it. I will bring you some food and vodka later. Just rest now. This is going to be a long journey."

As she left, we heard the click of the door being locked. We were now fully aware that we were prisoners.

"What does she mean? What will we have to do?" Galyna began to cry again. "We are kidnapped," she wailed as she wrapped her arms around Oksana.

I held back my tears, still hoping that somehow Sasha would appear and put things right. I wanted to run, to burst out of the doors and get as far away from this place as I could. I wanted to scream, 'Let me out, how dare you keep me here?' I was shaking, but I made myself walk to the window and stand still. I took a deep breath while I tried to process what was happening. *Can this be real? Are we unable to change this nightmare and go home?*

"I think we must try to escape before we get too far away," I said sadly as I looked out of the only tiny window into the dim street below. It had started to snow.

"How can we do anything? Even if we could get out of here, they have taken our passports and we haven't got any money. Do you have any Elena?" Oksana asked.

"No, nothing. I gave it all to Sasha to look after for me."

"We are well and truly fucked. We gave all of ours to Aunty Veronyka when we signed the contract."

"You signed a contract?"

"Yes, we are going to a club in London to dance. We have been practicing for months."

"Why do you think we are here?" Oksana asked me. "Do you think we are going to be working as prostitutes?"

I shrugged and felt the tears pool in the back of my eyes. I knew for sure that this was not as Sasha had promised. He had lied to me.

Uri returned to the house without mentioning where the other girls had been taken. When I asked, he just grinned and said, "They are in good hands now. It's all sorted so don't worry. Let's have a nice evening together here before we move on in a couple of days." He was in an exceptionally good mood, and I heard him tell Aunty that all had been signed and paid for. He had brought us a ready cooked Chinese meal and a large bottle of vodka. We sat together in the kitchen, where there was a small television which Aunty watched. We couldn't understand any of it, as Romanian is quite different to our language in Ukraine. Other people, mainly men, came and went as we ate and drank. They all seemed to be well known to Uri and Aunty Veronyka.

"Tomorrow we will take you out to see the city. Would you like that?" asked Aunty.

I felt that it was some sort of game they were playing with us, but Oksana and Galyna believed that perhaps it was a good sign that we were going out. All I could think was that it might be a chance to get away. By the time we had finished we were slightly drunk and ready for bed. We were taken to our separate rooms; my room was quite clean, but it had no windows and no carpet on the floor and the door was locked. I couldn't sleep, it was noisy and cold, and in my slightly tipsy state I had allowed myself to believe that Sasha would appear at any moment and change everything.

The following morning, we were ushered back into the kitchen to wait for the taxi to arrive and Aunty said,

"Come on, girlies. I want to see the Bucureşti Mall. I haven't been there yet. It was the first indoor shopping mall in Bucharest—lots of lovely shops I'm told. We will have coffee and our lunch there."

We were not allowed to be on our own, of course. Uri and Max were with us all the time. The shops were lovely, and Aunty bought us a silky negligee each.

"Thank you so much," gushed Galyna, stroking the deep pink one that Aunty handed her. 'They're so lovely." Oksana's was a soft jade colour and she looked as confused as I felt. Perhaps she too believed it was a gift out of kindness.

Regardless, I saw the look Aunty gave Uri as she said, "You are going to need pretty things to wear. I shall add it to your debt to us." Uri grinned as he saw my suspicious look, handing me the one they had 'bought' for me.

"Lovely blue one for you, Elena. To go with your pretty deep-sea eyes."

The feeling of apprehension and fear stayed with me all day. At no point could we have run away. Aunty held firmly on to Galyna, and Max and Uri held on to Oksana and me. We were led around like children—Aunty even accompanied us to the toilet in the restaurant while Max stood guard outside.

When we returned to our unsavoury lodgings we were taken to our individual rooms, given some magazines and left alone.

About an hour later I heard my door being unlocked. Uri stood there looking at me, his expression impassive, almost indifferent. He raised an eyebrow and ran his hand down the back of his head following the fall of his scratty ponytail. He remained still, watching me, with a sardonic look that I could not interpret.

"Have you enjoyed your day in Bucharest?" he asked.

"No, you are playing a game with us."

"Clever girl, aren't you?"

"Why are we staying here? What is going on? And where is Sasha?"

Uri let out a snort of laughter. "Not so clever after all. You silly girl, you belong to me for the time being. Sasha will be out hunting for his next bargain."

"No… he is… he told me he would meet us in Bucharest. Why isn't he coming?" I stuttered, still with the hope that I had been wrong about him.

"Why would he be coming?" Uri wandered over and sat on the bed. "Elena, come over here and be nice to me. You don't look so pretty when you are upset. I will look after you."

"Where is Sasha?" I demanded.

"Why would you think he is coming here?"

"Because… he promised." I raised my voice. I was not a stupid girl, and although it had only dawned on me slowly and painfully, I had realised that I had been tricked. I knew that I had to do something to get out of there.

"Let me go home, please."

Uri stood up, his expression changing. "No. You owe me now. I have taken on the responsibility of getting you to London. Sasha has done his part and now you belong to me." He took hold of my arms and swung me towards him.

"Let go of me. I don't belong to anyone," I shouted and twisted away from him, but he held me fast, so I turned, and banged my fist into his face. It felt as if I had hit a tree trunk as my fist cracked against his chin. He released his grip and gave me a ringing blow across my brow just above my eye. I lost my balance and fell hard. My nose and chin hit the rough floor and started to bleed. I rolled away and jumped up to face him again. I was panting, my face flushed. "Don't touch me, you creep."

Uri turned toward the door, opened it a crack and shouted, "Max, Viktor, come — I've got a wild cat here. I'll need some help to tame her."

Two grinning thugs appeared, Max, the one who could have been Uri's twin brother, and another who looked older.

Although I was fit and strong, there was no way that I could fight off the three men who proceeded to assault me. Viktor, the older of the men, knelt on my head and held my arms. The other two stripped off all my clothes and even though I kicked and screamed with all my might, both took their pleasure and left me lying on the cold floor bleeding and bruised.

In all my seventeen years I had never been physically hurt by anyone. The only time I had ever wrestled or fought, was play fighting with my brothers. Even though my father was a miserable and bad tempered drunk he had never once hit any of us. Until then I'd always felt in control of my life, but this had cast me adrift like a cork on a stormy sea.

"Give her some GHB to calm her down tomorrow, then let me test the merchandise," I heard the older man say as they left. "I can't be bothered with all this fighting anymore."

Uri laughed. "You're getting old, Viktor... I like a bit of a tussle with a wild cat, it excites me. She's worth the money we paid for her and we'll get a good price for this one in Germany if we can settle her down. Shouldn't take long," he said with a throaty laugh. "We'll help her along the way."

As they left, I heard the click of the lock and knew there was no way of escape. I moaned — misery trickled through my veins and tears sprang to my eyes. Not because of the pain, but because I was in this situation. I'd put my trust in Sasha — why? I loved him, and I thought that he loved me. It was becoming clear that he had sold me to these disgusting men. Other than a quick fumble with one of the farm boys, I had never experienced sex before Sasha. I was disgusted by the way I had learned what men do for their satisfaction. I sobbed into the rough bedding that they had left for me, and eventually, out of sheer exhaustion, I fell asleep.

The following morning when Uri returned with some thick porridge and a glass of water, my body was sore, and my head ached so badly that I asked him for some aspirin. He fished into the pocket of his jerkin and gave me two tablets. "Soon make you feel better, Elena."

The porridge stuck to my gums and made me feel sick, so without a thought I swallowed the pills and lay down. It didn't take long for the pills to set the room spinning. My breath became shallower, and a numbing sensation was spreading from my neck to my face and body. It was absurdly pleasant, and I felt my body heat up and slowly my breath lengthened. There was a moment, before I was completely swallowed into unconsciousness, that I couldn't identify what was real and what was not. My surroundings floated and I drifted into relaxation. The door opened and a cold draught hit me. I could hear voices as though I was in a tunnel, mocking and laughing. Suddenly I felt calm as a weight pressed on me, and my legs were pulled apart; the feel and smell of the old man washed through my senses – I remember nothing else.

Afterwards, I had no idea how long I slept, or what time it was, but when I woke my mouth was so dry that I swallowed the tepid water that had been left for me.

Across the room I could see the chest of drawers with a mirror above it, but there was no sign of my case or my clothes. I ran my hands over my stomach, then the tops of my legs and my inner thighs before slowly sliding my fingers between my legs. I felt raw. Dried blood had congealed around my vagina and anus — the whole area felt inflamed and painful. I lay quietly for some moments, listening to the sounds around me — there was loud sobbing from somewhere down the corridor, and I could hear the clump of rubber soles on the concrete floor amongst an exchange of voices. I felt that I was choking with tears, suffocating. My palms sweated against the rough bedding that covered my naked and bruised body. I lay there for the rest of the day and all evening. Pizza and a cup of coffee were brought in at teatime, and I ate and drank out of sheer hunger and exhaustion.

The next morning Uri returned. "Come on, get up. Let's get you cleaned up for the journey. You stink, little girl," he told me.

"I have no clothes," I wailed.

"No need." Uri took hold of me and roughly pushed me naked along the cold corridor to a shower room.

Aunty Veronyka was waiting for me with towels and a bar of soap. She tutted loudly when she saw the state of my bloodied nose and chin. "You have made a bit of a mess of her, Uri." She tipped her head toward my pubic area and said, "No need for that."

Uri laughed, as he backed out of the shower room, "Fucking wild cat, that one."

Aunty Veronyka handed me the soap and some shampoo. "Get into the shower and get cleaned up."

I was aware of my own stink as I stood shaking under the tepid water, slowly soaping my sore and achy body. I had bruises on my arms, my upper thighs and across my bottom. I carefully massaged the shampoo into my hair, aware that it would take more than a shower to make me feel better. Sour faced, Aunty Veronyka watched me throughout and turned the water off when I had finally rinsed my long hair. Handing me a couple of towels, she said, "Stand still, you need something on those." She waved her hand in the direction of my face and opened her own bag to retrieve a tube of antiseptic salve, which she tried to apply to my nose and chin. I wrapped a towel around my head and another around my body as I backed away against the door, trying to distance myself from her. I said as bravely as I could manage, "Don't you touch me, you fucking witch."

Yet Aunty Veronyka was strong and determined, "Do you want me to get Uri?" she barked as she held me against the door. "Perhaps you want to go on the trip looking like a war victim?"

I shook my head. "No, I thought not," she sneered as she liberally applied the salve to my painful grazes and bruises. "We are taking a cruise along the Danube. You need to look your best when we get there." She handed me my own bag of make-up, the one I had carefully packed back in Burlacha Balka.

"You look a sight young lady, make up your face. The sisters are nearly ready to go."

Wrapped in towels, I was taken back to the same room. My little case and my clothes were waiting for me, and an hour later Aunty Veronyka came back, wrapped in a big fur coat and hat, and collected me. Holding firmly onto my arm she pushed me into the corridor where one of the men was waiting. Uri was guiding Galyna and Oksana, the pretty Moldovan sisters, down the stairs. They no longer looked like the bright teenagers that had shared the boat trip out of Illichivsk ferry port with me two days previously. For a start they were either drunk or drugged, and heavily made up; they were the colour of newly mixed cement, but their lips were bright and glossy. Both girls had bruises on their wrists, and Oksana had a sore red welt across her cheek. Their pupils were dilated, and they wore nauseatingly forced smiles across their faces.

Neither spoke as they registered my own bruised and battered face – one that even the heavy make-up I had applied could not disguise.

CHAPTER 6

ELENA

Outside it had been snowing heavily, and Max had driven a big car to the curb that we were pushed towards. Our bags were thrown into the boot, and Aunty Veronyka said, "Get in the back, girlies."

Without a word Oksana and Galyna entered, and Uri got into the front. I still felt so sick and my head ached, but I stood resolutely without moving. "Where exactly are we going?" I demanded.

"Get in, Elena," growled Uri through the window. The threat was obvious, but I felt that I should at least try to get away before we got too far away from home. Surely, if I found a member of the police, and explained the situation, they would help us. I felt I had missed my opportunity on our day out shopping.

"No," I pulled away from Aunty and started to run, slipping and sliding on the icy path, pushing past a group of teenage boys, almost hitting a lamppost head on. My legs felt wooden, and I was aware of how sore my body felt. I swerved away from the pavement on to the road, but Max was too quick for me. He'd leapt out of the driving seat and caught up with me in a second, wrapping his big powerful arms around me. He twisted one arm painfully behind my back and marched me back to the car, grinning at the boys as if we were playing some sort of game.

"I don't think so, bitch," he muttered as he pushed me back to the car. Knowing that I had little choice but to obey, I got in.

"Stupid," muttered Aunty Veronyka as I started to cry with frustration. Within seconds we sped away. Oksana took my hand, laid her head on my shoulder and closed her eyes. The doors were firmly locked as we travelled out of Bucharest, and my tears turned into soft hiccupping sobs.

"Aşa că merge — o altă zi în România," muttered Max aggressively, as we passed a group of protesters that were shouting, waving banners and blocking the road. They had big painted signs — something to do with the collapse and liquidation of 'Bancorex'.

"What did he say?" asked Oksana opening her eyes.

"That's how it goes—another day in Romania," laughed Aunty. "Max hates being here in this country. He lost all his money in that bank back in '99. Although, I myself like Bucharest."

Max muttered something unintelligible from the driving seat.

"Although it is much better for us all in Hungary, much more stable," explained Aunty as she took off her hat, settled herself into the seat and closed her eyes. "Girlies you will like it in Budapest, lots of money there."

I couldn't imagine that I would 'like it' anywhere after the last few days.

I watched the city disappear as we passed the churches, the statues and fountains, the supermarkets and cinemas; we moved away from the endless bustle of people into the surrounding countryside. Galyna was either passed out or fast asleep in her sister's arms as we left the city and drifted through beautiful villages and towns. Oksana started to cry again but said nothing—I could see that she was hurting too.

We reached Giurgiu, a pretty place, where we stopped for lunch. Once again, both Uri and Max watched us closely all the time. Although we had hardly spoken during the hour and a half journey, both the sisters were now awake and distressed. Galyna had peed her pants, felt sick and couldn't eat. Aunty carted her off to the toilets to get her cleaned up. I drank some tea, but I ate very little despite my hunger.

Before long we were travelling the rather dull country roads that took us to the river. Aunty chatted occasionally, as if we were on a tour bus, and I couldn't believe that she was so insensitive and uncaring about what was happening to us.

"As we near the port you will see the old steel bridge that connects Romania to Bulgaria. The border runs through the river. Isn't that strange—that two countries are separated like that? We don't go to the other side, though. Terrible place."

As if we cared!

It was snowing heavily when we arrived at a place called Smârdan. It was a small port where we were to get onto a boat that would take us along the Danube to

Budapest — or so we believed. It turned out to be nothing of the sort.

Max had dropped Uri, Aunty Veronyka and the three of us girls with our luggage at the dockside, before disappearing without another word. It was freezing cold and there was a thick layer of snow along the banks of the Danube; great sheets of ice had formed around the boats and ferries. Very little moved along the river, except a few big cargo barges that chugged along, causing icy waves. Uri was busy shouting into his phone as we were marched along the riverbank, past a sandy beach to a jetty where our 'boat' awaited us. It was little more than a motorised blow up dingy, exceedingly small and quite unsuitable for a long journey. I couldn't believe this would take us to Budapest.

"Is this a joke? We can't go in this." I said trying to sound brave and back away, but Aunty held firmly onto my arm — she was very strong. Oksana and Galyna were pushed toward the dingy, and both were crying.

"We will only be on this boat until we get to the next border," Uri informed us, his voice rising in anger as he pushed his phone into his pocket, "then we will have a bus journey, so stop snivelling. Get in and do as you are told."

He turned to Aunty, "Bit of a hold up with Al, so we have to stop at the lock."

"S'not a problem, is it?"

"Nah."

We carefully stepped onto the dingy and huddled close to each other. It was open to the elements, and although we were given big blankets to wrap around ourselves, we still shivered with cold. Uri then got busy starting the motor as Aunty pushed herself down beside us.

"How long will it take to get to Budapest?" I asked her.

"Several days altogether, but this is the worst bit," she said with a grin.

We travelled along the grey river until the light began to fade. We were cold and stiff when we eventually got off the boat and onto the bus that was to take us to another part of the river.

We were all so distressed by the way we were being treated, none of us knew how to deal with what was happening. By now we were far from home, cold tired and frightened. Uri had sneeringly informed us that we would get no help if we ran away.

Later in the evening we boarded a private boat. The two men that took us aboard greeted Aunty and Uri as old friends, and we were given hot tea and packets of biscuits. This boat was much more comfortable, with padded sofas and blankets. We travelled all night, and I think that we all fell asleep eventually.

It actually took us four days to get to Budapest, because at some point we were stopped. After some discussion with the authorities at a lock, our plans were changed. Whatever was decided, it meant that we left the river, and took a long bus journey through a snowy landscape to somewhere called Arad, where we stayed in a hotel for the night.

All sorts of excuses about border controls and visas had been given to us, but in the end, we just did as we were told. We were so frightened and exhausted by then that we ate when instructed, showered and went to bed. The sisters and I shared a big bed, and we huddled together, crying and whispering for most of the night. We had no idea where we were, and no longer had any hope of getting home.

The following day we were kept locked in our room. Once again, we were left hungry and alone. Late that night, Uri marched us silently across fields and through woodlands, to cross the border into Hungary. We walked for hours in the dark, terrified and acquiescent. Aunty Veronyka did not accompany us, but she turned up in a taxi in the early hours of the morning at a railway station. Here we had breakfast, before we eventually got on a train to Budapest. We were all exhausted, and we slept for most of the long journey.

We arrived in the city in the early evening. By that time, we had all given up on any hope that we might've had. We knew that we were being trafficked into prostitution. Our destination was a huge, double fronted, three-storied house in Bonyhàdi ùt, which was a long leafy avenue not far from a huge, noisy nightclub called the 'Zug Bar'. Even though it was early evening, the street was full of street girls, drunken revellers and tourists. There was a buzz of activity, music and noise, and I heard several different accents. I had never seen anything like this place. Was this a brothel?

Inside the house we were told that this was where we would be staying for the next few months. The building consisted of an assortment of rooms and corridors, kitchens and shower rooms. It was much more luxurious than where we had stayed in Bucharest, and it was full of people coming and going. There was a huge, dimly lit bar on the ground floor, where people were drinking and dancing. A sign over the door said in jazzy gold letters 'Dizzy Days & Naughty Nights'. Lining the corridors were framed photographs and prints, depicting naked girls of all ages, colours and sizes, in every pose imaginable.

In a daze of fear and trepidation, we followed Aunty up an impressive staircase to the top floor and were shown into our own rooms. These were tiny spaces, where we'd sleep and keep our belongings. Besides the bedrooms, there were toilets and shower rooms, as well as a big communal kitchen, sitting and dining room—here, all the girls met during the day to eat and drink, or to just sit about and gossip. Big couches and tables were dotted around. There were several tall fridges, mainly full of beers, wines and vodka. Cigarette smoke, and a substance that my brothers called 'konoplya', hung thick in the room. The rooms for 'entertaining' were on the middle floor.

We collapsed with total exhaustion, and Aunty Veronyka told us that the following morning we would meet in the 'sitting room'.

"Go to bed now, because tomorrow you will start work," she told us with a wave.

CHAPTER 7

ELENA

The next morning, we met an assortment of women and girls, it seemed as if most had been in Budapest for many months. They drifted into the sitting room through the morning. Some spoke a few words of greetings, others slumped onto the sofas looking tired and hungover. Most of them drank pints of black coffee and shovelled down tranquillisers or aspirin.

"Hi, I'm Jeni," said a diminutive blonde dressed in baggy joggers and a 'Bon Jovi' tee shirt, who lay with her head on a cushion on one of the big sofas. It was 10 am and she was drinking from a bottle of vodka. "Hi, I'm Jeni," she slurred again. "You're new. Just arrived, have you?"

Aunty Veronyka came into the room. "Oh, you've come with her," said Jeni derisively. She wrinkled her nose. "Old bitch."

Aunty raised her eyebrows but did not respond to Jeni, who was obviously quite drunk. "Follow me," she said to Oksana, Galyna and I. "I want to show you around, mainly so that you know where you will be working. It's a big house, and you need to know where you are going." We followed her down the stairs.

All the 'entertaining' rooms were themed for every possible taste—from an underground crypt to an angelic parlour with fluffy clouds and angels' wings.

"We even have one with coffins," she laughed at my look of disgust. "We cater for all tastes here. In these rooms you will have your 'assignations'." She laughed and with a smirk said, "In every room there is appropriate piped music," she pointed to a switch on the wall, "and you will find a drawer full of condoms, all shapes, flavours and sizes, as well as a few French ticklers, butt plugs, cock rings, handcuffs and the like. Just go along with their fantasies, eh, girlies?" Galyna giggled nervously.

"In other words, we are common prostitutes?" I said.

"I prefer the term 'call girls' or 'escorts'. It's More upper class," she cackled. "May I remind you that you won't be walking the streets looking for clients, and we will be looking out for you all the time. There is always food and drink available in the fridges in the kitchen—you can help yourselves. You will not leave the house without a minder.

You will get paid and get a monthly health check – but I advise you to look after yourselves, too."

We had no way of leaving the premises. On every landing and at every door the minders waited and watched – even at this early hour of the day.

Late that afternoon, Aunty Veronyka came and told me to follow her. She led me into a room, with a notice on the door, which said 'Island Paradise'. It had great palm trees painted on the walls and a big bed with a pineapple decorated quilt. The floor was the colour of sand and the walls the colour of the ocean. Steel drums played in the background. It was disgusting, and my heart was pounding with the fear of what I was expected to do.

"You've got your first client later. He's a good payer, so you must be extra nice to him."

"What…? What do you mean? No, I will not be nice to him." I stuttered.

"I think you will find that you will. You need to earn some money to pay off your debts."

"My debts? Aunty I will pay Sasha what I owe him when I start my job in London." I said, without any real belief that I would ever see Sasha again.

"Sasha is not coming here. Forget Sasha," Aunty said in a whiney piss-taking voice. "You belong to Uri now and the job starts today. You owe us a great deal of money. If you pay it off, you will be free to go."

"Free to go home?"

"Of course, but we have already paid out a great deal on your behalf, so you must be a good girl and earn enough money to pay us back. So, dear, it's in your own interest to please your customers. That's the only way." She went to a long wardrobe and lifted out a floral skirt, a blouse and a pair of shoes. "Here are some nice clothes that you are to wear. This one likes his girls in heels." She handed me a pair of pink high heel shoes. "Oh, and I will give you something to make it easier. Just a little relaxant." She smiled her grim smile and reached into her pocket for a small pill bottle. I watched her fascinated. *How could I ever have trusted this evil woman? She pretended to care for us and promised to get us good well-paid jobs. In truth we are just common prostitutes.*

She handed me two of the pink pills. "Take them now if you want to get the job done. It will make it easier."

"No." I said, but she folded them into the palm of my hand. "Take them. I promise you it will be for the best. Believe me, they will help. We can't always vet the clients to make sure they aren't dangerous, so it's best to be prepared. Most of them only need a physically intimate, therapy session and that is easy money for you. Earn while you can, and pay us what you owe us."

She left and locked the door. I had butterflies in my stomach as I put on the awful clothes that she had given me. She returned very soon and as she unlocked the door; I heard her say, "You will like this one, Vladimir. She's new, so take it easy with her." She ushered a man into the room, glanced briefly at me to check whether I had dressed as I had been told, and left.

Through the door came a stocky man, rather overweight, in a shiny blue suit. He had a large, round face and thin, fair hair receding from a broad forehead. His big nose and his skin were lardy pale, as if he never saw daylight. He was a good bit shorter than my five-foot-nine. Initially, he was frowning, but as his gaze flickered over me, his fat lips widened into a broad smile. He took off his jacket and hung it carefully over a chair. He lit a cigarette and stood looking at me. I was dressed in the flashy skirt, the blouse and the pink high heels. Really, they were all too small for me.

He started to speak in a language that I didn't understand, but I assumed that he was Russian from his name. Realising that I had no idea what he was saying, he said haltingly in Polish, "Take off all your clothes, but leave the shoes on." This I did understand.

"I will not," I said lifting my chin in defiance but as he stepped toward me, I was suddenly afraid. He did not look so innocuous close-up, and his face hardened into a grimace rather than a smile. He looked dangerous.

"Take off," he said again. He raised a hand as if to strike me, and I dropped my eyes. Slowly, I undid the buttons of the gaudy blouse that Aunty Veronyka had given me to wear. By the time I had taken off my clothes, and stood in my flimsy underwear, Vladimir had his trousers round his ankles and was ready.

I was shaking and my mouth filled with bile, but I knew there was no escape. In my hand I still held the two pink pills that Aunty had given me. I put my hand to my mouth and swallowed — perhaps it would be better not to remember.

He pushed me toward the bed and kicked off his trousers. I could see his enormous cock, and I felt sick.

"No... no, please no," I cried as I fell backwards onto the bed. I was still sore from the men who had abused me in Bucharest. I swivelled and jumped up, but he was ready. His fist hit me directly on the top of my cheekbone, below my eye. As I lurched away from him, he grabbed me by my hair and shook me as hard as he could. My teeth sank into my tongue, and I could taste blood. I began to cry, although I knew that it would only make matters worse. He pushed me back toward the bed. Shaking uncontrollably, I began to feel dizzy and let my body relax. I was aware that he was taking off the rest of his clothes. I began to float, feeling as if my body no longer belonged to me, and I was aware that my knickers were being pulled off; only my shoes remained on, and the only sensation I could feel was the pinching of my toes as my legs were pushed apart. I opened my eyes, and the pasty face was leering above me. He lit another cigarette, inhaled deeply, and blew the smoke toward me with a laugh. Slowly, he took hold of it with his thumb and forefinger and stubbed it out on my hip. I was so shocked by the searing pain and the smell of my burnt flesh that I let out a howl.

"Shut up, cunt," he said in Polish, but I understood him well enough. Cursing, the man lunged toward me, and I felt myself being pushed back down again, his great weight on top of me, leaving me breathless. The fat prick was panting and cursing but he was enjoying the fray. As he entered me, he made a great wheezy sound and laughingly banged his fat, slimy body into mine. He stubbed out his final cigarette on my body again before he left.

As dawn broke the following morning, all I remembered was Aunty helping me back to my own little room and pushing me onto the bed. As I drifted into a drug-induced sleep, I tossed and turned — images of the evening with the fat Russian flashed through my mind for most of the night.

I tried to open my eyes. One was bruised and painful. On the floor lay the pile of clothes and the ridiculous high heels which that prick had made me wear throughout the abuse. I couldn't remember anything else, but the burns on my hip were red and painful.

Aunty Veronyka came in with a cup of weak tea. "What a shame, dear. Could've had someone a bit nicer than him as your first client in Budapest—eh, Elena? We will make sure that you get an easier one next time, but you must be a good girl. You don't have to fight." She smiled and patted my shoulder. "Drink this, dear, and here is some aspirin for your pain. I will bring you some food."

I ignored her, so she put the tea and aspirin down beside the bed, picked the clothes and shoes off the floor, and then thrust her hand into her jacket pocket. "Look how much you have earned from just one punter." She waved a bunch of Euros in my face.

She handed me a twenty euro note and pocketed the rest. "See, some of your debt is paid off already."

Twenty euros for what I had suffered!

When she left, I sipped the tea and swallowed the 'aspirin'. Everything hurt, and I cried with humiliation and anger. I was mainly angry at myself for being so naïve and stupid in believing Sasha and his absurd promises. When

Aunty returned with a breakfast tray I was sobbing uncontrollably.

"Please don't bring me anyone else like him." I knew that I sounded weak and pitiful, but I couldn't take any more violence.

"Don't worry dear, most are not like him. We'll not let anything serious harm you if you do as you are told. Now, stop snivelling and eat your breakfast. By the way, I am flying back to the Ukraine next week for the New Year celebrations. Uri will look after you from now on."

That was the last time we saw our Aunty Veronyka.

Good riddance!

Where the following day went, I will never know. The 'aspirin' that Aunty had given me sent me back into a dazed sleep, and I stayed in bed for both that day and the night which followed. I only awoke to take a gulp of the water that had been left for me. It was very early the next morning when I woke up. I had a splitting headache and a bruised face, whilst the burns on my hip were sore and seeping. After my experience with the disgusting Vladimir, I didn't want to move, but I was hungry, so eventually I got up and went into the living room.

There were a few girls wandering about in dressing gowns or baggy pyjamas, some eating toast, another boiling eggs on the old gas cooker. They all seemed to be in a world of their own and most looked tired and dispirited.

"Has anyone got any Germalene or disinfectant?" I asked, "These are oozing again." I opened my wrap and showed my burns to two of the girls sitting at a table.

One girl, who was idly flicking through a fashion magazine, lifted her eyes and gave an ironic half smile. "I've had far worse than that. Listen, hon, you really shouldn't fight the bastards. I learnt that a long time ago. Wait… I've got some ointment." She lifted a cavernous bag onto the table and eventually handed me a tube of cream. "I'm Tanya. Have you just arrived? I can see you have already been put to work."

I nodded. Tanya was a small and beautiful natural brunette with a solemn stance, a sulky mouth and eyes the colour of golden hazelnuts.

"This is not work." I said, carefully rubbing the cream into my burns and onto my bruised and painful cheek. "No one has the right to treat us like this."

"True…" she replied with a wry smile.

"Have you been here long?" I asked as I noted her hesitation.

"Two years," she replied, "but I do a bit of lap dancing and stripping as well now. Just a couple of nights a week, here or down at the 'Zug'. That *is* good money." She smiled, but it didn't reach her eyes. She could have been any age, from twenty to thirty-five. I was aware of an odd disconnect between her pretty face and eyes, as if her eyes were older, aged by things that had happened in her life.

"How old are you, Tanya?" I asked.

"Twenny-fucking-two, and I haven't done a single fucking thing in my life that was worthwhile." Although her eyes filled with tears, she lifted her arm and swiped her sleeve across her face. "What a bleeding life, eh."

"Can't we get out of it somehow?"

"Like how? What are you going to do? You think you can just walk away? I've tried that."

"Have you?" I asked as she lifted her hair and indicated a long white scar that ran down her neck from her hairline to her shoulder.

"You have no money or papers, and they will catch up with you eventually." Tanya took the ointment from my hand and led me to the other sofa in the corner. "You are going to have to get used to it. We get a lot of weird people in this business—expect it, and learn to deal with them. Most of them are okay, most of them don't knock us about. You just have to be exactly what they think they want. If you're not and they complain, one of the pigs will give you a hiding." Tanya frowned, "I was conditioned at a very early age to do what men told me to do. My own father started it... I never expect anything else from a man, so I might as well let whatever happens happen. I just don't fuckin' care about anything. Men," she said with contempt, "Are useless saddo's with a brain and a cock—but they don't have enough sense to run them both simultaneously. They give me the pills and I get fed. If I fucking died tomorrow, I would be more than glad. I just hope there are no fucking dicks in heaven," laughed Tanya bitterly.

"No, Tanya, somehow I will get out of this stinking life, or I'll die trying."

"More like, I don't know anyone who has got out alive and I've been at this since... God, I don't even know how bloody long I've been doing this. I actually started off on my own, on the streets in Belgrade—I had this idea that

I could earn enough to get me through college. I wanted to study Horticulture, you know, be outdoors growing things, but I couldn't cope on my own. I kept getting into trouble, so when I met this German cock-sucking charmer who offered to look after me, I got myself tied into this fuckin' life. He sold me to Uri, who takes almost every fuckin' euro I earn. Gives me a bit more now, but only if I do as I'm told and get enough punters."

I looked across at the girl on the other couch who lifted her eyes, nodded, and said, "My own father and brothers started abusing me when I was about five years old, in fact for as long as I can remember. Then he sold me into this. Sold me to a Russian first, who brought me here, before selling me to Uri. I'm Jeni, by the way."

"Yes," I said. "I saw you yesterday."

I looked around the room at the assortment of girls and women, and I found it hard to believe that we were all captives — captives with little choice about whether we stayed or left, to be used and abused as and when our minders wanted. It was utterly depressing.

"I fell in love with what I thought was a lovely, kind man who promised me the world..." I started to sob, thinking about Sasha, and Tanya handed me a clump of tissues out of her bag.

"And he sold you to Uri. Yes, we all know how they work. They get a few good-looking guys to cherry pick their targets and soften them up with gifts and sweet talk. Then they sell them to traffickers. Same old story the world over."

"But I really thought I was in love…"

"Who knows what love is," muttered Jeni from the couch.

Tanya sniffed. "Well, it's not real, is it? Love is in films, books and magazines. It's not in real life. Screwing and shagging are real—after a bit of spliff and a couple of vodkas, we pretend that love is real. We live life in a sham world, pretending that what's between our legs has something to do with love."

Over the next few weeks, I saw many tears. Some girls were hardened and believed they would eventually earn enough to leave, but most knew they were trapped. We wallowed in our own pain, our own individual miseries, our lost families and our lost selves.

Christmas and the new year of 2010 came and went. Budapest was in a party mood, and we were all kept busy with drunken revellers celebrating the new year. I took a great many of the little pink pills. I lived my life in a blur, guarded by Uri and his barrel-chested gorillas the whole time.

CHAPTER 8

KATE – 2010

Our New Year celebrations were spent at Jackson's sports club. I had never liked New Year's Eve, and in the past, I had generally drunk myself into oblivion on my own. This year however, I found myself enjoying the celebrations for the first time in my life. I had people around me, and my husband was at my side. I didn't even drink too much, and Jackson hardly drank at all. We danced, we sang, and then we went home and had sex.

After the London marathon in April, we had a week's holiday in Portugal. My adrenalin-fuelled husband found it hard to relax, so he went off running and left me on the beach or at the hotel. I was enchanted with the endless sunshine and swimming in the sea, something I had never experienced in my life (even though I had spent a good deal of my childhood on the northeast coast). I took loads of photographs, read my books and strolled along the beaches. I *was* lonely but that was nothing new. Mostly, I convinced myself that life was wonderful!

It was springtime and the garden was beginning to come alive. I was so looking forward to the summer, as I had planted a variety of bulbs and flowering shrubs. The previous year I'd had a crazy pathway lain to a shaded area of the garden where I could sit and read.

It was about the time that the tulips were beginning to bloom that I started being violently sick in the mornings. I bought a pregnancy test, just in case, never thinking for a moment that I could really be pregnant. We had been so careful.

I left it for a few more mornings but after a panic filled hour of vomiting, I peed on the stick and waited. My heartbeat quickened and sweat broke out on the back of my neck. Positive… I threw the test across the bathroom. I felt sure that I had not missed taking my birth control pill and thought somehow that this must be a mistake or a bad dream. I waited two more days and bought another two tests. Both showed positive. Methodically I wrapped the tests in toilet paper and hid them in the outside dustbin. The reality of my pregnancy didn't really sink in at first, but eventually despair kicked in—I started to panic, not only at the thought of having to tell Jackson, but about the decisions it would raise.

'Stay calm,' I whispered to myself as my heart started to race. I lay on the bed and stared at the ceiling. *'Jackson is not going to be pleased, and I'm not too sure about how I feel either. Do I want a child? Does anyone really ever want to give up everything in life to tend to a stinky, hungry demanding little being?'*

I lay alone in my room for about an hour, thinking about the reality of the situation. I thought about my life and all my struggles to find a place of meaning in the world— a place where I could be on the outside of what I felt inside, instead of denying that I had feelings at all.

I thought that I had found what I wanted—I had a successful career, and I was a wife with a nest of my own. Yet, to my surprise, I felt something that I had never felt before; a wave of pure joy welled up through my body—a baby! I had never, ever, considered having children. Not only would it be a huge responsibility, but I'd never been able to imagine what a child's life might be like if they were loved—after all, it was a sensation that I had never experienced.

My own childhood had been so unhappy and lonely, and my memories of myself as a little girl were so excruciating, that I didn't want to think of bringing a child into the world to endure anything that might be hurtful or unloving. But, as I rested my hands on my flat belly, I visualised my own baby in there; here was someone who was a part of me, someone to protect and love — someone who would love me.

The feeling grew, but it took me another month before I could bring myself to tell Jackson. I kept reminding myself of what we had laughingly agreed on when we first got together: to let each other have space and freedom. We'd agreed not intrude on each other's lives, to continue to live as individuals without the encumbrance of pets or children. But, in my head I was sure that he would come to love the idea of being a dad — perhaps not immediately — but as the fact of the pregnancy became a reality, I was sure that he would at least accept it.

After a particularly pleasant evening out, I plucked up the courage to tell him. He was reading yet another body enhancing magazine. I stood by his side and said, "Jackson, I think I'm pregnant."

There was a long-inhaled breath before he said scathingly, "I hope the fuck you are joking, Kate."

Panic gripped me. "Can we talk about this, please…? I didn't think I wanted a baby either but now it's there, in here." I indicated my already thickening waistline, "I feel different about it."

There was a long pause, he stood up and threw down his magazine before he answered. When he did his words were harsh. "You get shot of it right away. I don't want anything to do with the brat." His words stung me like a knife cut. I felt a sudden cold and clammy fear. I had wrestled with the belief that he would relent and welcome our baby into the world.

"We agreed that we didn't want children. It was part of the fucking deal." He glared at me, a tic moving in his jaw. "Wasn't it, Kate?" A tiny globe of sweat, pushed out from the skin above his lip. He was so angry, "Come on, you know it wasn't in the deal."

As he looked at me, I saw an utter absence of any love, affection or respect in his eyes. It occurred to me at that moment that our marriage has indeed been nothing but a deal. It was, in fact, asinine in almost every respect. There was no real sharing, caring or deep feelings involved. Had we kidded ourselves that we were in love? How do we even know when we are 'in love'? Perhaps all marriages were just a deal between two people who got along. Just a deal, so that each partner abided by the rules which were set out and agreed upon. I took a deep breath, trying to make my voice sound confident. "Yes, I know it was, but it'll be fine... we'll manage, and the more I think about it, I am quite liking the idea of being a mum. A baby isn't the end of the world. It might be just wonderful."

There was something about his face that made me falter. He was staring at me as if I had just arrived from Mars.

"No, no way. This is not something *I* want. Don't you get it? A child does not fit into my life in any which way, so either it goes, or I do."

I was hurt. "Fuck you," I hissed shaking with anger. A nasty little thought lurked that maybe he was right. Maybe I couldn't cope with it either.

I took a deep breath and calmed my angry thoughts. I said, "Fine, at least I know where I stand. I'm going for a shower, and I will think about it." As I left, I slammed the lounge door as hard as I could, leapt up the stairs, and stripped, dropping my clothes all over the bedroom floor. I allowed myself to sob my sorrow into the sound of the shower, not sure whether my feelings for Jackson were strong enough to get over this instant rejection.

Later Jackson looked at my naked body without the warmth and admiration that I was used to. He switched off the bedside lamp and got into bed, deliberately turning his back to me. A deep feeling of loneliness fell across me like darkness. I knew he expected me to abort this baby. Yes, I knew it had been agreed that we would not have children — my hope that he could be persuaded finally disappeared. Yes, it was a mistake, but accidents do happen. I knew that I was unexpectedly and secretly pleased, but Jackson was plainly furious.

Out of the blue, a week later, Jackson was offered a big promotion which entailed moving to London, so I suppose it was a bit of a knee jerk reaction when he asked me to go with him — but only if I was prepared to get rid of the baby.

"Just go away and quietly have a termination. No one need know and we can get on with our lives," he said. "We've been alright so far."

Had we?

"No, I'm sorry, Jackson. I have given it a great deal of thought. I've even paid a visit to the Marie Stopes clinic and discussed having an abortion, but I have decided I want to go ahead and have our baby. If you want to leave then you must, but I will not be coming with you."

A muscle twitched at the corner of his mouth, and he nodded slowly. He turned to face me, then swallowed, blinked and said quietly, "Right, if you have made up your mind, but you must know I will have no part of it, nothing at all, no contact, no support and no joint custody or any other malarkey… although I must say I am confused…"

"But you're not exactly heartbroken though, are you?" I said as I watched him carefully. I knew that this decision was mine and mine alone. If I were to have this baby, I knew I would be totally by myself.

CHAPTER 9

ELENA – 2010

The following weeks were an on-going nightmare with ten or more men every day. Some old and some young, some kind and gentle—others liked to be dominated, and some were just plain brutal. I realised that many of the 'customers' associated sex with violence and it turned them on if they knocked a girl around. Sad bastards! But, as the fear spread, the drugs became my desperate need: thankfully they blotted out or distorted what was happening to me. I was never paid directly, but Uri would hand me a packet every now and again, telling me that my debt to him was going down.

One lunchtime in March, after a particularly disgusting punter took me to the dungeon-themed room to be tied up and slapped about, I went into my room, curled up and sobbed into my pillow. I banged my fists against the mattress; I felt powerless and beaten.

Eventually, red-eyed and exhausted, I made my way to the lounge area. Several of the girls were sitting with bowls of soup, or wedges of readymade sandwiches (which were kept in the fridge). Miriam, a gorgeous Black girl from Somalia — one of the nicest people imaginable — had been in Budapest over a year. She was looking in the breadbox for something to eat. She smiled sympathetically when she saw my red eyes and bruised face.

"I've got to get out of here." I told her, "I'm going to take a chance tonight and get out. I hope that the police will help me."

"Don't be ridiculous," said Miriam, as she munched on a stale croissant. "Some of our best clients are police or government officials, I even have a barrister… comes regular. Do you really think we would have got this far? There are plenty of police involved in this business. I don't reckon you'd get any help from them. Where would you go anyway? Do you have a passport?"

"No, but I do have some money."

As usual Jeni was sprawled on the sofa with a bottle of vodka. Her skin was blotchy and her hair unwashed. She lifted her bleary eyes and said, "Yeah, but it won't do you any good. My best friend, Zoya, tried to escape when she was in Amsterdam, but her minder found her. He beat her so bad she could hardly walk. He told her that a couple of 'heavies' had been to her family home in Odessa. They had tied up her parents, her ten-year-old brother and raped her thirteen-year-old sister in front of them... and they killed all the family pets." Jeni lifted the bottle to her mouth and took a huge gulp. I watched as Miriam tried to take the bottle away from her shaking hands, but Jeni pulled it back and held it against her chest. "No... leave it. I need it. Zoya was my best friend... I miss her." She put the bottle on the floor and started to cry, sobbing into the sleeve of her sweater. "When he threatened to kill her whole family, she went back to work for him. I don't know where she is now... she was my friend..."

I went cold at the thought of Margo being faced with such a threat. It was unlikely that our brothers could deal with the heavies that they used.

"I have a younger sister," I whispered.

"Well, be warned, they will hurt her if you try to escape." said Miriam.

"Why are we expected to put up with being knocked about? I am always sore, black and blue and I have scars all over my body and look at this on my forehead. The bastard nutted me so hard that the skin has split open. I can't fight any more."

"The skill of a prostitute's life is learning to stay outside of herself for her own sake. Sometimes they are going to hurt you anyway, so it's not good to fight. Just freeze. It's the best way. We have no chance of escape. Here, this will help." She handed me a joint and I took a long drag. Within a few minutes the tightness in my chest and stomach calmed and I took the fresh one that she offered me. Even just the smell of the cannabis had a calming effect on me. I went back to bed and slept awhile before the evening rush began.

After the first few months I was almost resigned to the abuse. I hadn't become less disgusted but, as time passed, I did learn to disassociate myself. I closed my eyes to what was happening to my body. It sickened me through and through, but I forced a smile and a show of affection to those who wanted it and I learned to be more careful of those who didn't. I took the pills, smoked the weed, and let my days drift past without thinking about the next hour or day or week; I didn't think about the future, after all, nothing good could follow the sordid life that I was leading. I felt broken, lost and worthless; I hated myself, and I hated what I was doing. Everything merged together. The constant threats against Margo made me realise that I would have to endure whatever was demanded of me, or I would lose my little sister. Promises of freedom came and went, my debt to Uri seemed to grow, and I never saw my passport or any visas. I couldn't see an end to it.

I was haunted by the life I'd lost. I worried about Margo and how she would be struggling without me, how Nikki would be cooking his pancakes in his kitchen. I thought of Sasha travelling about, getting on with his comfortable life and — according to Uri — looking for his next 'sale'.

Uri still came occasionally and took his pleasure with me.

"I want to go home." I pleaded drunkenly one night when he came to tell me that I was doing well and that it was time I went to work in the club downstairs. "No, I won't...You can't keep me here."

"If you do as you are told you can earn more in the clubs, dance, go topless, smile and get your debt paid off.

Or you can even go and pick up your own clients in the bars and hotels. There are some pretty good pickings in the hotel bars — businessmen, tourists and even a few top blokes with plenty of money. You are a good-looking girl; with some decent clothes you should be able to make 20,000 HUF for an hour or so. Pretty easy money, eh? You could soon earn enough to go home."

That sounded like a fortune to me, and better still, it would allow me to choose my clients, but I also knew that Uri would take over sixty percent of what I earned.

"How much do I still owe you?"

"It depends on what expenses you incur. You are being fed well and you get any new clothes you want, medical treatment if you need it."

"Rubbish. I am here against my will and you know it."

"Elena, I have to remind you that *you* are here illegally, and no one will listen if you tell anyone that you are being kept against your will. Prostitution is legal here, so you won't get much help. At least you are not a highway or street girl. They have a much harder time. Here you get your clientele inside in our nice entertainment rooms. I know some of them are a bit rough, but our boys are here if things get out of hand. Just earn while you can."

If I can save enough, I can help Margo and go home, I thought. "Okay I will try it then, but is it more dangerous for me to go out on my own?"

"What do you think the boys are for? You will always have a minder on hand. They watch all the time and look after all our girls. Ask Oksana and Galyna, they have been dancing in the club and are doing well. You'd better decide soon."

It was only about a month later that Jeni was found dead in her room. We had police and officials snooping around for about a week. Even the IOM sent an investigator from their headquarters in Switzerland. Documents of identification were produced and the few police that were involved accepted them as originals—I was told that they also took a few bonuses. It turned out that Jeni was born in Hungary, so she didn't qualify for an investigation from the IOM. Once a verdict of drug overdose and alcohol addiction was reached everything quietened down. But we had a week without punters while the investigation took place, so we earned no money and were encouraged to learn new dance routines, although mostly we sat about smoking and reading magazines.

We were all upset, and we were worried that she had been deliberately overdosed. "She was a beautiful and spirited girl when she first came here," Miriam told us, dabbing her eyes. "She didn't deserve to die like that. All alone too! She had her problems, but don't we all?"

I fingered the scar on my forehead and thought about how much I relied on the drink and drugs now, as did so many of us. Miriam was one exception. She never took the drugs. She smoked a little marijuana occasionally but rarely drank alcohol. I asked her why she didn't need to blot out what was happening to her.

"While it's happening, I've learned to shut my mind off, and try to disassociate myself from what is going on. I let them do what they like with me. It's the best way. I take myself away to somewhere else where I can breathe good clean air and see the sunshine, then I pray. I believe that God will protect me. I know I can't run away, so I make my mind take me wherever I want to go. I try to concentrate on something else, silly things like a crack in the ceiling, a spider or a shaft of light. Sometimes I listen to the music. I make up a scenario in my head that takes me away from what is happening to me."

Great, I thought, but I can't do that. I need to blot it out completely. I didn't care that much anymore. Why should I? Even though all I wanted was to get away from such a sordid life, I realised that escape was only a dream. *What would I do? Go back to Ruzhyn and poverty?* I could not imagine that Nikki would want to hire me again. Apart from learning English and a smattering of German and Russian, I had achieved nothing but disgrace in the past year. Even Uncle Gregor would be ashamed of what my life had become.

Soon after the conversation with Uri, I started going to the bars in some of the nicer hotels (of which there were many, and they were growing all the time). I frequented the Intercontinental, the Four Seasons Hotel Gresham Palace and the Kempinski, and I met men who were looking for a bit of fun or just a quick fuck—men who were willing to pay well. I tried to be selective, but I often found that even the most innocuous were the most difficult. Some were travelling salesmen or tourists, and I often slept with stag night guests—I took groups back to the house and made them pay extra for the privilege. I knew that I was being watched all the time. Even so, it was a relief to get out, to get away from the club and walk outdoors in the sunshine. I was thankful to be away from the smell of desperation, stale sex, cigarettes and marijuana. Just feeling the fresh air in my lungs felt like a privilege. It was a busy city, and I would pretend I lived there amongst ordinary people — people with families who had happy get-togethers, outings, regular meals, pets, loving relationships, fun and laughter in their lives — normal people. Yet, however bright the sun, I couldn't forget the fear and misery of my life, and it made no sense to me. I found myself watching people, asking myself if I could ever return to my expectation of 'normal' instead of living in the dark corridors of the city. I was always aware that the 'minders' were close by, and my next client could be anything but 'normal' — I knew I had to accept that.

In May, Uri informed me that I was having a change of job again and he introduced me to Silvia who was going to be with me in a new massage parlour that they had recently opened further along the same street.

"We'll see how you get on there," said Uri. "I think you need a change."

"I know nothing about massage," I wailed.

Silvia laughed. "You don't have to. Don't worry, it's not bad and the money is good. Our working rooms are better than this shit hole. We often get punters that only want a rub and a blowjob. And you get a uniform." She held up a tiny black plastic skirt and a white, scoop-necked silky tee shirt. "It'll suit you."

So, within days I became a masseuse. Silvia was right: generally, it was less dangerous than the themed rooms at the brothel or touting for business in the hotels and bars.

All through the summer — June, July and August — I massaged, kneaded, wanked, sucked and mostly avoided being penetrated. I took more and more tranquillisers, smoked more spliffs and every evening I drank enough alcohol to put me to sleep. Nonetheless, I didn't get any bad punters all through the summer. I was still tired, but I found it easier not to complain. I was earning more money than I had ever seen. I was reasonably well fed, I had a bed to sleep in at night and I had some extremely nice clothes.

I had also managed to wire some money back to Margo, but I sent no message. I didn't want anyone at home to know where I was or what I was doing.

Weeks passed, and as the summer came to an end, I knew that Uri would want to move me on again. I still occasionally worked in the club, and it was around September at lunchtime when the club was almost empty that I heard Uri talking to Carl Melnyk. He was a tall blond, overly tanned, but good-looking German who had turned up in the nightclub the night before. They were leaning on the bar, and I was collecting bottles to restock the upstairs fridge when I heard Uri say, "We don't like to keep the same merchandise for too long. They get to be known and we need new faces here for regulars, if you know what I mean. I've got some really good girls I want to sell on. Are you interested?"

"I am." I heard the German reply. He had an air of natural superiority, haughty almost, and he was obviously wealthy. He made a reference to how many girls he 'ran' and how much he was willing to pay for 'good merchandise'.

"Where are you heading?" asked Uri. I had never heard Uri be deferential to anybody, but there was definitely a note of submissiveness in his voice as he said, "May I ask where you are going to take the new stock?"

I dropped down behind the bar so that they couldn't see me and started to move away when I heard the German reply. "I've got quite a few places in Berlin, two in Brussels, Amsterdam, London and some in Scotland and Wales. I move the girls around. I am looking for new, interesting girls for the British market. Depends on how many good girls I can find on this trip, but I am willing to pay the best prices if you have anything special, Uri." He leaned forward and said quietly, "I have about a hundred thousand to spend on this trip. I want some Russians or Ukrainians, blondes preferably but I like a bit of swarthy myself. Any coloureds?"

I heard Uri take a breath as he said, "Yes, I've got a couple. Miriam's a good girl, not so young now, but does a good job. Customers like her but she has been here a while now. Got a nice tall blonde from Ukraine that you would like, a good girl. Used to be a wild cat, but not anymore. You should try her out yourself." said Uri.

I knew he was talking about me, as he had suggested that it was about time that he got rid of me a few weeks previously when I'd told him to piss off.

I went upstairs and told Tanya what I had heard.

"Yes, I know him. Carl Melnyk. Nasty bastard. Hope he doesn't buy us. He's bloody wealthy though, he's got places everywhere. But he's a mean bugger and a big man in this business. People are scared of him because he's got a vicious streak—he never makes empty threats. He does what he wants, when he wants, and he's got some influential friends as well as a team of thugs who do his bidding."

Ultimately, he bought us and before we knew it, Mija Belous (who I didn't know very well), Tanya, Miriam and I were in a private car on the long journey to Berlin. It took many days, and we slept in seedy hotels along the way.

When we arrived, I wondered if perhaps I might find my friend Anca from Vinnytsia there. I had never heard from her again, and I assumed that she too had been tricked into a life of prostitution. That was now over a year ago. There were also the girls I had travelled to Bucharest with,

Lilia, Natali and Yeva. Were we all prostitutes, making money for the evil bastards who treated us like animals?

CHAPTER 10

ELENA

I really didn't see much of Carl Melnyk, or Berlin for that matter, as we were kept hard at work and rarely went out. All through the autumn we worked in his biggest, smartest club, the aptly named 'Palace of Dreams'. I rarely had time off but earned quite a bit more than we had in Budapest, so I managed to send more money home to Margo.

The clients were different too. There were a lot of tourists, police and government officials, as well as the usual motley crowd of oversexed teenagers and the odd pervert. We catered for local businessmen (who were all there on the pretext of liking the lap dancing) after their corporative lunches or meetings.

There were so many girls working in and around Berlin who 'belonged' to Carl and there was a vast team of minders that kept us all in check. It wasn't unusual for us to see girls with bad cuts and bruises, burns and broken fingers—sometimes these were afflicted by our minders rather than our clients.

Carl was rarely seen at the club but, when he was there, everyone was on their toes.

All of us knew he wasn't a man to mess with. He always got what he wanted. He was clever, well-educated and ruthless. We'd heard many stories about how he dealt with misbehavers.

"Keep well clear if you can," advised Tanya, "If he takes a shine to someone, he's the kind who takes what he wants and hurts along the way. Stay below his radar if you possibly can. He's a very attractive bloke, so some girls fall for his charm and don't take the warning — they think he is going to take them to Hollywood or something."

It wasn't until early November that I had any dealings with Carl at all. I had noticed him come into the club early one evening to watch what was going on. I was on a podium, dancing to Kylie Minogue's hit 'Spinning Around' with a crowd of after-work drinkers — all fairly good-natured — and I was doing well; money was being stuffed into my sequined pants. Carl had spent several hours talking to the managers and the female supervisors (these were two older German madams; one was in charge of the front desk and the other worked with the girls at the bar—both women were always heroin-charged and I kept well away from them).

I had been warned not to cross Carl, but I'd had a long, boring night and I was so tired I could hardly walk. When he approached me, he indicated that I was to follow him. 'Destiny's Child' was thumping away in the background. My heart dropped into my aching feet. I turned and walked behind him into the hall. He had a private apartment on the floor above and he took my arm and guided me up the marble staircase. I was still wearing my skimpy dance outfit.

As he unlocked the door he turned and ran his eyes over me, from my feet to my head. It was a humiliating inspection, and I felt like a piece of meat—of course, that's all I was to him. I took a step back. "I've just finished a long shift Mister Melnyk. Please let me go to bed." I said, my heart bouncing in my chest.

"I have been watching you tonight." His accent was smooth and cultured. "You are a good dancer and a beautiful girl. I just want to talk to you."

We stood on the landing, and he leaned forward and caressed my cheek. His eyes looked kind and concerned. "I know you are tired but just give me a few minutes."

My body responded to this unexpected show of affection, and I half hated myself for it. I had been told how he could turn on the charm and I knew it was dangerous to allow myself to be seduced by it.

"I would like a little of your attention." He slowly ran his fingers down my neck and across the top of my breasts. "I am going to take you to London in a couple of days, so I would like to get to know you better." I knew what that meant. He took a firm grip of my arm and slowly moved me towards his apartment.

I hesitated. "Please let me go, I need to sleep." His grip only tightened, and he pushed me inside the room. He turned me toward him so that his face was inches away from mine. He lifted his hands to the sides of my face and smiled his sexy smile. "But I want to get to know you, Elena. You are coming with me. I want to know about you, whether I can trust you — I want to know that you are good enough." He moved his hands back behind my ears and with each, he took hold of a length of my hair and twisted it. My body shook visibly, as he said, "Just do as you are told. Now stand still and wait. When I tell you to do something you will do it." He released my hair and walked away from me. He picked up two whiskey glasses and poured a good measure in each. Smiling he offered me a glass. I took it. "Drink," he said, and I obeyed. I bloody well hated whiskey, but I drank it quickly and he did the same. He repeated this three times, and I knew that I was ready to collapse with alcohol and exhaustion, when he said. "Get on your knees, Elena." I obviously didn't obey him fast enough because in a single movement he crossed the room, ripped off my scanty top and took hold of my nipples and rotated them with his thumb and forefinger. He twisted and pinched and smiled.

Detach yourself, I could hear Miriam say, *allow yourself to go away to somewhere beautiful and calm.* I couldn't, he was bloody well hurting me.

"You are hurting me. Please…"

He let go of my nipples and held both my hands with one of his, the other he wrapped around my neck and pressed his thumb into my throat so that I could hardly breathe. Harder and harder he pressed, and I pushed and twisted with all my might, but Carl was strong. I choked to the point of near unconsciousness, but I could feel his excitement.

My heart was beating madly in my chest as he said. "Now Elena, do as I tell you. Be a good girl and get on your knees." His expression had darkened, and all traces of the sexy smile disappeared. He loosened his grip and with one hand he loosened his belt.

I knelt and wanted this to end as soon as possible, so I waited, hardly being able to swallow. I knew here was a man who loved to hurt and humiliate. Men like him don't like women, they only want to dominate and control them. He grabbed my hair and pulled my head back. I kept my eyes closed. His cock was so hard I could feel it pushing against my face. He kept tight hold of my hair and forced himself into my mouth. I started to panic as he pushed his cock deep into my throat. He was still holding the back of my head with both hands so I couldn't pull away. It is hard to describe the nauseating horror of this act of domination by a man against a woman. The fear, the gagging panic, the flashing lights as you nearly pass out through lack of oxygen and the total humiliation. As he finished, he pulled me to my feet, and I caught a glimpse of the look of pleasure that the power he had over me caused. I spat as hard as I could and landed what remained of his jism across his smug face. He laughed and wiped a hand across his mouth. "Elena, what a spirited little wild cat you are!"

As I lurched away from him, he grabbed me by the throat again. I started to choke and gasp for air. "Learn to do as you are told," he said quietly.

With all my strength I pushed him, and losing his grip, he fell back heavily against the wall. From then on everything seemed to happen in slow motion. He held me and kneed me in the stomach, he then punched me so hard across my head and chin that I collapsed onto the floor. I thought I swallowed blood and sweat poured off my head and body. I kept my eyes tight shut and lay still, praying that the pain in my ribs, my throat and my stomach would stop.

After a few minutes he came and picked me up and dragged me to his bed. Most of what happened next was done in a haze of pain. From his hip pocket he pulled small knife, which he held to my neck. "This is just a little reminder of me," he said as he flicked it across my throat.

He pulled off my dance pants and relieved himself again without a word. He left me where I was and for a while I couldn't move, aware only of the dribble of blood on my neck where the knife had made a small wound.

Eventually, I staggered naked back up to my room, coughing and spluttering, the amount of blood from the tiny nick on my neck had made it look a lot worse than it actually was. I took a big dose of painkillers, and something called Zopiclone to put me to sleep. I sobbed into my pillow until I finally dropped off. I wasn't sure how much I had slept because every time I moved the pain in my throat, head and stomach kept reminding me of what had happened.

The next morning, steeling myself, I swung my legs round and out of the bed. As my feet hit the floor, my head pounded and every muscle in my body throbbed with pain. I pushed my hair back and took a deep breath. The beating that I had received from the German had left its mark. I was bruised all over, and my throat and neck were so swollen and sore that I found it hard to swallow the tea that had been left beside me. It was almost cold, but as the liquid hit my throat it gave a little relief. I pulled on the thin robe that was lying on the floor and made my way into the sitting room where there were three other girls.

It was a dull, wet morning and the room was dimly lit. I could see that one girl was asleep on the couch, another was staring out of the barred window and the third was perched on the table — the third girl glanced at me, and then ignored me.

I went to make some coffee. I had a handful of painkillers and anti-inflammatories, so I threw them into my mouth. I stood and surveyed my surroundings as others came and went. Nearly all the girls were young and broken. The room smelt of despair and sex. I felt myself in a pit of sorrow.

Tanya came in, took one look at me at my bruised and tear-stained face, and led me to the sofa. She wrapped her arms around me as I started to cry again. "Another bad punter?" she asked.

"No, it was Carl," I croaked, "the bastard who calls himself our protector. Some fucking protector! He's the prick, who takes almost every penny we earn, and then fucks us himself. He said he is making sure I am good enough for his clientele."

"Fucking bastard." Tanya went to the sink, found a flannel, and soaked it under the tap. As she was squeezing it out, she said, "He's taking us to England tomorrow. There are six of us going." She nodded toward another door with a turn of her head. "One of the other girls is in there. Elsa Gottenburg. She arrived here last night. She's very young and only speaks German. Mija Belous, the small pretty blonde — the who looks much younger than eighteen — and Miriam are coming with us. There will also be one more."

"Who is the other one?" I asked.

She indicated the other door that led off the sitting room. "Don't know her. She's in there."

Tanya stroked the wet flannel across the nick on my neck and gently wiped my face and hands. She sat down and put an arm around me. She was a genuinely kind person, and I leaned my head on her shoulder as the tears cascaded down my cheeks.

"Surely if we get to England, the English police will protect us, and we could get out of this… get some help? That bastard could've killed me." I sobbed.

Tanya laughed out loud. "I don't reckon the police in England are any better than the rest of them, but let's hope to God that London is better than this slimy hole. Do you know we are going to be transported in a bulb and flower delivery waggon? I've just met the English driver who has come to collect us. Called Gareth Lombard. Another creep! And Carl is coming with us — to 'protect' us no doubt." Tanya scoffed.

CHAPTER 11

KATE—NOVEMBER 2010

Jackson had disappeared almost without a backward glance, and I didn't really miss him. He had informed me of his address, as well as his intention of getting a divorce as soon as possible. I thought that I would've had regrets, or that I would've had trouble getting over the feeling of abandonment, but in fact I felt fine. I realised that my marriage to Jackson was what I had needed at that point in my life. It wasn't by any means bad, but it just wasn't good. I accepted that we both had purely selfish reasons for being together, but that the time had come to an end for us. The fact that there was no possibility of having a fight about the house or access, custody and child support made me feel that there had never really been a marriage at all. It made little difference to my life, except that I was now completely responsible for the household bills, and I had to get the bus to work—even so, I liked buses!

I also resolved to revert to my given surname, so that the baby would be mine and mine alone.

At work people were kind, and I suppose that because I was glad to get back to my job as normal—as well as the fact that I wasn't sobbing into my tea—nobody had much to say. Some were surprised, and a few probably considered me a bit cold. Mr Howard Kendrikson, however, was concerned when he found out that I was pregnant. He insisted that I sat down more than before and that I took regular pee-breaks.

"My wife had terrible bladder problems when she was pregnant. Couldn't go anywhere unless there was a toilet handy," he confided with a wink.

"Thank you." I *was* grateful because, I found as I grew larger, my bladder did seem to get smaller.

"Will you come back to us after the baby is born?" he asked me kindly.

"Of course, as soon as I can make arrangements, I'll be back. I'm on my own now and have bills to pay, besides, I love my job." I was sure it would be that easy.

As time passed, I found myself holding my stomach more often, and as the funny little bubbling feelings turned into someone playing football in my belly, I flushed with excitement at the thought of this new life that I was growing. My breasts felt heavy and sensuous and I visualised myself with a downy haired baby, sitting in a rocking chair as it suckles at my breasts.

By the time I had my first scan I was already irrevocably attached to the little being that had invaded my body. I had surprised myself with my growing joy at the thought of being a mother. I felt well after the first couple of months, and although I tired easily, I still continued with my job as before.

Mollie and her husband Bill were horrified that I was on my own and went out of their way to look after me. Bill mowed my little lawn and saw to my bins when he was home, and Mollie drove me to work quite often as I'd found the bus journey straining in the preceding months - she always managed to find an excuse to go into town.

We both laughed when she said, "I always knew Jackson was too self-centred to have a family. Body overdeveloped at the expense of his common sense."

"I know Mollie, but we had agreed not to have any children. I did know that, but I didn't expect him to leave me — I'd hoped that he might change his mind. I don't even know whether I should tell his family that I am pregnant. What do you think?"

"Kate, wait awhile and see if Jackson has a change of mind when the baby is born." Mollie advised. "Don't you... mind him not being here?"

"No, strangely I don't. I've spent so much of my life on my own, no family, no ties and now I'm ready... He won't come back, you know... but I will have someone of my very own to look after and love."

All in all, I had an easy pregnancy, but I was still desperate for it to end. I felt huge and invaded. Feeling the kicking of the tiny vengeful little feet as they pummelled my insides, I was only briefly afraid. There would soon be a baby person, a tiny thing with endless needs. It should be a shared experience I thought, but I had already resigned myself to coping on my own.

I was relieved when I left work on December first, precisely two weeks before Thomas was born.

I took myself to hospital by taxi at the first sign of labour pains. As I clamped my teeth together in the taxi, holding my breath and trying not to cry, I noticed that the taxi driver increased his speed when he noticed me clenching and holding my enormous belly.

Mollie would be furious, I thought. She had made noises about being with me, but I really thought it was something I should do on my own. I wasn't being brave — I was afraid that I wouldn't be strong, and I wanted this experience, good or bad, to be mine and mine alone. After all I was used to being on my own.

I had my baby within four hours of arriving — a lovely little boy! Absolutely perfect too. An 'easy, happy birth', I recall the midwife telling me.

The baby's cries rose as the cord was cut and he was quickly wrapped and placed in my arms. His face was red and furious, and he was yelling heartily at being thrust into the world from the warmth and comfort of my womb. I could only stare in wonder at the little being, the pain forgotten, swept away in the giddying rush of tenderness that swept through me. I marvelled at the tiny, perfect little body and held him close. From the moment I pressed my mouth against my baby's dark little head, I adored him.

When I got back to Harlow Crescent, my divorce papers had arrived, and just for a moment I was saddened that Jackson wouldn't meet his beautiful son. Nevertheless, a new era of my life was beginning, and I was happy.

CHAPTER 12

ELENA - November 2010

We were told to pack one small case and get ready for the journey early in the morning. It was cold and wet when we left 'The Palace of Dreams', and clutching a bottle of water and a packet of sandwiches each, we six: myself, Tanya, Mija, Miriam, little German Elsa (who couldn't have been more than fifteen), and a beautiful young black girl called Calaso who had been brought in from Belgrade. We were herded towards a truck waiting in a side street. Painted in a bold red scroll on the side of the big white Daihatsu Hijet Jiffy Catering Truck were the words: *'Floral Days'. Florist Network, Belgium – Fast deliveries to your door – Guaranteed quality bulbs and flowers.* The van was decorated with pictures of huge tulips, daffodils and hyacinths.

The driver, Gareth Lombard, looked us over and warned us that it would be a long, boring drive. He said that we would have to do as we were told, be quiet and that we would not be let out until we reached our destination – although we would have one stop in Brussels for the toilet.

He was a nasty looking, pale-faced individual with a strange accent and he pushed us in like animals. We had each brought with us a small case, which basically held a bit of underwear, clothes and our make-up. I also had a spare purse with all my savings in and the pretty negligee that Aunty Veronyka had bought me in Bucharest. The cases acted as our seats, and we were packed up hard against the cabin of the truck. We were surrounded by big, heavy boxes and had little space to move. I was still in pain, and I hurt all over from my beating from Carl. The concertinaed doors were slammed shut and locked.

Tanya and I clung together. We had no idea how long we had been travelling and were all in different ways broken and frightened. Each of us had been warned that there would be consequences for our family and loved ones if we didn't do as we were told. We knew that we had left Germany in the early hours of the morning; after some time, we got out of the truck in Brussels to go to the toilet, before getting straight back in. Miriam had a watch, which told us that we had left Belgium at 4pm—it was now 11pm, so we reckoned that we had been locked up for about nineteen hours.

All we'd had was a bottle of water and a packet of sandwiches each (which we'd eaten when we set off); we'd eaten no other food all day. It was freezing cold in the truck, and even though we all had thick puffer coats and warm boots we were shivering. We were tired, exhausted and dehydrated, so we packed ourselves together like sardines to keep warm. We'd crossed the English Channel on a ferry and little Elsa had been sick on the floor in front of us; the smell of vomit and the overpowering, oniony smell of the bulbs was so awful it made me retch.

"We must be on a motorway," muttered Tanya, "we are travelling so fast. Does anyone know where the fuck we are going?"

We all thought we were going to London but when we were in Brussels, Mija had heard the Englishman say that they were going to drive west from the capital; she didn't hear any more however, so our destination remained unknown.

The sound of the crash was enormous. Suddenly we were thrown back, then across the small space of our confinement — the truck had tipped sideways and careered onto the tarmac. I felt myself and Tanya fall backwards, and we hit the truck's cabin. Elsa and Mija were screaming loudly as they landed on the floor. I couldn't see Calaso or Miriam at all.

There was another series of jolts and the big cartons that had been placed at the back of the truck hit the rear door. They were full of spring bulbs and the earthy, onion smell was nauseating as they crashed and split.

I felt my head hit the roof of the vehicle as it bounced and rolled, then one final crash back onto the road caused the side of the truck to cave in towards us as the door at the rear buckled. Suddenly the end of the truck split apart and released several of the big boxes that had obscured the back door out onto the road, creating a gap. The space was just big enough to escape from. I couldn't see where my case of belongings had ended up, so without a second thought, I pushed past the boxes and the scattered bulbs and squeezed my body through the concertinaed panels that the crash had created.

I had no idea where I was, only that the truck that we were travelling in had crossed the English Channel and was now somewhere in England.

Having jumped out of the back of the truck, I landed heavily on a wide, tarmacked road amongst the debris of plants, bulbs and boxes.

My head was spinning as I pushed myself away from the vehicle. The road was wide, and traffic zoomed along the other side of the motorway. The front of our vehicle was crushed and the lorry in front had jack-knifed across the road, blocking it completely.

As I was about to run across the road toward the wide bank, another vehicle flew past and crashed into the front of the lorry.

Gathering all my strength I immediately turned, ran in the opposite direction, jumped across the central barrier and, avoiding the speeding traffic, I ran across, eventually falling headlong into a muddy ditch. I saw that at least two of the other girls had jumped clear behind me and were running away from the crash in the other direction. I could just see the back of Tanya's dark hair and pale green anorak as she headed off in a different direction. I was pleased that my deep blue coat was less visible in the dark.

There was just enough light to see that our truck had run headlong into the back of the lorry, and the front of the cab was completely crushed. There was another vehicle, a white car, which looked as if it had caused the pile up, squashed almost flat under the lorry and it was obvious that at least three other vehicles were involved.

I waited no longer. I knew that the scene would be covered with police and ambulances within minutes, which would lead to my discovery. Turning away from the road I could see a ploughed field with an area of forest across the other side. I decided that it was probably the best bet. I needed to find a place to hide, so I ran as fast as my stiff legs would carry me. I ran across the field, through the dark woods and a stretch of farmland onto a narrow country road. I ran for about another hour, with no idea where I was heading. I was cold and shaking, my legs burning with pain, and my hands and face were covered with mud – only blind fear pushed me on. I was terrified, although of what I wasn't sure.

Keeping to the shadows, I made my way through a village. I passed a few shops and a petrol station before I eventually found a sign: 'A432 Chipping Sodbury and Bristol'.

The small wound on the top of my head throbbed and my legs hurt, but I kept going to get as far away as possible; nonetheless, soon I was so tired that I had to stop. I halted for a short breather in a bus shelter before setting off again toward the town. I passed more fields and small areas of woodland, housing estates, factories and roadside inns. Traffic zoomed past all the while, and I was tempted to beg a ride; I decided against it in case I was being pursued (even though it seemed unlikely, as I must have been far away from the crash). I had no idea where I was, and I thought that I had run due west the whole time. My fear of the unknown had made me run, although I had little idea of what or whom I was running from, but every step brought me closer to gaining more control of my life.

Eventually I came across a small park, where the paths were surrounded with trees and shrubs, and it looked like a good place to stop for a while. At the far end there were public toilets, but upon investigation I soon realised that they were all thoroughly locked up. Fortunately, the men's toilet had a window with a broken lock, and after a tussle with the rusty catch, I climbed inside. In the dark, I relieved myself and washed the majority of the mud from my hands and face using bunches of toilet paper. The place was cold and stank of urine, but I found a large sheet of plastic in a cupboard and decided to go back outdoors and find a place to hide, so that I could rest for a while.

I was exhausted and frightened, but I was free, and no one would be stripping me and abusing me that night. I wondered briefly what had happened at the scene of the crash. Had any of the other girls managed to escape? Were the men that had bought me still alive? If so, would they, or others, be searching for me?

I had no plan, only a few euros and a packet of tissues in my pockets—even worse, I had no clothes other than the coat I was wearing, a small woolly hat and a pair of gloves. I had absolutely no idea what would happen to me, but what could be worse than what I had already endured? The terrible gut-wrenching fear had vanished, leaving me weak and shaky, as though I had just stepped off a roller coaster. A memory briefly surfaced of the day in Gorky Park with Sasha. How could I have been so stupid to put my trust in him?

I was hungry, not having eaten since the previous morning.

It was already the early hours of the day when I wrapped the plastic tightly around myself and eventually fell asleep tucked under a large rhododendron bush, well hidden from the path.

I woke less than an hour later, stiff and hungry. It was still dark, but I was so cold that I needed to move, so I left my hiding place and jogged along the vacant footpaths towards the village. Lights flickered and went off along the streets; other than an occasional early morning dog walker there were few people about.

At the far end of the street, I found a completely deserted supermarket. As casually as I could manage, I wandered through the car park to the back of the store, knowing there were often bins laden full of discarded food — I was right. I even found a large, linen bag with the supermarket logo on it. After a quick rummage, I found that there was little in the bin that morning, but eventually I found a couple of apples, a piece of cheese and a pork pie — it was all out of date, but I knew from experience how to sniff out anything that wasn't suitable to eat. Amongst my findings there was a bruised melon and a packet of broken shortcake biscuits — breakfast!

Throwing the whole lot into the linen bag, I jogged back along the street to the park where I had spent the night. Despite the early hour, the fresh breeze made me feel free. As the pale, wintry sun rose, I could see that there were benches along the paths and a small duck pond in the distance. The park was deserted, and I realised how beautiful my surroundings were. Golden leaves covered the pathways and the early morning frost made everything look clean and bright. As the sun rose the frost began to disappear leaving a glistening landscape. What a perfect place to stop and eat. I sat on a bench and ate the pork pie and a piece of cheese. The melon had proved a bit of a challenge, as I had no utensils, but eventually I managed to pull off part of the skin and the over ripe fruit sated my thirst. The shortbread biscuits tasted stale and mouldy, so I crumbled them up intending to feed them to the birds.

I was totally exhausted, so I returned to the bush where I had left the plastic sheet. With my hunger sated, I fell asleep again within minutes, waking an hour later to the sound of heavy daytime traffic.

I rose quickly and looked around, but I could see no one; nonetheless, I soon became aware of a voice somewhere fairly close by. Pushing myself slowly out of the foliage, I pulled my hair back into a tidy tail. The cut on my head had stopped bleeding and was forming a scab, so I coiled my hair over the wound, straightened my clothes and wrapped my scarf to hide the small cut and the bruises on my neck. I pushed the polythene back under the bush in case I needed it again and crept forward toward the park bench. A tiny wizened old lady in a fur coat and red woolly hat occupied the seat by the path. She was feeding the pigeons and chatting happily to them. I found I could understand her words quite well.

"Come on, little one... No, buster, give the others a chance... you are a very greedy boy." She made a small clucking noise. "Are you a boy? Perhaps you're not a boy but you look like a boy. Behave now."

Fascinated, I approached slowly — the old lady turned and beamed as if she recognised me. "Hello dear, I do like to make sure the little ones get some too." She threw another handful of crumbs and turned toward me.

I reached into my bag for the shortbread biscuit crumbs and began to throw them for the birds. The old lady smiled her approval.

"Did you want a sandwich? We've plenty here." She indicated the plastic box on her lap. "We always make too many. Here take one… these are the egg ones, and these are the cheese."

"Thank you ver' much," I said as I perched on the bench next to the old lady. "May I 'ave the egg?"

"Whichever you like my dear, give the birds the crusts, and then we'll go home and get a nice cup of tea. I've got your favourite, Earl Grey. I know how you like it."

"I don't know you, do I?" I inquired as I munched gratefully on the sandwich. It was delicious and better than anything I'd had since leaving Nikki at the café. "Vat shall I call you?"

"It's Peggy, dear. Of course, you know me. You've been looking after me for… how long… must be nearly a year."

"Have I?" I gazed into the rheumy blue eyes, and said, "I think it's time to go home then, Peggy, don't you?"

"Yes dear. I need my medication and today the window cleaner is coming."

I found myself wondering if this was the best stroke of luck ever. This delightful old lady really thought that I was someone else, someone she knew well enough to take her home. My only thought was that if I went home with this woman, I could get warm and have a shower — besides, it would give me time to plan what to do next.

Peggy led me across the park to a three-storied house in a leafy avenue, and she chatted brightly all the way, talking of people that I obviously didn't know. She even mentioned that today was fish and chip day, and that nice Mister Braithwaite always brought them to the door for her.

"If you warm the plates and do the bread and butter at 5 o'clock we will be ready for him. We will have soup for lunch though, as Daphne Jones brought a big pot full round two days ago and it needs finishing up."

"Lovely, Peggy," I said, thinking that this delightful old lady had no idea that I was a stranger and was quite happy for me to accompany her home. As we entered the front door, I was aware that it had been left open, and that the hat stand was overloaded with a multitude of coats, scarves, hats and umbrellas. On the floor lay an assortment of footwear, bags and socks, all rather dusty. Amongst the bags was a backpack that had seen better days, but I thought it might be just what I needed.

"You haven't locked your door, Peggy," I told the old lady as I pushed the front door closed and dropped the mortise lock. "You really shouldn't leave it open; someone might come in and steal from you."

Peggy seemed not to hear me, and I followed her through the hall into a large kitchen that looked out onto an enormous, overgrown back garden. No one else appeared to be in the house.

"Pop the kettle on, dear," Peggy said as she deposited her scarf and bag onto a table that was already covered with an assortment of dishes, a bag of knitting wool and old magazines, letters and newspapers. "Sorry, my dear I can't remember your name. I do get forgetful about names. Always remember in the end…Are you Kathy or Hannah?"

I hesitated only a moment and said, "No Peggy. It's Margo, my name is Margo." I wasn't feeling confident enough to tell Peggy my real name and had no idea how long I could hang on to the pretence of being someone that Peggy knew. I boiled the kettle and found the sugar and tea bags in the cupboard above the worktop. Looking around to find the fridge I saw that Peggy had already produced a jug full of milk from what looked like a walk-in pantry.

"Margo, shall you read to me a bit after we've had our tea? I liked the one you started last time," said Peggy.

"Vich one vas that?" I asked not sure whether my knowledge of English was good enough to read aloud.

"The one about the girls in the convent, Spanish author, I think. We'll find it in the sitting room." Peggy had already taken her tea and was sitting at the kitchen table pushing the papers and magazines aside. "I think some of these can go in the recycling Melody…"

"Margo. It's Margo. Do you vant me to sort them or take them all, Peggy"?

"Yes, dear take them all out. We need to tidy up a bit." She gazed distractedly around. "I'm not sure where they all come from. I thought I'd cancelled all the papers last year."

"Do you vant me to check for you? Tell me the place they come from and tomorrow I vill get them stopped for you."

"Good girl. You can go to the butchers too and tell him I don't want any more meat from him—I didn't like what he sent last time."

I smiled and began to relax as Peggy chatted on. My leg muscles hurt from running and my back ached from the rough nights and the journey in the truck. The cut on my head was sore from the accident and my headache had become worse as the day wore on. All I could think was that I felt safe for the first time in over a year—it was such a relief.

After a bowl of homemade soup, I built a fire in the sitting room from logs collected from the outside shed, and then attempted to read to Peggy. Before long we were both fast asleep. Peggy told me that she had risen early, and it was an afternoon ritual to have a nap after lunch. With the warmth of the fire and the sheer exhaustion of the previous days I too found myself asleep within minutes.

At five o'clock we ate the delicious fish and chips that had been duly delivered by Mister Braithwaite. There were two portions and apparently that was the regular delivery. I had kept out of the way and hidden in the pantry so as not to be seen by the said Mister Braithwaite, even though Peggy had asked me to answer the door when the food arrived. I started to relax and found that Peggy was not only delightful company, but that she was generous and kind.

Later that evening, after watching television for a couple of hours, I helped Peggy up the stairs to the first floor and got her undressed and ready for bed. I found Peggy's bathroom and encouraged her to have a wash and brush out her hair. I felt a wave of affection for the old lady.

"Peggy can I ask something of you," I said as I helped Peggy into her nightgown.

"Yes, dear. What is it you want to know?"

"Do you 'ave a family?"

Peggy paused to consider. "I think I do."

"Do you know vere they are?"

"No dear I don't."

"Do they come and see you?"

"Who?" Peggy asked as she lifted herself slowly onto the high old-fashioned bed.

"Your family."

"I never married."

I had tidied some of Peggy's post when we had our tea and had noticed that all her letters and bills were addressed to a Mrs E. Grimshaw.

"Are you sure Peggy?"

"You are my only daughter left now. Melody?"

"I am Margo… But never mind… I vill see you in the morning Peggy. Sleep vell."

Here I am, I thought, *in this beautiful but slightly neglected old house with a delightful woman who now thinks that I am her daughter rather than her regular carer.* After the nightmare of the last year, I found my tears close to the surface and I wanted to tell Peggy how grateful I was. However, all I did was carefully close the bedroom door, and whisper, "See you in the morning, lovely Peggy."

CHAPTER 13

ELENA

Now that Peggy was in bed, I was free to explore the rest of the house.

I went down to the kitchen, locked all the doors, washed the dishes and cleared the kitchen table. I cleaned all the worktops, the cooker and the kettle and laid the table for breakfast.

Eventually I discovered a room on the top floor that had a made-up bed as well as a wardrobe that had a selection of female clothes in it. They obviously belonged to the live-in carer but someone a lot shorter than I, so there was very little that would fit me comfortably. However, I did find some clean underwear and socks, a couple of sweaters and some toiletries.

Across the landing there was a large bathroom, so I ran myself a bath. Finding soap, towels and a bottle of bubble bath I carefully slid my sore body into the luxurious water. I wallowed in the sheer comfort and safety of being there, savouring the soothing sensation of the warm water on my skin. Back home in Ukraine, hot water was a luxury and during the past two years I'd had to make do with endless quick showers in tepid water between clients.

I tried not to think of the horror of the past few months but, as I washed and soaked my body, I realised how much evidence of the cruelty that I had suffered was visible from the scarring and bruising on my body. My right hip and buttock had cigarette burns and bruises. There was a scar on my forehead and one under my eye. The nick on my neck had an ugly scab and my ribs, stomach and throat were covered with bruises from the disgusting bastard that had almost strangled me in Berlin.

I lowered myself deep into the water and carefully shampooed my sore head. I found myself wondering about Margo and Uncle Gregor and if they were worried that they hadn't heard from me. My brothers would certainly be concerned, as I had promised to send them money as soon as I was settled in London. It was now over a year since I had left Vinnytsia. I wondered too about Tanya and Mija.

I stretched out and turned on the hot tap with my toe, reviving the tepid water. My mind was drifting so I tried to focus on a plan. I knew I would soon be discovered if I stayed in Peggy's house. *I think I will have to leave very soon. Someone is bound to come tomorrow, but where shall I go?*

My skin looked taut and stretched and I had dark rings under my eyes. The long hours of seediness, the drugs, the sadness and the late nights had taken their toll, but I felt so much better. I found a pair of pyjamas and a soft blue bathrobe hanging on the bathroom door — as I gazed at my reflection, I wondered how long I could stay in this cocoon of peace and comfort.

I made up my mind.

Just for tonight I will stay in Peggy's house and enjoy the peace. I was in a comfortable room, clean, well fed and safe. Peggy had no idea who I was or where I had come from, but I knew I couldn't stay there for long. So far, we'd not had any visitors other than Mister Braithwaite with the fish and chips, but Peggy must get regular callers and she had neighbours. She was old and was obviously well looked after.

Waking the following morning I couldn't believe my luck. I had slept soundly and felt relaxed and refreshed for the first time since leaving Ukraine.

Peggy had risen early too and was dressed in a colourful combination of clothes: thick red tights with a grey skirt, a blue and orange fair-isle knit jumper, all topped off with a large red silk scarf around her neck. Her wispy white hair was coiled into a bun on the top of her head. She was looking at the newly cleaned kettle when I went down into the kitchen

"Look at this dear. We have a new kettle." She was smiling happily.

"Shall I make the breakfast, Peggy?"

"Yes, that would be nice, dear."

"Shall I see to the newsagents and butchers today?" I asked her as I prepared boiled eggs and toast for our breakfast.

Peggy seemed distracted as she moved about the kitchen, pushing things around the worktop and opening and closing the cupboards.

"Do you need somesing, Peggy?"

"I do. I have some medicine..."

I found her bag of pills on the floor in the pantry and carefully read the instructions before I would let Peggy have them.

Later with directions and money in my pocket I went to the local shops. I found that Mrs E. Grimshaw was indeed Peggy's name, so I cancelled the papers and magazines, and paid the outstanding bills with the money she had given me. Only the newsagent commented on the fact that mine was a different face to whom he was used to.

"Hannah on holiday, is she?" he asked and before he could say more.

"Short break. I am filling in for her," I replied.

So, Hannah was Peggy's regular carer. Where was she?

As instructed, I bought Peggy her favourite mints. Just as I took the change and was about to leave the shop the local papers were being delivered. They plopped down beside my feet and I caught sight of the headlines, *'Local pileup kills three people'*. My heart banged in my chest. Who had died? I picked up the top copy. "I vill take this please." I handed the money to the newsagent, and as soon as I got out of the shop, I opened the paper to read about the accident. On page three there was a photograph taken at the scene of the crash, but it was dark and therefore difficult to identify each individual vehicle. Next to the photo of the crash were Tanya's, Mija's and my own passport photographs. I hadn't seen my passport since Aunty Veronika had taken it from me on the ferryboat in Constanta.

I read quickly:

'On the westbound M4 road into Bristol last night, just a few miles outside Dyrham, three people were killed in pileup of with a delivery truck, several cars and a lorry. Three other cars were involved, one of which was overturned between the vehicles. The English driver of the delivery truck is still in a serious condition. The German co-driver however was pronounced dead at the scene. Another woman from the accident died an hour after being admitted to Bristol Royal Infirmary. Her relatives have yet to be informed. Police are looking for three girls who are said to have left the scene of the crash and who were travelling in the delivery truck: Tanya Moro and Mija Belous from Moldova and Elena Shevchenko from Ukraine. They are asked to come forward and report to the police immediately.

So, Carl Melnyk was dead, and the Englishman badly hurt. What of the other girls I wondered? Was the dead woman one of them? Had Tanya and Mija managed to get away?

The newsagent was picking up the bundle of papers and was about to display them on his counter. I realised that the second he saw that article and photos he would know who he had just served. I found myself trembling and my knees felt that they would give way, but I started to run back to the relative safety of Peggy's house. *They know who I am and are looking for me. The newsagent knew Peggy and her regular carer, so it wouldn't take long.*

As soon as I arrived back at Peggy's house, I decided that I would have to leave straight away. Entering the front door, which Peggy had left open for my return, I grabbed the dusty rucksack and rushed up the stairs shouting to Peggy that I had returned.

Over the next hour, I packed the backpack with things I thought that Peggy wouldn't miss and would be useful: a plastic cup with a lid, a sharp knife, a pair of scissors, candles and a torch with extra batteries, a box of matches, a toilet roll and a packet of tissues, two towels, a flannel and enough underwear and sweaters to see me through a couple of weeks. I found a cheap watch with a broken strap and tucked it carefully in my pocket. I had no idea where I had lost my own watch, but it had disappeared during my stay in Berlin. Unfortunately, the trousers and shoes were too small for me, but I liked the thick blue bathrobe and stuffed it into the bag. From the bathroom cabinet I took aspirin, cough medicine, a sewing kit, plasters, diazepam, some antibiotics and some anti-inflammatory tablets.

I undid my hair, pulled my long blonde plait over my shoulder and made a decision; if I were going to get away undiscovered, I would do better by changing my appearance. It wouldn't be difficult to pass as a young boy if I cut my hair really short. My breasts were small and my hips straight. I could get a job, stay off the drink and drugs and make a new life somewhere else.

I found some scissors in the dressing table drawer and lobbed off as much of my hair as I could. I folded it into a plastic bag and stuffed it into the rucksack. *Mmm not bad,* I thought. I really did look like a boy! Quickly checking around, I carefully pulled the bedding back into place, and raced down the stairs. I grabbed a thick, dark woollen hat, a baseball cap and a scarf from the hat stand as I passed. I jammed the woolly hat onto my head and the scarf around my neck and chin. I tucked the baseball cap into the rucksack. I couldn't see or hear Peggy but sent her a silent 'thank you' as I pulled the front door closed behind me. I hoisted the full rucksack onto my back and set off at a brisk walk. I still had two twenty-pound notes and some change in my pocket that Peggy had handed me for the shopping, and I knew that she wouldn't even remember giving it to me.

CHAPTER 14

Less than an hour later, Melody, one of Peggy's daughters, arrived with a large bag of shopping and was pleased to see that the front door was firmly closed. So often she arrived to find it open. She only lived two streets away and called on her mother regularly. She had her own key so carefully opened the door whilst calling to her mother. "Ma, where are you? I've brought you some fruit and veg from the market."

Peggy appeared from the kitchen drying her hands. "Hello dear, how nice to see you for a change."

"I've been every day while Hannah has been away. Missed you yesterday though. I guessed you had gone to the park, but I couldn't hang about, as I had to pick George up from the airport. Everything all right?"

"Of course, dear. My life is splendid."

"Has Peter been?"

"Peter who?" asked Peggy.

"Your son, my brother Peter. Only I noticed when I came in that his rucksack, cap and scarf were missing. Has he been?"

"No, I don't think so."

Melody knew that it was probably impossible to expect her mother to remember and although her dementia had accelerated slowly lately, she was still doing well living on her own. She just hoped that Hannah, Peggy's regular live-in carer would be back soon.

"Have you had some breakfast today, Ma?" she asked as she was putting the vegetables into the pantry.

"Oh yes," said Peggy, "and it was very nice too. Margo cooked the eggs to perfection."

"Margo?"

"Yes dear. She's gone shopping for me."

"Oh, right."

Just as Melody was stacking the fruit bowl and about to continue with her questions, there was a knock on the door. A tall, smiley, policemen who introduced himself as Constable Dean Moore of the Bristol police and wondered if he could ask Mrs E. Grimshaw some questions.

Melody showed him into the hall. "You do know that my mother has dementia and is often very confused. What is it you need to ask her?"

"I will be very brief, but we think she might have some information about someone we are looking for."

"I very much doubt it. Be warned, any info my Mum gives could relate to her childhood, an old love, my long dead heroic father or the local vicar. They have all been confused at some time or another."

"Ah," said constable Dean Moore, new to the job and not sure what his procedure should be. "I have a photograph that I would like to show her."

Melody led him through to the kitchen. "Constable Moore has a photograph he would like you to look at Mum."

"Good. Would he like a cup of tea?"

"Thank you, no. Do you recognise this girl, Mrs Grimshaw?" He pushed a copy of the passport photo of Elena across the table.

"That's Margo."

"Where is she now?"

"Left last week, didn't she Mel?"

Melody watched her mother carefully as she lifted the teapot and poured quite a bit of the tea into the saucer. Taking the teapot from Peggy's hand she said, "I think you are thinking of Hannah, Mum. She went home to Ireland because her father was ill. Remember? She will be back tomorrow."

"Ok, that's good then. Was there anything else?" Peggy picked up her cup of tea and carefully tipped the tea from the saucer into her cup and wandered off.

"Who is Margo?" the constable asked Melody.

"No idea." Melody replied laughing. "Just a figment of Ma's imagination, I guess."

CHAPTER 15

ELENA

Over the next hour I put as much distance as I could between myself and Peggy's, wondering all the while from what and whom I was running. I had heard so many stories in the past year of corrupt police and officials that I was more afraid of turning to them for help than being caught by the German who had bought me. I had no ID, visa or passport, so I would be treated as an illegal immigrant. Were the British police as corrupt as those in the Eastern countries? Would the police lock me up or protect me or send me home? Would they expect me to tell them about the people involved in the trafficking, the prostitution, the beatings and the threats? If they did, what would be the consequences back in the Ukraine? Would my traffickers send someone to beat up or kill Margo as they had constantly threatened? Carl had even told me that they would kill good, kind Uncle Gregor and his family if I ever spoke to anyone about them.

I was terrified by my circumstances. I stumbled blindly on, caught up in shreds of doubt like cobwebs in my brain, with no idea which way to turn or where I could get help.

The next few days and nights I kept moving and eventually became aware that I was in a big city called Bristol. It was relatively easy to stay unseen during the day, as there were so many people about doing their Christmas shopping. Decorations were being strung across the streets and huge Christmas trees had been erected everywhere. With the money that I had from Peggy, I bought a good meal for the first four days. At night I usually managed to find an outside garden shed or covered patio where I wrapped myself in Hannah's fluffy robe and slept as best I could. In the evenings, I looked for a busy pub where I could lose myself in the crowds of people. The best ones were where there was music and sometimes people would get up and dance. I managed to purloin several drinks and packets of crisps, chips or nuts.

One day, I found myself in a part of Bristol that was new to me. There was a building in the process of being built behind a shopping mall called the 'Galleries', and I wandered around to the back of the scaffolding and discovered that I could get undercover there. That night I slept under a big tarpaulin that was part of the half-built building. Further along inside, there were already some shops filled with stock.

The following morning, I had to get out fairly quickly, as some of the shops were being opened, and the workmen arrived at the back to continue work on the extension to the shopping arcade. The next two nights I slept outside in an alley with another homeless man who was so drunk that I was quite sure he was no threat to me. He thought I was a boy, so almost completely ignored me, even though I tucked myself next to him and his big woolly blanket.

"Got any spliffs, mate?" was all he said, took a swig from a bottle that he kept close to his chest, closed his eyes and fell asleep again.

One day clicked over to the next and before long I realised that I had been on the run for nearly two weeks. I was filthy, cold and hungry all the time. Not once did I contemplate the future, I just continued from hour to hour, day to day thinking about being warm, fed and safe—although I knew this was unlikely unless I found some help. The strange thing about misery is how it expands to take over every thought and feeling, until you have nothing left but the next moment. Regardless, things change from day to day and the next night it was snowing and freezing cold. I found myself amongst another group of homeless men and women who had a brazier burning. I settled myself against a wall as close to the fire as I could manage. No one spoke. They were all immersed in their own misery. At three o'clock in the morning a fight broke out between two of the homeless men, both had been drinking since early evening. They rolled around in the slushy black snow, punching and kicking, blood splattering and forming pale pink puddles in the dark road. A few late-nighters full of drink themselves, gathered shouting and jeering. It quickly turned into a free for all. I hoisted my rucksack on my back and legged it as far away from them as possible as I heard the wail of the police sirens. I was trembling and cold, and I knew with certainty that I couldn't go on living on the streets all winter. Perhaps I should go to the police after all, and make up some sort of story, without telling the truth about how I had come to be living on the streets of Bristol. But hard as I tried, I couldn't think of any explanation.

It was the next day that I started to feel ill. I stole a pie from a supermarket but found I couldn't eat it. My throat was so sore, and I was trembling with fever. I needed a drink, so I abandoned the pie and took a bottle of vodka from the shelf of a posh delicatessen and stuffed it into my rucksack. I had been sick most of the previous night and now felt as if I had some sort of infection. My body was hot and sweating and my nose running. I looked and felt filthy.

I had three pounds left in my pocket, so I made my way to the nearest coffee bar, took the antibiotics that I had taken from Peggy's and decided it was time to make a decision about what I was going to do.

I eventually staggered into a churchyard where I found a group of homeless men and women. Nobody took much notice of me so I found a space against a wall and wrapped myself up as best I could, opened the bottle of vodka and drank half of it straight down. I slept for a while, but the weather was really bad, and it had started to snow again. A soup wagon came, and I lined up with the others, got a bowl of hot soup and a lump of bread. Eventually, as the weather worsened, a group of people from the Salvation Army came along and took us all (me, three men and two women) to a hostel called 'Logo House' for the night. I hadn't even given a thought about not going with them, as I felt so ill. I hoisted the rucksack onto my back and followed them. I was by now not only exhausted but hung over.

At the hostel I had a shower and was shown to a bed with all the other males. Despite the snores and snorts, I had a good sleep, but the next day the warden asked me questions that I couldn't answer.

"I have to keep records, lad," he said. "You can stay here for a bit if you need help, but I have to know who you are and why you are on the streets by yourself."

"I am on my vay to Scotland," I said blindly trying to think of some excuse, "just run out of money tha's all."

It was obvious that he didn't believe me as he laughed. "You've a long way to go then, me boy. I will have to make a report."

I told him a few lies and, totally unconvinced, he said, "Okay, stay a couple of nights."

As I hadn't had a decent meal since Peggy's money ran out, I stayed for lunch. There was quite a friendly atmosphere, but I tried not to talk to anyone. Most of the men had several days or weeks of growth on their faces and I had not a whisker. I had already been touched up a few times by a couple of the men, and I began to wonder whether I was in as much danger looking like a fresh-faced young boy as I would have been as a girl.

The food was good, some sort of stew that was hot and spicy and I began to feel a bit better. I slept there for one more night but didn't feel that I could stay any longer as I was sure someone would clock that I was a girl and not a boy.

The snow had all but disappeared, but everywhere was still wet and icy cold. I left anyway and the next day I walked all day. I was cold, despondent and shivering when I found a scruffy backstreet pub that had a motley group playing and singing really old-fashioned blues songs, which I liked. I sat in a corner with a half pint of beer and let myself relax and get warm to the noisy rendition of 'Have Yourself a Merry Little Christmas' and other similar country type, Christmassy songs. The music was good, and the three boys played with enthusiasm and good spirits, missing a note here and there but enjoying themselves immensely.

In a break, the singer—a pale, skinny, dreadlocked, monkeyish boy—sat next to me. Someone had bought him a drink, which he lifted in the air, with a 'thank you' to the person at the bar. He regarded me with some amusement. I must have looked a mess.

"D'you like de music, man?" he asked.

"Yeh, I do," I managed to croak. I had hardly had any sort of conversation with anyone since leaving Peggy's and I was finding it hard to be pleasant. I was shivering uncontrollably.

"Are you okay mate? You's don't look too good to me."

"I'm okay. Get back to your music."

He loped off for another hour of swing songs and blues melodies, and I allowed myself to sit still and try not to think about how bad I felt or what I was going to do.

I realised that it was well past midnight when they finally packed up and I knew I would have to get up and leave. The thought of another night in the cold made me want to cry. I leaned back against the tatty upholstered seat and thought I might be sick again. My eyes were watering, and I pushed myself forward and attempted to get up. The boy with dreadlocks came over and plonked himself down beside me. He wore an odd assortment of clothing, but in comparison to me he looked clean and healthy. The rest of the band were dismantling the sound equipment and getting ready to leave.

"Hey, mate. You's not alright, are you?"

"Yes… no. I'm not sure. Need to go… " I stood swaying and dreadlocks put out a hand to support me.

"Don't touch me," I hissed as I attempted to clamber past him, my rucksack swinging on my shoulder. For a brief moment I was back in Berlin or Budapest and I jumped away from him.

"Hey, wait on, mate. Are you ill? Sit down for a jot and I'll get you a brandy or sunfin'." He waited. "Name's Jingo and I ain't a fool, mate. You's not looking good."

I really couldn't move, and I found it hard to swallow but managed to answer, "No, sorry…"

"I'm trying to help you," he said gently. "I can see that yo' is frightened and ill. If you need to hide for a while, I know the perfec' place. I'll show you."

I knew that I needed help but was not sure that any man could be trusted, certainly not someone like Jingo who obviously lived life by the seat of his pants.

Jingo had a quick conversation with the other members of the band who looked at me suspiciously, but they nodded and headed off to their battered van that was parked across the road. I stood outside trying to make up my mind what to do.

"Come wid me. I'll show you somewhere where you will be safe. I can't stay because we 'ave a gig in Manchester next week an' we's leaving tonight. I'll probably stay ther an all."

I watched Jingo with narrowed eyes, not sure whether to trust him or not—I decided I had too. I couldn't spend another night in the open feeling as ill as I did.

I pulled myself up and followed him down the road. I insisted on carrying my rucksack and walking on my own even though I was unsteady on my feet. We passed the churchyard and a big housing estate and headed back towards town. There was no one about except some bin men and a few dog walkers. We seemed to have walked for miles. We passed the shopping arcade called 'The Galleries' where I had slept a few nights before. I followed him to the end of Union Street, turned into Wine Street and we made our way to a small row of derelict buildings. The shops were all boarded up, except the second to last one that was still occupied by an Oxfam charity shop. There were a couple of small alleyways between some of the shops and it was obvious that they were being used by the homeless and druggies. The smell was rank, and piles of rubbish intermingled with the detritus of collected useful boxes, bedding and plastic sheeting.

As we plodded down Wine Street, Jingo motioned for me to follow and led the way through one of the narrow alleyways. We weaved our way through the old bits of furniture and the black dustbin bags that had split and scattered their contents across the ground. There was a small loading yard at the back of the shops covered with mountains of rubble and rubbish; there was part of an old car that had been abandoned there and several broken shopping trolleys. The place stank of rotten food and muddy puddles. I fished Peggy's torch from my pocket and followed carefully. A high wall surrounded the whole area with the original entrance boarded up. The back windows of all but one of the shops were smashed and graffiti crawled up every wall. There had been an attempt to block off the back of the shops with a tall wooden gate, but Jingo knew how to get in.

"There it is." He pointed to the unbroken window. "I'll show you how to get up there." We crossed the yard and Jingo pulled a sheet of mouldy corkboard away from the bottom step of a zigzagging, weed-covered fire escape. He warned me that the fifth and sixth step were broken so he leapt up to show me: "Don't put yo' weight on these or the very top one, okay? The rest are fine. I stayed here for about nine months, and no one ever came near. I even put a lock on the door of the room so yo' can lock yourself in." He held up a key. "There's running water and a sink, but no loo up 'ere so yo' 'ave to 'ave a pot or go elsewhere." He laughed, "I peed in the sink, of course, but there is a public bog in the arcade so go there when you need a shit. The place's got electric because I linked it up wid the shop at the front, but I wouldn't put the light on at night in case anybody sees it. Actually, nobody can see it anyway unless they come round the back — just make bloody sure nobody sees you comin' and goin'."

The rickety stairs took us to the door at the top and Jingo pushed it open. It led onto a small landing, which had two doors and a staircase that ran down two flights of stairs to the ground floor. Jingo had a key to the door on the right and as he beckoned me in, he said, "The place is due to be demolished so if I were yo' I wouldn't stay too long. I think the charity shop has another year here and then it will close so yo' will need to find somewhere else before then." He handed me the key.

It was dark, as an old blanket had been tacked up across the window, but as my eyes adjusted, I could see that there was not only a makeshift bed on the floor but an old armchair, a rickety table and a wooden chair with duct tape holding the back together. The sink in the corner was full of an assortment of pans and crockery.

"Thank you, I vill be okay now."

"Can I do's anything else to help you?"

"I need to earn some money… get a job. Do you know anywhere…?

"Go see old man Chioti at the garage on the roundabout. The one at the bottom of Dexter Street. It's an all-nighter. He's always looking for help an' he's a good bloke. Tell him Jingo sent you. I 'ave to go now and catch up with the boys."

"Thank you so much, Jingo. Hope all goes vell for you in Manchester."

"Good luck mate. Stay safe." With a grin he dropped a handful of coins onto the table. "Not much… sorry." He had disappeared in an instant, his dreads swinging and his long legs taking him speedily down the broken fire escape.

I looked around. It was pretty grim, but I sank into the battered old armchair with relief. I noticed that there was an electric fire and I leaned over, plugged it into the protruding socket and turned it on. Jingo was right, it had electricity and my shaking body soon felt warm — I was so grateful.

After a brief rest, I tried the tap in the sink and after a short burst of rusty looking water it ran clear — what a relief — it even tasted good. I had the rest of the bottle of vodka in my rucksack and I drank it all before falling into a deep exhausted sleep on the mattress on the floor.

The following few hours were a blur, but I woke during daylight, rested but hungry. I felt a good bit better. It was time to find some provisions.

I practised going in and out unseen, and only on the third day, a Thursday, I heard a noise that disturbed me. Standing on the landing on the outside of my door I became aware of movement at the bottom of the internal flight of stairs. I leaned back into the shadows and watched a woman come through from the front to a cupboard under the stairs. She pulled out a vacuum cleaner and a box of cleaning materials and disappeared back through the door, which swung backwards and forwards for a few seconds. Three hours later she came back and returned the things she had taken out, went back through the door and locked it. I heard the lock click. I made a note of the time and the day of the week because it was obvious that she was the regular Oxfam shop cleaner; other than her, no one came near.

The following weeks gave me time to contemplate my life. I learned to find the things I needed and got really quite good at shoplifting. I rediscovered the pleasure of isolation. I was no longer forcibly confined, rather, I had the freedom to be on my own. Over the past year every moment had been spent with others, on call and in fear, unable to make any decision about my life.

Each day I felt the power of my new freedom: there was a time that I hated it, but now it was a choice, and being on my own was liberating. I found myself reviewing images and experiences I'd had in the previous year: the ideal of love that I thought I had found with Sasha but turned out to be total fantasy; the places I'd been and the sordid misery of having to sell my body and pretend that I enjoyed it; the journeys from one bar, massage parlour, hotel or brothel to another; the pain inflicted by callous men; the drugs that we had increasingly depended on to cover our loathing; the girls with their fear and disgust of themselves and their lives; the filthy pimps and minders who made a fortune buying and selling us. But now, except for the hours spent at the garage, I was free to dream — I felt that I would somehow be able to redeem my life and my self-respect; perhaps I could eventually go home.

For the past year I had forgotten how to dream. When you are constantly faced with the consequences of being abused and manipulated (worst of all, having to be drugged enough to pretend it's enjoyable) it is so easy to become hardened and cynical about any hopes or aspirations that you once had. There were times when I knew it was essential not to think about what might change in my life, nor what the consequence of change might be. Sometimes it is better not to think.

I cleaned up my 'room' as best I could, and it became my retreat. No one ever came near, but I remained careful when I went in and out. I always took my rubbish to the park bins, used the toilet in the shopping arcade and stole only what I needed. It had only taken one visit to the garage that Jingo had told me about and I had got a job. I was very careful to look like a boy; my hair was so short, and I wore jeans and a man's sweater. I removed the baseball cap as I entered the garage office. Mister Chioti badly needed staff to cover the night shift, seven nights a week, so with very few questions asked, he offered me a job starting at ten thirty pm until the morning shift, which started at seven.

"I only want your name. I will pay you minimum wage in cash, because I know you have no bank account or papers, and you will not cheat me. If you do, I will call the police. Right? Name?" His eyes glinted behind his bottle top glasses, but he was a kind man, and I was so grateful to him for giving me a job.

"My name is Eric and I vill not cheat you." I had chosen the name because the barbers across the street from the Oxfam shop was called Eric's and the name sounded particularly masculine, going by the pictures in the window.

Mister Chioti was pleased with how quickly I—or 'Eric'—picked up the job: I ran security checks, worked the automatic car wash and handled the new till; I also learnt about when to restack shelves, refill the coffee machine and how to keep the place secure. A burly Jamaican giant called Winston was in charge of the pumps as well as all the breakdowns and inquiries, and we made an interesting pair; I was slight and pale, whilst Winston was dark and muscular. Winston was a man of few words, which suited me, and I liked him a lot.

CHAPTER 16

KATE

It was so much harder than I had ever imagined — being the mother of a screaming little demon like Thomas both exhausted and frustrated me. On Christmas Day 2000 I had been invited to have lunch with Bill and Mollie and their family, but I had to leave immediately after eating because of the constant wailing of my new-born son, Thomas James. I don't think I'd had more than an hour of sleep each night since he'd arrived. I had intended to return to work fairly soon after giving birth, but as time passed his endlessly frustrating wailing made me feel I couldn't leave him or ignore the fact that he wasn't content.

"Some babies just need to cry and make a noise," Viv, the health visitor, told me. "He is healthy and beautiful. It will pass, you'll see. Sometimes you just need to leave him and let him cry."

I hated leaving him alone to wail his pitiful protests — I couldn't even begin to guess why he made them.

At first Thomas cried that incessant, gasping, repetitious cry of a new-born. At six months old it had developed into a loud, full howl that drove everyone within earshot into panic. Not that many people were often in earshot, however, as I only had one regular visitor and that was Mollie Burton.

A couple of girls from the bank had popped in for coffee when Thomas was about six weeks old, but they made a fairly quick exit when the noise of his howls made conversation nigh on impossible.

I had few friends — I had never been able to make them easily, but Mollie was more than just a neighbour, she had become like a mother to me, the mother I never had. She'd been wonderful and I'd come to rely on her, especially after I'd had Thomas. She was the only person, other than those I'd worked with at the bank, who knew about Jackson leaving because of the baby. When my grief was overflowing, mainly with self-pity at the thought of being alone again, it was Mollie who had made an effort to comfort me. She was often alone, as her own children had grown up and left home, whilst her husband worked on the oilrigs, so we had become quite close — insomuch as I never got close to anybody! She had been the one who I had confided in about my pregnancy. It was she who helped me through, took me to antenatal classes and collected me from hospital after Thomas was born on that cold, sleety December day just before Christmas. She had been an endless source of support as she had produced three sons and a daughter herself. I guessed she was only in her fifties, so she had started her family at a young age, whereas I was thirty when I had Thomas.

Viv came regularly on health visits for the first few weeks and Mollie popped in almost every other day, so Thomas and I were mostly alone. I'd rock him for hours, sing to him and massage his hands and feet until he finally settled and slept. It was only then that I could marvel at his beauty. He looked so much like Jackson with his pale silky skin, his dark eyes and hair. I would gaze at his perfection for a few moments before I left him to grab a meal, a shower or a short sleep. My baby was only lovable when he slept. I was so tired all the time and the only time I left the house was to go to the clinic for Thomas's jabs or to collect food and nappies.

"You look exhausted," Mollie told me when Thomas was six months old in June and I was trying to encourage him to take a bottle at night. "You need to have a break from him and get out and have some 'you' time. I'll sit for you. I can give him his bottle and put him to bed."

The previous day I'd received an invitation to an engagement party at the weekend from Leanne, one of our junior clerks at the bank. It was only going to be few drinks with a disco at a village hall.

"Go, I'll sit with him," Mollie said when I told her. "He'll settle for me. My middle boy was a crier, so I know how to handle it."

"Are you sure Moll? I won't be late back; I'll leave by eleven."

"Stay as long as you like. We'll be fine," she assured me.

As I headed away in a taxi that Saturday evening, I could hear Thomas's wailing echoing in my head, but as we turned the corner we got away from the sound and I was mostly relieved.

It was a good feeling to be going out, to be nicely dressed and smelling sweet. Such a nice change from the sour smell of breast milk or the baggy jeans and sloppy sweatshirts, which was all I'd worn throughout the months since Thomas was born. Even though I'd managed without a social life I was looking forward to seeing my old colleagues and eventually returning to work.

With no husband, no family, my maternity allowance gone and not a great deal of my savings left, I knew I would have to find a nursery very soon and start earning again.

I *had* contacted Jackson when Thomas was born but I hadn't had a reply and I knew I wouldn't see him again. I had no regrets where he was concerned. The whole marriage had been a terrible mistake.

I'd enjoyed my evening out much more than I'd expected and it was great to see some of the people I'd worked with when I joined the team in Bristol. Most of them knew that Jackson, my dear husband, had left to go to his new job and that I hadn't gone with him, but no one asked about him and I was grateful. Of course, they all wanted to know about my baby, Thomas, and asked when I would go back to work. I had originally planned to go back after the first three months, but realised that, without support that was totally unrealistic.

I'd drunk three glasses of some sort of punch and felt some of the tension of the last year drain away, but I had experienced sudden flashes of Thomas and a longing to feel his small, soft body in my arms; at about ten forty-five I called for a taxi so that I could be back home soon after eleven. As the taxi drew up in front of the house and I was fumbling for change, I could hear Thomas crying and my body reacted involuntarily as all the tension returned to my body. Once inside the house, I rushed into the lounge where Mollie was sitting whilst holding Thomas over her shoulder. She was stroking his back and as I entered, she raised her eyebrows. "Good party?"

I nodded as Mollie handed me my sobbing baby. "Has he been crying all evening?"

"No, I think he saves it for you," she laughed. "He's been fairly quiet until about an hour ago. I've fed him, changed him and played with him, but he won't stop so in the end I just let him cry."

He turned his shrivelled face to me, and for a brief moment stopped his howling, but within seconds he roared again with renewed vigour. It was difficult for me not to take it personally. I felt tears pool at the back of my eyes.

"What am I doing wrong, Mollie?"

"You are not doing anything wrong, love. He's tired. Put him down and he'll probably sleep now he's had a good bellow," she assured me—but I knew differently.

Mollie left and I put Thomas into his cot at 1 a.m. still howling, and when he eventually stopped, I cried myself to sleep, waking only at 5 a.m. to go and check on him. My eyes were puffy with fatigue but as I gazed at my baby he was once again my beautiful, lovable, peaceful boy. I carefully pulled the blanket up and sat whilst watching him in the pale morning light. I loved him so much.

220

CHAPTER 17

ELENA 2011

It was springtime when I realised that I was pregnant. I hadn't had a period for over a year, but I'd put that down to a lack of food and exhaustion. I had felt a popping sensation, which eventually turned into definite movement. My stomach only looked slightly swollen and because of my tall, thin frame, I kidded myself for a while that it wasn't true. In the following weeks I had to wear bigger and bigger sweaters to cover my blossoming belly.

I wanted to go home so badly, but I realised that even if I could get back to Ukraine, I couldn't manage without a job. I would get no social assistance as I was not an orphan, and I was of full legal age. I could not be registered at the labour exchange and receive unemployment benefit either, since I'd not worked there recently. Nor could I receive any family allowance, as this is paid only after the child is born. I wasn't even registered with a GP—for that, I would need my documents. I missed my home and family so badly, but I knew it was pointless to imagine that I could ever return.

It was less than seven weeks later that I felt the contractions begin, slowly at first but with increasing severity. It had been a windy, wet night and I was just leaving my Wednesday night shift at the garage when the pains began in earnest.

I was so distracted by the pelting rain and the flashes of lightning that it took me a few minutes to register the waves of pain that washed through my belly. In minutes I was soaked and as lightening branched across the black sky, I carefully crept around to the back of the shop and moved the rotten wooden plank that covered the bottom of the fire escape. I was shaking so violently that I clung to the rail as I ascended the rickety steps, taking care to avoid the broken ones. It was a dark, cloudy morning, so the light was poor. Pain threatened again, and as I reached the top step, I carefully lifted my foot to balance on the slippery platform outside the heavy door. I was so afraid of falling that I had to stop and lean against the wall. With the intense pain I found it particularly difficult to get inside.

Eventually, dripping wet, I got into my room, locked myself in, turned on the electric heater and abandoned all my clothes. I found Hannah's bathrobe and collapsed onto the mattress on the floor. Panic flooded through me as my waters broke. I was terrified. I wasn't ready to have a baby.

God help me. I didn't want to bring a child into the world and the thought of it sickened me. *How can I take care of another human being when I can't even take responsibility for myself?* I closed my eyes, not daring to believe that I was about to give birth. Terror, along with the pain of the unknown almost stopped me breathing. *It is not possible to be in so much pain and not die.* I thought. *What if I do die, here, all alone? No one would find me. The baby will probably be so small that it will not survive. What will I do? I haven't looked after myself and I have smoked and drunk vodka almost all of the time I have been here.*

I was shaking violently, and the pains were repeating faster and faster. A tremendous crash of thunder outside accompanied the extraordinary experience of agony that was attacking my body. It seemed like an eternity, but it was in the early hours of the afternoon when the pain of pushing finally ceased.

I looked down with horror at the tiny alien-looking baby, slippery with vernix and blood, that I had pushed from my body onto the grimy mattress.

I knew what I needed to do, but I had little strength to move as I absorbed the enormity of what had just happened. It took several minutes for me to realise that the tiny infant, although he seemed quite small, was not only alive but looked quite healthy. And it was a boy. He began to cry, a soft mewing noise that stirred me into action. I picked him up and cradled him carefully as I reached for a clean towel and wrapped him firmly. I knew what to do. I needed string and scissors or something to cut the cord. I couldn't remember where the scissors were that I had used to cut my hair, but with difficulty, I stretched across to a box of knives that lived under the sink. They looked blunt and old, but I eventually found a piece of string, and cut the cord with the sharpest knife I could find.

It took another painful hour before I managed to push out the afterbirth and another hour before I could clear up the blood and urine. I had no idea what I was going to do, but the best plan was to leave the baby somewhere where it would be found and looked after.

Exhausted, I carefully laid the towel-wrapped baby on the bed and tucked it under the soft blanket that I had taken from Dunelms previously. The opportunity arose when someone had stolen a velvet headboard from one of the display beds and the security staff were heading across the road in pursuit. I had picked up two blankets from the pile near the door and walked out. I thought it must be my lucky day!

One of them was always laid across the smelly old armchair and I often wrapped it around myself when it was really cold. I pulled the blanket around my shoulders as I was shivering with shock. I lay down facing the baby and looked at the little miracle that I had just forced out of my body. I could only stare in wonder, the pain forgotten, swept away in the giddying rush of tenderness that swept through me. I marvelled at the tiny perfect little body and pulled him into my arms and held him close. From the moment I pressed my mouth against my baby's tender little cheek, it felt as though I was being brought back to life. As the scent of him filled my lungs, I felt myself revived, my blood flowing, and my back straightening. Here was something to live for, but how could I care for him?

I fell asleep exhausted and hungry and woke with a start as the baby cried in the early hours of the morning. I knew that I had to try and feed him but my tiny, undernourished breasts had little to offer despite the baby's soft whimpering cry. I felt such a surge of love for the strange, quiet little being that I had produced, and sang softly in my own language until he finally fell asleep again.

It was dawn by the time I carefully washed in the cracked old sink and ran my fingers through my tufty locks. I knew that I would probably lose my job for not turning up for my night shift, but by then, it was almost a full day since the baby had been born and he had not yet been fed. I knew exactly what I needed, and I knew where I could get it — I'd spent so many hours wandering through shops to keep warm, that I knew exactly where I could get anything and everything.

I pulled on an over-sized mac that I had found in a bin. It was old and faded but it had been washed — its best feature was that it had two huge inside pockets. I pulled my dark cap onto my head. Although it was a warm morning there were great puddles from the previous storm and the fire escape was slippery and dangerous.

There were a few early-risers milling around waiting for the shops to open. I was extra careful when I emerged from the alleyway. I skirted around until I found a route away from the building that wasn't cluttered with the homeless.

It didn't take long to lift what I needed from Boots chemist shop, as the assistants were busy gossiping as they refilled shelves. I managed to get a packet of sandwiches, three baby bottles, some sterilising tablets and two tins of formula. Getting nappies would prove to be harder because of the size of the packets, but I knew that I could make some towelling and linen nappies from what I already had. I had become quite adept at lifting bags from charity boxes and there were plenty dotted around Bristol.

Returning back was more difficult, as my pockets were full, and I had a large bag of assorted clothing that I'd picked up outside the 'Help the Aged' shop. Someone had conveniently left it on the doorstep before it had opened.

The baby was asleep, so whilst I carefully boiled water on my little primus stove, I explored the bag that I had picked up outside the charity shop. It contained some extremely large hoodies, two pairs of boy's jeans that I thought I could alter to fit me, several men's shirts and a pair of Doc martins that were only one size too big (I knew that with a pair of thick socks they would do me a good turn). There were also some books—quite a haul!

The water had boiled, and I knew that everything had to be sterilised, so I set about making up the three bottles that I had purloined from the chemist shop. I waited for the little boy to wake, and carefully tested the temperature of the formula. I lifted him into my lap and held the bottle to his tiny mouth. Instantly he started to suck, and I sighed with relief. He was beautiful with blue eyes and tiny wisps of white hair. He looked so very much like Margo, that tears erupted, as I thought of her back home in our village.

I knew I would have to find a way to let go of this little person who had invaded my life. In the meantime, until I'd decided how, I had to feed him and take care of him. He was so quiet, and when he was fed, he settled down again easily.

I finally slept, and when I woke, the baby was awake again. I made three nappies out of an old towel and found a large safety pin in the sewing kit that I had brought from Peggy's. After cleaning him and feeding him again he slept peacefully and seemed to be warm and comfortable.

My first thought as he snuffled into sleep after the second bottle, was how was I going to be able to go to work and leave him. Perhaps, if I fed him really late, he would sleep until I returned from the garage when the day shift arrived; nonetheless, I was so unsure whether that was realistic or whether he would cry all night—maybe he'd even die. I felt physically sick at the thought of leaving him.

Most of the rest of the day I slept and got up in time to give the baby another bottle before I left for work. I made myself a cup of tea and ate two apples with a digestive biscuit. I switched on the electric heater even though it wasn't particularly cold, but I knew babies had to be kept warm.

Carefully locking the door and still feeling sick I crept down the fire escape. What if he woke up and wailed? What if he died in the night? My shift was from ten thirty pm until 7 a.m.—could a new-born wait twelve hours until his next feed?

I told myself that if he cried, someone might hear. It was unlikely though because no one came around the back of the shops anymore. Many of the homeless had gone to a new hostel that the local authorities had opened during the winter months. I was sick with worry as I ran through the early morning mist to the garage.

Mister Chioti had been concerned when I hadn't shown up for work but as it had never happened before, he accepted my excuse of a twenty-four-hour bug and all was well. Winston had coped.

All through the night I felt sick with worry. How could I leave my baby alone for so long? Would he cry? Would he lie in a soiled nappy? I fretted and promised myself that the following day I would deposit him somewhere where he would be found and get properly looked after. I was in no position to keep a child and that baby deserved a decent life.

The night was busy at work and before I knew it was morning and time to leave. I ran the short distance back to the Oxfam shop as fast as I could. I always stopped to check if anyone was around before I made my way through the hidden entrance to the yard that Jingo had shown me. It took seconds to get back into 'my' room. I couldn't hear any sound coming from the bundle on the mattress but when I picked him up his little eyes were open. The tiny rosebud mouth puckered and made a sucking noise. I was shaking with relief.

"You are ready for your next meal eh, little one?" I whispered, feeling so pleased that the baby was quiet and not visibly distressed at being left on his own. Within minutes I had cleaned him, boiled some water and made up the three bottles for the day. I found it hard to believe that the baby was so content when he was fed and comfortable. I lay on the bed with him and we both slept. As the day wore on, he only whimpered if he was hungry or wet. I settled him close to my body and he took the formula without a problem every time. I was careful to sterilise the bottles and keep him clean.

In those first few days I intended to look after 'the little boy' until I had decided where would be the best place to take him; it had to be somewhere where I knew he would be found and looked after.

I couldn't decide, so the days turned into weeks, and although I knew that I would have to give him up, he had given me a purpose to every day.

Each night, I left for work as usual, and I felt sure that the baby mostly slept until I arrived home in the morning a few minutes after seven. He always appeared calm and contented.

The first time he smiled at me I was enchanted and whispered to him in my own language how happy I was to have him. My days were spent looking after him, although he would often settle back into sleep after his bottle in the morning and I'd take the opportunity to go out and shoplift what I needed for him (stealing a little food for myself whilst I was out). That day I stole a bag of rice and some tomatoes, although I did buy an onion and two bananas as well as some disposable nappies — keeping the towels clean was an almost impossible task considering the circumstances in which we were living. I dumped the used nappies in different bins daily, whilst on the way to the garage.

The little boy rarely cried, and I found myself enjoying his development. During the day I slept when he did, and I learnt to manage on only a few hours of sleep every day.

I think I will wait a little longer until I am sure he is well enough to leave somewhere.

CHAPTER 18

KATE August 2011

The day that Thomas died started like any other, with him howling for his breakfast. I was still breastfeeding him in the morning and it was really the only time that he seemed at peace with me and the world. I loved this time of the day, and when it was warm enough, I would sit outside the French windows and watch the birds and squirrels in our tiny back garden as Thomas filled his belly. It was August, he was eight months old, and as I still had plenty of milk, I continued to supplement his meals with my breasts. I worried about the day they would dry up and I would lose this precious time with him—besides, he never seemed to be as content after a bottle.

Every time he cried a part of me felt like it was being eaten away; when he was unhappy, I was unhappy. I loved him so much, but his dissatisfaction with life made me question everything I did.

We'd walked in the park, and he had grizzled for a while and finally slept. I tried to relax and enjoy the balmy evening sunshine. Thomas was snug — he snuffled a bit in his sleep, but he seemed content.

It was quite late when we returned and just as I was gently lifting the pushchair through the front door, Mollie appeared holding a parcel for me that had been delivered to her. I had ordered a blue potty and a drinking cup with elephants on the sides, which I'd seen in a sales catalogue. Thomas didn't need either yet, but I liked them so much; they were good value, so I'd ordered them on a whim. I was being deliberately careful with my savings because I'd decided not to go back to work yet.

"Is he still asleep?" Mollie asked as she handed me the parcel.

"Yes, I am going to make the best of it, have a sandwich and a glass of wine. Do you want to join me?" I whispered. "I have to take advantage of the peace and quiet."

Mollie responded quietly. "Glass of wine? Why not? No sandwich for me though, I have to cook dinner for Bill. He's leaving to go back to the rig in a few days."

"Okay. How long is he away for this time?"

"Just the usual — he'll be back in the autumn."

Less than half an hour later Mollie got up to leave, so we tiptoed through the door and past the pushchair in the hall. It was the silence that alerted me. I leaned over and gently pulled back the light sheet that was covering him — I instantly knew that something was wrong — there was absolute silence. I held my breath as I waited to hear his own. I listened and heard nothing.

"Night then, Kate. Kiss Thomas goodnight..." Mollie was about to leave.

"Moll, he's not breathing." I screamed. I could feel the cold panic of realisation washing through me. Mollie was instantly by my side. She leaned over, scanning his chest, hands and face for movement. I pulled out his tiny hand but there was no response — he was cold. I knew he wouldn't wake. It was my fault for leaving him there. I lifted his soft little body and held him close. My throat constricted and I could feel myself making a noise. I would have collapsed in a heap if Mollie hadn't wrapped her arms around us.

"Turn him toward me and I'll try to breathe into his mouth." She sounded calm and professional.

"He's gone." I wailed but Mollie clamped her mouth across Thomas's pale, little face and tried mouth to mouth until it was obvious that he would not respond.

I remember little of the sequence of occurrences after that: the blue flashing lights, the noise of people coming and going, the paramedic who looked like a schoolboy, Bill's arms around me, the doctor arriving and the little yellow pills that sent me into another realm. Then the police arrived, a man and a woman. The woman sat close to me on the brown sofa and said quietly, "We need to ask you a few questions, Kate."

"It's my fault. I have done something wrong I know I have."

"What did you do?" asked the woman.

"I left him in the hall to have a glass of wine. His blanket was too heavy… or too light — was that it? Perhaps he got too hot… too cold… I shouldn't have left him… What happened? I did do something wrong…"

My words tumbled about, made little sense and I repeated myself over and over. The young policewoman wrote into her notebook and said to her older colleague.

"I'll stay with Kate. You talk to Mrs Burton; she was here when they found Thomas."

He left the room and the girl said gently, "We will try to find the cause of death, but I can assure you that SID, or sudden infant death, is not uncommon. Often there is no clue as to what the reason for it was. Kate, mothers always feel responsible, and this isn't the first time I have heard a mother say it is her fault. It's unlikely that you did anything wrong at all—listen, if there was a reason, it's unlikely to have anything to do with you. He could have something else wrong, but we will wait and see, just don't blame yourself."

What have I done to deserve this?

Later Mollie came in and held my hand, her eyes red with crying. "Thomas has got to go now. Will you hold him for a moment and say goodbye?"

Mollie's husband Bill came in and was cradling Thomas. He held him toward me, and I could see he was crying too. "Take him, Kate. You need to hold him. Take your time."

I took him, and whoever else was in that room disappeared. I held him and studied his beauty through my tears, knowing he wasn't there. He was like a little dark-haired doll, a waxwork, but he was at peace. He was quiet, no longer charged with whatever it was that he thought he needed from me. At that moment there was a release for us both.

When I finally looked up, I saw that Mollie was in fact there. She held out her arms and took away my love, my baby, my Thomas.

If I let myself think about it, Thomas's death seemed like a recurring dream that repeated itself so often that I found it hard to remember his short life at all. That moment when I found him limp and pale, the comprehension and disbelief, the shock of holding him and knowing he was no longer there, repeated itself over and over in my memory. I had thought myself an incompetent mother. I remember the constant feeling of panic when I couldn't subdue my baby's harsh crying. I had no idea what he needed. I loved him, I fed him, changed him, rocked and stroked him. Sometimes the noise would cease for a few minutes but suddenly his back would arch, and he would roar again with renewed vigour. He always seemed unhappy to me, but now he was gone.

Some days I could hardly make my body function at all. My legs didn't want to walk, my arms didn't want to put on any clothes and my stomach didn't want food; I didn't care whether I lived or died. I often found myself standing, looking out of the window, not really seeing the street, just standing there in a state of vacancy and unawareness. I could remember nothing of the days that followed Thomas's death or the arrangements for the funeral. Only the image of the tiny white coffin stayed imprinted on my mind.

I often sat in the dark until the sun rose and realised that I hadn't been to bed. Then I would sleep all day. It was on one of those early mornings in September that I found myself curled on my couch with a blanket wrapped around me. The television was still on from the previous night, and it showed a programme of world events that had occurred that year: Osama bin Laden had been killed in Pakistan, there'd been an earthquake in New Zealand, an attack by a right-wing terrorist in Norway killing seventy-seven people and a Japanese tsunami. The appalling news of happenings around the world and the horror of what those thousands of people suffered only added to my feelings of desolation and disgust; nevertheless, it did make me realise that life still went on and that the practicalities of every day were still possible.

By the time I returned to work in October 2011, out of sheer necessity, I was already relying on daily antidepressants. Each night I popped a couple of pills, which were designed to help me sleep and take the sharp edges off my bouts of depression and darkness — they didn't work, and my insomnia worsened.

My sleep had become fractured by vivid dreams and abrupt awakenings. My relationship with sleep had always been strained. When I was in care with other children all the time, the noise was always disturbing at night: the babies cried, the toddlers wandered, and others sobbed in distress at being wet or the lack of a loving arm around them. Being fostered with strangers was worse. There, I was constantly listening for the sound of a door opening or the creak on the stairs. I often lay awake praying, dreaming for a normal life where I would be loved and could live in a happy family.

Memories came flooding back. *'You are going to be a good girl for me aren't you Kate?'* I would stare at Henry Gladstone with fear coursing through my body. He'd sit down on my bed and peel the blankets away from my trembling fingers. He'd lean down toward me while his fingers explored my thighs, then moved around my buttocks before coming to rest on my pubic bone. When he pushed his bony fingers inside me, I would hear the intake of his breath.

How could I sleep? During my later days hiding in the squat in Reading, an odd variety of people came and went every night, I never felt safe enough to sleep. Even all those years on, I'd often wake up sweating and crying — people with secrets rarely sleep soundly.

When I moved to Bristol, and settled down with Jackson, my sleeping had improved, but now that I had lost Thomas, I reverted to the quivering mess I used to be; I spent most nights in a drugged stupor, waking early and filling myself with caffeine and antidepressants to get through the day.

Howard Kendrikson was kind and lightened my workload, so I just about managed to drag myself through each week, although I was barely fit for purpose. Since Jackson had left, his assistant had been doing the job, so there was plenty to keep me busy. I had been away from work for ten months and the computers had been upgraded so I needed to catch up. I tried hard to put on a good face, to stay alert and focused on my job — I congratulated myself for being able to get on with life. What an actress I became!

CHAPTER 19

ELENA — SEP/NOV 2011

The baby started to sit by himself and was gaining weight, and before I realised it nearly six months had passed, but still I hesitated parting with him. As he grew, I wondered about Carl Melnyk, the brutal German who I knew must be his father — but he looked nothing like him. He looked more and more like my beloved sister Margo. I hoped and prayed that she was being taken care of. I berated myself endlessly for being so naïve as to leave her for Sasha's promise of a prosperous new life.

I thought and thought about what would be best for the little boy. He needed more than I could give him, but soon it would be wintertime again, so I wasn't going to leave him just anywhere. I realised how much I'd grown to love him. He had become my purpose for every day. I hadn't even given him a name, always referring to him as 'little boy'. Every night, after a good feed, I settled him down to sleep and went to work, confident that he would wake as I returned the following morning—and he did.

As he grew, I would sometimes arrive back and find him playing with the plastic bowls and the one soft toy I had stolen for him (a small green dragon with a smiley face). My 'little boy' always had a smile for me, and my heart would skip a beat with pure love; I'd lift him and hold him close. He was the one and only precious thing in my life.

I knew the time would come when we would have to leave the room, not only because of the little boy's needs, but because a date had been set for the buildings and shops to be demolished in the New Year of 2012. That gave me over a year to save enough for a deposit on a flat of some kind. With that in mind, I hesitated about giving away my child and started saving a few pounds every week, which I hid in a biscuit tin under a loose floorboard. I thought that if I had a proper address, I could probably get a full-time job.

I still continued to shoplift for most of our food, and occasionally stole small items of clothing, sanitary towels, soap and deodorant. There were so many shops in Bristol, and I always made sure that I didn't always go back to the same ones. I never stole money, nor anything else, from the garage. Mr Chioti was a kindly man who had got to know several of the Eastern Europeans in the area and he liked me. He told me that his grandfather had come to England as a penniless Greek after the troubles there. He knew what a difficult time immigrants often had. He'd give me the odd out of date loaf of bread, overripe banana or pint of milk.

"Eric," he would say, "while you are on duty you can drink as much coffee as you like and eat any doughnuts or fancies that are left over, but if you ever steal from me… police… do you understand? I will not tolerate that."

"Yes — of course, sir," I had replied.

The only time I knew anything about what was going on in the world was from the radio in the garage and I had usually left before the news. When I arrived for my night shift people were always talking about how shocked they were by world events: tragedy, tsunamis, riots in London, people being shot, killed and terrorised. All I could think was that I had brought a child into this dangerous world. There were talks of massive repercussions from the withdrawal of US troops from Iraq and I was afraid that we would have no future at all. My only thought was, *what a staggering capacity the world has for the drama of pain and self-inflicted misery.*

Mister Chioti offered me a bottle of vodka for Christmas, which I politely refused; I no longer drank any alcohol. He gave me a ten-pound note instead. I grinned happily — it was just what I needed.

"You're the only Polack I know that doesn't drink," he grinned. "They all like vodka."

"Not me but thank you for the money. It is better for me, I not Polack, you know," I replied.

"Buy yourself something nice then, boy," grinned Mister Chioti.

I knew exactly what I was going to spend the money on. I had seen a sturdy circular playpen in a charity shop and although it was a struggle to hide it in the yard without anyone seeing me, I eventually got it up the fire escape steps and into my room at 2 a.m. in the morning on my night off for Christmas Eve. My 'little boy,' was now over seven months old and was fast asleep.

I would watch him sleeping and knew that I wanted to keep him. How could I part with the only thing that brought joy into my pathetic life? We had a little world of our own that was so different to anything outside. I still lived with the fear that I would be found by the traffickers, or that I would be arrested and imprisoned for being illegal — but my joy was in this room with my 'little boy'.

The playpen and some plastic bricks were his Christmas presents. I bought a pot of ice cream as a special treat, which we shared on Christmas morning.

He thrived, and within another couple of months was eating jars of baby food, bananas, rusks or soaked oats. He played happily, but when he started to move around, I was worried that he would hurt himself. There were exposed wires where Jingo had rigged the electricity and some of the floorboards were rough, so the playpen became his home at night or if I went out during the day. He also slept less, which meant that I didn't get enough sleep during the day; I often found myself dropping off on my night-time shift. I kept convincing myself that I could manage — nobody died of lack of sleep, did they?

I kept my little treasure as clean as possible, fed him as well as I could manage, and watched him like a hawk. I knew that his development was slow, but he was an angelic child; as long as I played with him and fed him during the day, he slept well at night and never seemed to be distressed when I arrived back in the early morning.

CHAPTER 20

KATE

I hid away over Christmas, and in the new year of 2012 I struggled through work every day; I knew that I was often unapproachable and moody.

During the next eight months, through spring and summer, I found everything becoming more and more difficult. I knew I was changed—I never used to cry, but now a television play, a story of depression, cruelty, or a news story about the needy in the world would make me sob; even a touching advertisement had me bursting into tears. One day the floodgates opened, and I cried for a whole day about the loss of my brother Alex, which was something I had never allowed myself to do before. Any story of the old or young in pain or distress reduced me to a quivering pulp, sniffing and grabbing for tissues.

It was the anniversary of Thomas's death in August, and I was barely hanging on. The facade that I was okay was now slipping away. I know how close I was to having a breakdown; my sanity was slowly leaking, at work I increasingly missed clients and made wrong entries or calculations. I would walk around the bank forgetting where I was going and my colleagues often covered for me.

At weekends, I'd buy a microwave meal, a large bottle of gin, a few tonics, a piece of cheese and some crackers. I spread my drinking from Friday night until Sunday night, so that I stayed in a state which straddled the line between drunkenness and sobriety. I locked my doors and closed the curtains; I didn't want to talk to anybody in my own time and usually nobody came. I didn't have the capacity for idle talk anymore; if my phone rang, I ignored it or unplugged it.

I was a ravaged, war-torn island and the horizons were bleak. Mollie tried to see me and would often shout through the letterbox, but I wouldn't let her in. I know that sounds mean, as she was always so good to me, but I had used up all the talking that I could manage at work. After a few weeks she stopped shouting and sent motivational cards through my letterbox. One, an affirmation, 'I AM IN THE PROCESS OF POSITIVE CHANGE', made me laugh hysterically—I tore it into pieces. All the other cards sat on my mantelpiece unopened.

There were times when I asked myself whether it was worth the pain to go on living. I began to believe that the world was a disaster, that the greater part of humanity was hopelessly stupid — and that included myself.

What had finally pushed me into making the decision to change my life was an ordinary interaction with a nice customer in the bank, who insisted that her account had been closed and that she still had money owing. It was a genuine inquiry — of that I have no doubt — but I felt that it was delivered in a slightly accusatory tone, as if it was my fault. That was the straw that broke the camel's back. I started to shout, "No, not me, no…" The unfortunate woman watched me walk away as I suddenly felt as if all the blood was rushing out of my body — I was empty, I was drowning. In that moment I didn't know or understand anything, I was in a tangled mess of conflicting emotions. I couldn't stay still, and I began to run, but I wasn't going anywhere, and suddenly the floor rose up to meet me. I only remember Mr Kendrikson, my manager, holding me close and saying softly, "You're alright Mrs Ingram." I didn't know who he was talking to. I was aware only of a man smell, which sent a shivering memory of Henry

Gladstone through my already panic-stricken body, but a strong arm was holding me up, and for that I was grateful. All my thoughts and actions from thereon were lost to me until I woke up in the local hospital corridor, shaking uncontrollably. I stayed in the psychiatric ward for four weeks.

Each day, I felt stronger and when I eventually returned to my dusty little house, I knew that things would have to change. Despite the months of trauma, I made a decision. I was lucky to be in a financial situation which gave me a choice. I could stay a victim or turn into a survivor. I had worked damned hard all my life to be a survivor, so I decided to go back to Scarborough, or somewhere on the northeast coast to face my fears and look for my brother, my only blood relative.

Although I loved my house, and it had been my first proper home, I couldn't wait to leave. The memories crept around me like haunting tunes, voices and sounds of weeping and sorrow and loneliness. It seemed to retain a sense of the things that had happened in it, a residue of pain and distress.

I set about trying to sell as much furniture as possible, and tearfully got rid of all the baby equipment and clothes to a charity shop. I had made some decisions — I would rent somewhere close to where I'd lived in the northeast, partly because I knew I was born there and partly because it was beautiful. I had loved living close to the sea, with the vast expanse of windy beaches and the bluff kindness of the people there. I would find my brother Alex, and I would look up my last foster parents, Mary and John Lambert who had lived near Filey — I wanted to apologise for my behaviour when I'd lived with them. They did not deserve the uncontrollable monster that I had become, living in York with the Gladstone's. I had run away from Filey and I think now that it must have been a relief for them. For six months I hitched and slept rough, thieving to eat, eventually ending up in Reading in the squat. But that was all history now. I would try to get a job and start to look for my brother, the only living relative that I knew of. He had been adopted out of care when he was four and I was six, whilst I was fostered out but never adopted.

CHAPTER 21

ELENA

Soon it was springtime again and it was only when the 'little boy' was a year old that he wanted to be out of the playpen all the time so that he could explore and climb. He often tried to look out of the window, even though I had pinned a large piece of hardboard over it. I became more and more undecided about what to do. I had woven a curtain of protection around us, and I struggled to engage with the outside world at all. Even so I knew I could not keep him contained for much longer. I was saving well, and in another month or so I would probably have enough saved to find us a flat. In the meantime, I found big rolls of sticky tape in a DIY shop and covered the wires and prickly floorboards so that he could wander the whole room.

All through the summer months I kept him in the dark room, only lifting the hardboard occasionally to let in a little sunshine. My 'little boy' had not been exposed to the outside world at all; he had not had any sun on his body and I knew that he needed some sort of vitamin that you got from sunlight. I made inquiries from a book in the library and bought some children's Vitamin D capsules, which I squirted into his food.

Also, he had not been registered at birth, so he didn't officially exist. Every day, I felt guilty that I had been so selfish to keep him in that room without friends or relations, without a family or the stimulation that most babies need and get from their surroundings but, as I watched him, I saw a happy and contented child. He never really cried, he was quiet, loving and he was mine. He was what made me smile, what made me want to live in this world that I had not found to be kind to me, but I knew I had to find a way keep on. I constantly thought that perhaps I could get another job; I knew that was being unrealistic, but I was still unsure whether I could keep the child a secret for much longer. I had been in England in hiding for nearly eighteen months, and other than Mister Chioti and Winston, I hadn't communicated with anyone at all. I was constantly afraid of being found.

My 'little boy' deserved to be an ordinary little boy with playmates, with a proper home and garden to play in. He deserved to have parents that explored the world with him, but the thought of being without him broke my heart. He was the only thing in my life that made living worthwhile, but I constantly berated myself about my selfishness. Perhaps, I could find someone to look after him for me until I found us somewhere to live? Perhaps, I should really let him go? What I eventually decided, was that I could not keep him contained in that room for any longer.

He was walking with ease, so perhaps I could take him to the local nursery and enrol him, but I needed an address and there would be fees. I could even leave him amongst the other children in the garden; I had watched the children at the local playschool and nursery and seen it had an outside area where he could play with the other children. There would be lots of people around and there would be teachers and mothers there. He would definitely be found. Could I walk away from him? It would give him the chance of a decent life, but mine would be over. My mind changed with the wind.

Another few weeks passed. He was nearly eighteen months old.

I'd picked up a bag of children's clothes left beside a charity bin weeks before, and although there wasn't a good coat in it, there was a woolly hat, a lovely and chunky blue jumper and some dungarees that would fit him. I could make him look good and well cared for.

It was Thursday the 18th of November and I made the decision to at least take my little boy out for a walk, to get him used to the idea of the world outside of our 'room'. I dressed him carefully in the blue jumper and dungarees and pulled the little red woolly hat over his blonde hair. He looked lovely.

"I'm going to take you for a walk in the shopping arcade where you will see lots of other people. You hold my hand, and we will walk to the shops and see if we can get you some shoes."

I pulled on my boots and unlocked the door. Apprehension filled my body and I found myself shaking at the thought of what we were going to do. *Would he be frightened or excited?*

Suddenly, I realised that I would need to take some money with us, so I turned and went over to the window to where the loose floorboard hid my biscuit tin of savings.

There was a strip of tape over the top because of the splinters in the wood so I tried to pull it off. I had done such a secure job that it took a little longer than I had anticipated, but eventually I carefully tugged it free.

"Won't be long little one—I just need to get in here and then we can go and buy you some nice boots." I yanked at the floorboard and eventually it lifted, and I took out my precious tin. "How much should we take?" I counted the money and folded sixty pounds into the pocket of my padded jacket. "That should be enough," I said as I stood and turned, ready to take his hand and begin our adventure.

My heart contracted and panic flooded through me.

The door was open, and the little boy was nowhere to be seen. I had never left the door unlocked before. I heard my breath come in little ragged gasps, the prickle of panic rose in my throat and for a moment I couldn't move. Sudden realisation of the danger hit me. He had never seen stairs before. I leapt up and stumbled out onto the landing. No, he wasn't there either. I moved toward the banister and leaned over to look down the internal staircase. I couldn't see him, but there at the bottom of the stairs was the red, woolly hat that he had been wearing. Leaning just a little further, I noticed that the door that led to the corridor beside the Oxfam shop was swinging—of course, it was Thursday. The cleaning lady came to the store cupboard on a Thursday to collect her cleaning things.

I must hurry and find my 'little boy'. He can't have gone far. I turned to run down the stairs, but I tripped and fell forwards against the banister.

That was the last thing I remember as my world crashed and swirled and came hurtling down around me.

CHAPTER 22

KATE - THURSDAY 18th NOVEMBER 2012

My house sold almost immediately, and on the 18th of November, I was ready to leave the following Sunday. Bill had helped me load the hired van with the bigger items that I was taking with me, and he and Mollie had said a tearful farewell to me on Wednesday, when they left to go to Wales.

I needed to get some cash and some provisions, so although it was cold and windy, I decided to go into town.

I'd collected what I needed: just a few snacks for the journey, a couple of ready meals and a bottle of gin. I was feeling cold, so a hot cappuccino beckoned before my return home on the draughty bus. I reached the covered shopping arcade, part of The Galleries, where I knew I could get a good hot coffee. I hurried along, past the dry cleaners and the chemist. Next door to the coffee shop, I noticed a children's clothing store, and couldn't help myself and I stopped to look in the window. It would have been Thomas's birthday soon, and I could see things that I would have wanted him to wear; I wondered if the red padded coat on the model would be too small for Thomas. I twisted my neck to see the price and the recommended age on the ticket before deciding that he would probably have needed a bigger size to get through the winter. My beautiful little boy would have been two in December, but he was quite a big baby and the ticket stated that it was for two years plus. I swallowed as the loss hit me anew - he would be a toddler now, walking and chatting. I wondered whether Thomas would have liked the colour.

Suddenly I felt my body tense. A wave of shock passed through me as if I had suddenly been pulled into another dimension. I shivered, felt dizzy and held my breath. Was my mind playing tricks on me? I didn't dare look down. Was I imagining something that seemed so strange and impossible? Had I lost all sense of reality? Perhaps I really was going mad — or perhaps it was a result of all those damn pills I was taking. A small, very cold hand had taken hold of my fingers. I kept my eyes fixed on the bright red puffer jacket and woolly hat on the torso of a toddler sized model in the shop window, as a soft little hand pushed its way into mine.

My heart was banging in my chest as I turned. The tiny fingers curled around my hand and tightened. I glanced down at the upturned face that belonged to a small child. Whether it was a boy or girl I couldn't tell, as the child's hair was long and uncombed. Pulling myself back into reality, I quickly bent my knees to come down to the level of the sweet little face. A smile appeared and I could see a few front teeth. The eyes were blue, the colour of the sea on a sunny day, and it had straight, tangled hair and a little face that was as pale as clotted cream. I supposed the toddler to be about twenty months old or so, possibly younger. The child was small and quite well dressed, wearing a chunky blue sweater and denim dungarees, but no coat. The blue bootie slippers that adorned the small feet were muddy and tiny bits of tarmac clung to the soles. The odour of nappy was quite strong

"Hello. Where is your mummy?" I asked finally. The blue eyes gazed at me but didn't respond.

"Do you have a name?" Looking around at the passing shoppers, no one appeared to be looking for the child and as I waited, I asked, "Do you live nearby? Can you show me where you live?" Although the child nodded, she or he didn't move or point, so after about ten minutes of getting nowhere, I said, "It's cold here, let's go into the café and get a drink, shall we?" The little head tilted to one side, eyes wide and steady, gazing up at me. I wasn't sure, but I thought I saw a slight nod.

With the child still holding tightly onto my hand, we walked slowly into the café next to the children's clothing shop. I ordered a cappuccino and a milky hot chocolate for the child. We sat in a seat by the window so that I could look out for anyone searching for this little person. Someone must have noticed that this child was missing. Perhaps I should find the shopping centre security, but as time passed, I found myself drawn to this sweet, silent, little person and I didn't want to just walk away and leave him.

Over an hour passed, and although I chatted and tried to encourage the child to talk to me, it had not spoken at all, but sat gazing at the surroundings wide eyed, whilst attempting to drink from the fat cup. I eventually asked the waitress for a straw and before long the cup was almost empty. The child smiled at me often as I continued to ask questions, so I found myself intrigued with this little blue-eyed angel.

On that ordinary, seemingly normal Thursday afternoon, the life that I was clutching onto with all my might changed completely. Looking back, I realise that I had felt that God, or whoever it was who was in charge, was giving me another chance. It was irrational I know, and I did worry — of course I did. The child did not belong to me. The child must've belonged to somebody, but no one had claimed him. By then I had decided he was a boy and as far as I could ascertain he had been discarded like an unwanted parcel just waiting for me to find him. I knew I couldn't part with him. If I took him home and cleaned him up a bit, perhaps I would take him to the police station. Surely I couldn't be expected to just leave him? What would they do if no one had reported him missing? Social services would be called, of course, so he would be faced with another set of strangers. He would be distressed, whereas at the moment he was smiling happily as he sucked the last remaining chocolate off his straw. He seemed totally content and anyone who looked at us would assume that I was his mother. I decided at that moment that this little dimpled treasure would be better off if I looked after him — after all, he had obviously willingly attached himself to me.

I wondered about his real mother: was she somewhere close by, looking for him? Was she ill or drunk perhaps? Surely by now someone was looking for him. Another half hour passed, and it was beginning to get dark outside and colder too.

"Come on then, little one." I lifted the child out of his seat and wrapped my woolly scarf around his soft, cold, little body. "Let's go look for your home, and if we can't find it you can come home with me."

We walked the length of the arcade and then out along the main shopping street and saw no one looking for him, so I decided that I was going to take care of him. He still hadn't spoken—perhaps, he couldn't talk. I knew that most toddlers at about this age could say about fifty words or more, use phrases and be able to put sentences together. I had read a great deal about child development when I was pregnant with Thomas. I understood that children varied, but no matter, when they say their first words, it's a sure bet they already understand much of what is said to them long before that.

On the bus going home he pointed and cooed. His eyes widened in alarm as a large lorry whooshed by — perhaps he hadn't even been on a bus before.

"Lorry," I said as I held him close, "Make a big noise, don't they?"

I discovered that he was definitely a boy when I carefully undressed him and popped him into a warm bath. He seemed overjoyed at the sensation of the bubbles that I had added, and he allowed me to wash his matted hair. I even took the scissors to the tangles at the back, so that by the time he was finished he looked beautiful and smelled clean and fresh. I have to admit that the smell of urine had increased as we had travelled home on the bus, and I could see that he'd obviously had the same nappy on for some time. His little bottom was red and sore. The only thing I had in my first aid kit was a jar of Vaseline, so when he was clean and shiny, I gently rubbed some into his bottom. I popped all his clothes and his slippers into the washing machine, found an old towel that I fashioned into a nappy and pulled on an old pair of my smallest pants, which I knotted at each side. I couldn't find anything to put on his little body, but I eventually cut up a pink tee shirt and tied it around his middle with an old silk scarf. He smiled and giggled throughout this activity—he seemed perfectly content. He was quite thin and incredibly pale skinned, so I guessed that he was younger than I had first thought. His tiny, dimpled hands reached for me at every opportunity, and I felt a wave of pure joy as he wrapped his arms around my neck—I loved the feel of him. Dressed in his odd assortment of clothes, I held him tight to my body. I felt a surge of emotion, it was a good feeling. *My Thomas*, I thought, knowing in my heart that it was not true. The pretence worried me, but it warmed me too.

Later I watched him happily eating scrambled eggs and toasted soldiers. I had little food left in the fridge, as I was leaving at the weekend.

"Is that good?" I inquired hoping that he was going to speak. He smiled and nodded so I knew that he had understood me.

"Are you going to tell me your name?" He nodded slowly again, dipping his chin up and down, but still did not answer.

"Okay, you finish your supper and tomorrow we will go back to the shopping centre one more time and see if anyone is looking for you. If not, we will buy you a warm coat and some boots."

His clothes were drying on the radiator. The tumble dryer had been sold but luckily the washing machine was still in place as the purchasers had asked to buy it.

I watched his bright little face as he gazed at me.

"Would you like a biscuit when you've finished your egg?" He nodded again and lifted his last piece of toast toward me. I laughed, feeling delighted at his offer. I leaned forward and ruffled his now shiny hair.

After a biscuit and a glass of milk, we sat on the sofa together and listened to the radio. His soft, warm little body leaned against me, and I wrapped my arm around him. He seemed to be perfectly content as he laid his head on my lap. By 10 p.m. he was fast asleep, so I wrapped a blanket around him and carried him up to the second bedroom. I carefully covered him with a spare quilt.

In the early hours of the morning my bedroom door creaked open. The child stood silhouetted against the door with my pink tee shirt hung loose around his legs. I couldn't see his face, but I knew he was quietly sobbing.

"Come here, darling," I sat up and he walked toward me. He was still half asleep. His thumb was pushed into his mouth and his face was wet with tears. I lifted the duvet and he crept in beside me and curled up against me. My heart exploded and I kissed his little head. "You can stay with me. You'll be safe here." I stroked his back and within minutes he was asleep.

The following morning after a bowl of oats and honey, I dressed him in his clean clothes and wrapped him in my big woolly scarf and some small fluffy socks that someone had given me in the Secret Santa two years past. We took the bus back to the shopping centre where I'd found him, and it occurred to me that by now there would be someone looking for him—surely there would be a notice about his disappearance. What a devastating thought that I should have to part with him so soon.

We walked through the park and the little boy held onto my hand and made no attempt to move toward the playground as I had expected. When we came to damp areas, I picked him up and parked him on my hip. The blue slippers that I had pulled over the fluffy pink socks only had soft soles and I didn't want him to get them wet.

We made our way through the road works and the big tarmacking lorries that still closed off an area of the high street and several of the side streets. We went straight back to the coffee shop, and as we drank our coffee and chocolate milk, the child solemnly watched the passers-by: families with loaded shopping bags, teenagers play fighting, a courting couple laughing into each other's eyes, oblivious to the world. A trio of gum-chewing, tattooed girls arrived and sat down at the table next to us, shopping bags bashing the chairs, chatting about someone they obviously disliked. "Did you see the state of 'er hair?" one of them asked, aghast. "What sort o' colour do you call that?" Between them they made quite a lot of noise, and my little boy watched them with a serious wide-eyed look on his face, keeping close to my side. Then there was a slight kerfuffle as two paramedics sped by, dividing the crowd in their hurry, and the girls lost interest in their conversation. "Been an accident somewhere, looks like," said the youngest of the group..

Still, no one had taken any notice of us, and the little boy sat quietly drinking his chocolate milk—he made no move to leave me or wander off.

As we prepared to leave, I heard a new customer tell the waitress, "Big hoo-ha down Union Road by the Oxfam shop. Some bloke had a fall out the back. Fell down some stairs. They think he's broke his neck."

"Oh dear," the waitress replied. "There's always something dodgy going on down there. It's all the yobbos and drug dealers that hang around outside those old derelict buildings. Them old shops should've been knocked down years ago."

"They are coming down in a few months, after next Christmas I've heard. Going to be a car park." The new customer informed the waitress as she plonked herself on a seat by the bar.

"About bloody time, parkins become a nightmare here," she replied. "And the bloody roadworks all the time. Can't drive down there anymore. Drives me mad in the mornings. No wonder the ambulance can't get down there." She picked up our cups and swept a cloth over our table. "Alright, love?"

"Thanks, yes, lovely. Come on, little one," I said as I lifted the boy on to my hip. We headed straight into the children's shop next door, and before I realised it, I had bought not only the red puffer coat and hat from the window but also two pairs of boots, an assortment of vests, pants, socks, two sweaters, two pairs of dungarees, two pairs of pyjamas and a dressing gown. The shop assistant was kind and helpful, when I asked for a packet of nappy pants she turned and looked at him to assess the size. "Just for nights, are they? How old is he? Should be out of them soon by the looks of him."

I nodded and smiled, not sure what to say. "He's getting there."

She assumed that we lived above one of the arcade shops because the boy had no boots or coat on, so I said as coolly as I could manage. "We'll put the coat and boots on. He's off to stay with Grandma." She pulled the little red woolly hat onto his head, and he beamed his dimpled smile.

"What a picture! Your Grandma will love your new clothes… What is your name little man?"

Before she could say another word, I picked him up and stuttered, "T…T… Thomas but we call him T.J. I sped out of the shop into the crowds with my heart fluttering. We only stopped to buy a colouring book and some crayons, a couple of newspapers, crisps and a big bag of jelly sweets. Within half an hour we were back in the house and I was exhausted with relief. I made us a sandwich lunch and prepared some potatoes to mash for supper while the boy loosely coloured a red bus in his new book. Now in my head he was T.J., not Thomas: was I deceiving myself that he was the child I had given birth to? No, but from that moment on he was definitely mine and I was going to keep him.

Practically everything was packed, and the fridge was almost empty, but I found a tin of baked beans and some cheese. It was Friday and we were not leaving until early Sunday morning, but I still had eggs, bread and a big box of porridge, milk and some fruit, so I didn't need to go out again.

Of course, I couldn't sleep, and rising early on Saturday, I continued with my packing in between chatting to T.J., trying to encourage him to talk. He followed me around gurgling words I couldn't understand and pushed boxes and tried to lift things. We ate porridge with brown sugar and grated apple for breakfast, and as he now had his warm clothes to wear, I took him over to the park to feed the ducks with some stale biscuits I'd found in the back of a cupboard. It was a typical November day—really cold with a bit of watery sunshine; nonetheless, T.J. ran and skipped along beside me, only wanting to be lifted when several ducks came flying toward us upon seeing our food.

I still felt that I was walking in a dream, but I was so happy and couldn't wait for the following day when we would leave for a new life together.

Shit. I really was going to kidnap a child!

CHAPTER 23

KATE - Sunday 21st November 2012

I tried to focus and anchor my spinning thoughts but part of me wanted to scream with the sheer terror of what I intended to do, and part of me wanted to sing with joy at being given this chance of being a mother again — I knew it was now or never.

It was time to leave; the beds, chests of drawers, the sofa and the carved coffee table that Jackson and I had bought together, had already been collected by their new owner that morning and the van that I'd hired was almost completely packed. As I pushed the last cushions, bedding, bags and cases into the back, I had already made the firm decision to take T.J. with me. In the last two days I had scoured every newspaper and listened to every radio and TV channel, but there were no reports of a lost child. Surely this little angel, this precious little person belonged to somebody. Why hadn't it been noticed that he was missing? Why were there no appeals for his whereabouts? I'd decided that he now belonged to me. Why not? No one had claimed him, so it stood to reason that his parents didn't want him, but I did, and I knew that I could love him and care for him. No one had seen him with me and challenged me, besides, he had shown no desire to leave my side.

From the moment of my decision, I was anxious that someone from the bank or perhaps a neighbour might see me with this child and know that he did not belong to me. Luckily, Bill and Mollie were away in Wales visiting one of their sons; we had said a tearful goodbye to each other on Wednesday, the day before I'd found the boy.

All through the day another part of myself asked, *was I really prepared to kidnap him and take him with me? Would I be able to keep him? Surely someone, somewhere was looking for him.* My thoughts changed from hour to hour as chaotic as a cloud of flies. *No, I couldn't keep him. I will take him to the police. But what would happen to him if no one claimed him? Undoubtedly, he would go into care. He would be sent to a home, some disgusting place that fed and clothed him but didn't protect him or want to love and keep him like I did. Or, he could be fostered out to scrupulous money grabber, with little love for children, as I had been.* The next minute I wondered: *Perhaps I could pass him off as my own Thomas. He was about the same age as my boy if he had lived. I still have Thomas's birth certificate. Would I be breaking the law? Was there a law against loving an unwanted child?*

Everything I thought about myself was wavering, slipping away. Now all I wanted to do was to leave as soon as possible. I adapted a pile of cushions and a strap so that T.J. was secure in the passenger seat of the van, and I hoped and prayed that I wouldn't get stopped. I was sure there were laws about having such young children in the front seat. Luckily, he was really too small to be easily seen, and very soon he slept.

With every mile we got away from Bristol I felt calmer; the anxiety that I felt started to dissipate. I became aware of my vertebrae unknotting and my shoulders relaxing. The relief of knowing that having made the decision it was going to be a fact. T.J. was mine from now on. When he was awake, I sang some of the songs being played on the radio, a new song by Adele as well as a couple of old favourites; the little boy giggled and made a few strange sounding noises, but nothing that I could understand.

We stopped to go to the toilet and buy some snacks, drinks, fruit and essential wet wipes for sticky little fingers. The distance was long and the drive boring until we got off the endless, grey motorways. Luckily, the weather had been quite bright all day and when we reached the winding roads of the countryside the sun was shining.

I felt as if I was coming home.

We headed toward the coastal road that led up to Scarborough and we soon found the B&B that I had booked for two nights. It had taken nearly all day to drive the two hundred and sixty miles.

When we arrived, it was late, so we ate our snacks and fruit, had a bath and went to bed. T.J. had slept quite a lot on the journey, so he took a while to settle. As he did so, I told him about the wonderful life that we were going to have together; I told him how we would find a lovely place to live, how I would take him to the beach and look for crabs, about how he would go to playschool or nursery and then to big school, how we would make friends with other children, how we were going to find his Uncle Alex — my brother. He gazed at me as if he understood and made a word that sounded like 'aness… es… es' He grinned and cooed but said nothing else.

Early the next morning, after a huge breakfast, we set off to find the local letting agent in town. It wasn't far and I carefully parked and locked the van.

Although it was sunny, it was bitterly cold, and our breath hung in the air like drifts of smoke. T.J. was well wrapped up in his new clothes, but as we looked for the letting agents he struggled and wanted to be carried after the first hundred yards or so. I decided that I would buy a buggy at the first opportunity. I thought again that he must be younger than I had first estimated. He was still wearing nappy pants at night but in the last two days had used the toilet without a problem.

We found Anthony in the estate agent office, who was a delightful and enthusiastic help. He found us a property that he was sure would be perfect, a two-bedroom cottage in Mill Lane, Osgodby, a village just off the Filey road. It was so easy. I had a good reference from the bank and plenty of savings. Anthony told us that the cottage was empty, and I signed a six-month lease on it straight away. I didn't even go to see it, but once the agent had taken my references and I had paid the required deposit he handed over the keys and instructions for finding it.

"It's in good order and has a new heating system, it's rural but fairly close to the town. I think you will need transport as the bus service is not too reliable," he told me when I explained about the van. "Go and see Mick down the road, good bloke and he's got a couple of right little bargains at the moment. He'll give you a good price and a guarantee."

I was overjoyed because, within the next hour, I had not only found somewhere to live, but had purchased a lovely little blue VW that had only had one previous owner and was in good condition. I'd never owned a car before, but Mick had promised help with any problems and arranged the tax and insurance cover there and then. I was overjoyed and T.J. had been as good as gold as I toted him around, only whinging a bit because of all the walking. I gave Mick the address of the cottage and he promised delivery on the following day when I planned to unpack and release the van back to the rental company.

It was lunchtime so we found a little local café and ate fish and chips with a cup of tea and a glass of milk for T.J.

"Let's go and look at our new home," I said as we left. I needed to turn the heating on and perhaps unload some of the van. T.J. was tired by the time we found the cottage. It had a small, secluded driveway and I told him to stay still in the van while I got out and had a look. Initially it seemed dark and dreary and after struggling with the door that obviously needed some oiling, I got inside. Next to the front door stood a large mahogany coat stand and a boot box, a dark blue and green rug covered most of the floor space and a big soft caramel coloured sofa sat in front of an open fireplace which was stacked with logs and ready to be lit. There was a bookshelf, a pretty standard lamp and a good-sized TV. The cottage smelt musty and damp, but it had been empty for a while, so that was to be expected. Although the living area was small, it was cosy and there was a door to the narrow staircase, which took me up to a landing where Anthony had told me to find the heating controls inside a large airing cupboard.

The cottage had two bedrooms with only a small bed and wardrobe in one and a double bed and chest of drawers in the other. By the time I got the heating on and taken the bedding, a few towels and some clothes into the airing cupboard ready for the following day, my little cherub was ready for his nap. Without exploring further, we returned to the B&B where we both curled up in bed, and with a sigh of relief, I joined T.J. for a short sleep. Everything was going so well.

We spent the evening in our room watching the television. T.J. stared at the screen, totally transfixed; I don't think he had ever watched Peppa Pig or Blue Peter before. At one point he got off the bed, walked toward the screen, and put his little index finger against the picture. He turned and his smile was one of delight—he looked so happy. I had to turn the TV off so that we could get ready for bed. In his pyjamas and little blue slippers, he walked around the TV set several times looking for the picture before I could get him into bed. I wondered again at the mystery of his life and where he had come from.

The following morning the weather was bright and fresh so, after breakfast, I packed our belongings, fastened T.J. into the van, and set off for our new home. I told him happily, "Not long now, my baby boy. Just you and me together." His eyes widened as he picked up on my excitement. I jumped into the driver's seat and clapped my hands, which made T.J. giggle. I rolled my shoulders to ease some of the tension that had built up between my shoulder blades over the past few days. We set off, and to my surprise T.J. started to clap his hands and made a singing noise.

We called into a little supermarket shop, and I bought two huge bags of groceries plus two storybooks, a TV guide, a newspaper and an orange teddy bear.

Upon arriving at the cottage, I lit the fire and was delighted to find a good large fireguard folded in the kitchen. I hooked it firmly around the fireplace, lifted T.J. into our new home and settled him on the sofa with his new storybooks, while I started to unload some of the boxes.

Unpacking took far longer than necessary, but each and every box was played with, inspected and folded up as we emptied them. Unexpectedly, in an unopened box we found the blue potty and the drinking cup with elephants on the sides that I had bought for Thomas and never used. My heart skipped a beat or two, but T.J. was delighted, and we had to stop to make use of the cup for orange juice, and then the potty for a long sit down.

I also found my box of treasured photographs: pictures of my garden in bloom, Mollie and Bill at a barbeque, a clutch of pictures of Thomas, mostly with his mouth open wailing, and one favourite photo of Jackson ready to set off for a run in a new set of lycra attire. He was laughing and flexing his biceps and he looked happy and handsome. His dark hair was quite long, and a quiff lay across his forehead—for a single moment I remembered him with affection. I carefully packed the box away and took the photographs to the top shelf of the wardrobe upstairs. At that moment, I didn't want any reminders of my past life—I was so happy.

The cottage had a lovely, tiny kitchen, with a back door that led across a small patio into a long, lawned garden. Someone had looked after it well and I could see signs of a vegetable patch and a garden shed at the far end.

It was a busy and satisfying day. Later, when T.J. was fast asleep clutching the little orange teddy bear, I knelt on the floor beside the bed that we were going to share and watched him. His chest rose and fell with the gentle rhythm of his breath and his eyes fluttered in his sleep. I sat back on my heels and prayed that I had done the right thing in bringing him here with me. I would make us a good life and wherever he came from would be irrelevant because he would become mine.

That first night felt strange; although the cottage was silent, if I listened carefully, I could hear the water circulating through the radiators and pipes so that the wooden floorboards gently creaked as they reacted to the change in temperature. There was a single streetlight on the corner of the road and a pale eerie shaft of light lit the far side of the room. There was a moment when I thought I must have been dreaming. I lay exhausted in my little bubble of strangeness, and wondered at the fact that life had changed irrevocably in the past few days; I felt a wave of sheer joy pass through me.

CHAPTER 24

KATE

By the beginning of December, I had registered both T.J. and I with a local doctor. It had been easy until the doctor asked for our previous doctor's address and our medical records.

"Oh. I don't know... I think we might have a problem there." I had anticipated being asked and I said, "I don't think they will be able to supply any. They had a big fire recently and I understand most records were lost."

"Mmm, well never mind..." said the doctor without even looking at me as he was busy trying to get T.J. to stand against the height marker on the wall. "Have you got Thomas's PCHR?" Noticing my blank look, he continued. "Red book — Personal child development record book."

I tried to smile but my mouth feels tight and frozen. "Oh, yes... Sorry, I seem to have lost track of it in the move. It will probably turn up." I tried to sound confident but when the time came for T.J. to be weighed the Doctor looked concerned. "Thomas is tall for his age but... two years old in December... let me see... he should be more like 26 - 27 pounds and he is only 19.6. Is he eating well? Has he been healthy?"

"He is eating better than he used to." My insides were quaking as I realised that T.J. was probably quite a bit younger than Thomas would have been, but I tried to be confident as I told the doctor, "In fact in the past few weeks he is doing better than he has ever done. He never was a good eater, and I *was* worried, but I think we will find that he will catch up the way he eats now. It must be the sea air," I lied. "He is healthy, though - isn't he?"

"Seems so," the doctor replied with a smile as he watched T.J. scooting his dog on wheels across the surgery floor. "Has Thomas had all his jabs?" I nodded, hoping and praying that he had. Perhaps he hadn't and I started to panic, surely every child had them nowadays. I tried to remember which ones Thomas had.

"I think he might be due for his flu vaccine though," I said knowing that it was recommended for two-year-olds.

"I'd like him to gain a little weight first," said the doctor checking his chart. "Come in after his birthday and we'll see where he is then."

"Okay doctor." I was so relieved, but he continued, "I think he should be talking more than he is too. I've checked his mouth and he isn't tongue tied, so if his speech doesn't develop soon, we will need to investigate why he is a bit behind."

I was sure that there was nothing wrong with T.J., but I had wondered whether he could speak at all, because initially he'd said nothing that I could understand. He often made noises or tried a few words, but mostly I didn't know what he was saying, so I decided it was time to teach him. On the way home from the doctor's surgery, I bought cards and blocks, books and educational toys.

Every activity or outing became a game of naming things and colours and places, and I encouraged him daily with new words. It wasn't long before he would ask for things, like milk or potty or his most favourite thing of all, the little wooden pull-along dog. It usually accompanied us everywhere. I had bought it when we had first arrived here on a shopping trip to the main street where we had found a charity shop that sold endless toys and clothes for toddlers. I had also purchased a second-hand buggy, a car seat and a small outdoor trampoline.

T.J. was a constant source of fascination for me, his pale silvery hair, his chubby dimpled cheeks — every new word or task achieved seemed like a miracle. My boy, the child I never thought I would have. Love and pride swelled in my heart with his every smile. He was a joy to watch and over the following week he began to say a few sentences and seemed to understand me well enough. He improved daily and smiled happily at every new word he mastered. He ran and played, and he would laugh at me when I chased him or tickled him. I often gazed at him in disbelief. It was almost as if another child had emerged from the quiet, withdrawn little person that I had found on that cold Thursday afternoon in November just a few weeks ago.

I had reduced my medication and no longer needed the sleeping tablets; it was liberating to be free of the bleary haze that I had been living in for so long. I'd existed in a state of lethargy since losing Thomas, but now I found it hard to believe that, in a few short weeks, I had moved from that struggling unhappy woman, incapable of doing the simplest mundane tasks, to feeling renewed; I was bursting with energy and enthusiasm and I was restored and happy.

It was all because of this beautiful, sunny little boy who clung to me with such a sweet loving need.

I made T.J. the centre of my world, read every parenting book I could find until I convinced myself that I could do this on my own. As each Thursday passed, I counted another week of happiness with 'my boy'. Some days I was plagued with worry and knew that a woman somewhere had given birth to my little angel and must know that he was missing — I constantly pushed this thought away.

I decided to make a proper room for T.J. so, with the landlord's permission, I went to the local DIY store and bought paint and blinds, a big toy box and some free-standing shelving. I thought that I could assemble the shelves myself, not because I was particularly good at that sort of thing, but with my new enthusiasm and energy, I decided it was worth a try. I set about repainting for an hour in the afternoon when T.J. took a nap, and then sometimes in the evening after I had read him a story and tucked him into bed. I was inordinately pleased with myself. A decorative strip with elephants and giraffes in blue and gold was the next step. The blue blinds needed a bit of help, and I discovered Mick from the garage had a brother who would do small jobs on his day off. I bought a colourful duvet from a charity shop, and it soon looked so beautiful that T.J. decided that he would sleep in there, rather than in my bed. Occasionally he would wander in for a cuddle, but I knew he was beginning to feel safe.

My Thomas would have been two on the 15th of December, so that became T.J.'s birthday; in the morning the weather was mild and windy, so we drove to the coast at Scarborough and watched the seagulls.

I remember thinking, *one day soon I would take him down onto the beach*. Before long the tourists would be arriving onto the now deserted beaches, clutching their deckchairs, windbreakers, buckets and spades. It was a vibrant place in the summer months: fish and chips, donut and ice cream stalls, amusement arcades and tacky novelty shops all creating the atmosphere of holidays and fun. I couldn't wait to join in.

As we sat together in the car watching the waves, I asked T.J., "T.J. say 'I am two years old'. It's your birthday today."

"Two... birfday day," he grinned happily, and I was overcome with pride.

"Let's go for a walk and learn some more words, shall we?"

"Yeth, go walk."

We headed along the seafront holding hands and I pointed to things along the way, the rusty gate, the pebbles and the waves rolling along the shoreline.

"Just look at those birds in the sky and how they fly on the wind."

"Wind an' sky an' birfday today," said my little Thursday angel.

It was icy cold and too windy to stay out for long so with pink, glowing cheeks and cold fingers we headed home for lunch. I'd bought T.J. some little coloured cars and a toy garage, which he played with, happily making brum brum noises and scooting the cars into the skirting boards. I watched him with pride. In the last five weeks he had changed so much — he was no longer quiet and withdrawn but happy and exuberant as any other two-year-old. I'd even attempted to make a chocolate cake and blown up some balloons. I was more excited than I had ever been for my own birthdays, which had basically all been non-events. This little boy was going to get everything that I had missed as a child.

A few days before Christmas we returned to the doctor who was pleased with T.J.'s weight gain.

"There is no denying that Thomas is thriving," said the doctor when he weighed T.J. It startled me a little when the doctor referred to T.J. as Thomas, but I had to get used to it as that was bound to happen especially when he went to school. "I still haven't managed to find his records," he said but didn't show any concern.

When he asked my boy how old he was T.J. giggled and said, "I's two an' 'ad choco' cake on my birfday."

"Well, that's wonderful," said the doctor. "Now let's get this little flu jab done and you're good to go and enjoy your Christmas."

T.J. had his flu jab and his little face crumpled, his mouth puckered, and his eyes filled with tears. He turned to me and reached his now chubby little arms, so I lifted him and held him close. "It's done now, darling, don't cry." I hated to see him distressed in any way. With my boy in my arms, fitting his body into mine, he stretched his fingers to my face and stroked my cheek. I felt such intense pleasure and at the same time a fleeting pain. I had convinced myself that he was mine, but I knew he was not and wondered yet again at where he had come from.

By the time we reached the 25th of December 2012 I had made the little cottage our home. We had developed an easy routine and each day I helped him with his words, and together we played games. I bought and wrapped presents, set up a small Christmas tree and decorated it with baubles and lights. T.J. was thrilled with it, and as I worked putting up shiny stars and glittery ropes of tinsel, I told him what they were called. He started to copy the words and before long had increased his vocabulary yet again. I no longer had any doubts about his ability to speak. A rare peacefulness washed through me and with it I gave thanks to the events that had brought us here. At that moment there was nothing else I could wish for.

I took T.J. to the church nativity, and he gazed solemnly at the singers and the decorations.

We watched funny films on television and ate nuts and chocolates in front of the fire - I couldn't have been happier.

All through the following weeks we enjoyed our cosy little world. The cottage had proved to be perfect, as we could walk along the country road to a farm where they sold free-range eggs and an assortment of essentials, as well as home grown vegetables. Even though our home was small, I loved every nook and cranny of it. It smelt different now, with the help of a good clean and a diffuser full of sweet-smelling essential oils; the log fire that had dispelled any lingering damp. To me it now smelt of peace and happiness and love. T.J. blossomed and his speech was as normal as any other two-year-old.

In February we were snowed in for a couple of days. T.J. had never seen snow and it was a joy to watch him. I took photographs of the cottage and the garden and of T.J. with the snowman we had built. I watched my happy little boy, his eyes shining and his cheeks pink with cold and as we played, I felt like a happy child myself. We cleared the front path and threw snowballs at each other until we were so exhausted and wet that we stripped off all our clothes and soggy boots, changed into our pj's and built up the fire.

We sat drinking hot chocolate and T.J. said, "I likes the snow — s'good Mummy."

Could life get any better?

Sitting comfortably by the roaring fire I had a fleeting memory of a snowy day in York back in 1980 when I had hidden in the garden shed, freezing cold and hungry after running away from Henry Gladstone. He had been drinking and I was terrified. It was two days later that I was found and taken from York back to the children's home in Scarborough. I was ill for nearly a month and interviewed several times about why I was hiding. I told the social worker everything, and although she was kind and wrote a long report, I never knew what happened to the Gladstones. It was nearly six months later that I went to live in Filey with Mary and John Lambert.

I closed my eyes so tight that I pressed my eyeballs back into my skull. I needed to push these images away and set aside all those thoughts of my past to concentrate on the love and warmth of my life with T.J.

The following day was dry and frosty, but we needed some eggs and milk. We trudged through the snow to the farm. It wasn't far and we were greeted with a cup of hot tea by the owners, Geraldine and Fred King, who let us get warm while we sorted what we needed.

"We have some kittens for sale if you would like to see them." said Fred as he filled a box with fat brown eggs. I raised a questioning eyebrow to Fred, but he only grinned at T.J. and said, "Well, they all need a good home with someone to play with an' I thought you might be just the fella."

"Yeth, I would," answered T.J. excitedly — of course he would!

T.J. was so enchanted with them that we obviously had to have one. His little eyes lit with excitement when I told him he could decide which one to take home. He picked a little grey tabby and instantly named her Lena, although where he had heard that name before I never knew.

With my rucksack full of food and tins of kitten meat and biscuits, I zipped the little kitten into my puffer jacket, and we raced back home. She soon transformed our lives with her activities. It was the best thing that I could have done as T.J. adored his new pet and spent hours chasing and playing with his little Lena, she followed him everywhere and slept close beside him every night.

When the weather was good enough, we drove into town to the big supermarket; we often stopped for a drink and occasionally had lunch out. T.J. was growing fast, and his energy and enthusiasm were wonderful. It was time to let him out into the world.

Spring had arrived overnight abruptly, shrugging off the coat of winter. There seemed to be something miraculous about seeing the relentless optimism of new growth after the long cold of the winter months. The cottage garden threw up crocuses and daffodils, and as April approached the garden blossomed. Everything looked green, the hedgerows were full of springtime's wild-flowers, and they were bathed in watery sunshine. The air was suddenly balmy; seagulls, white and squawky, reeled across the pale blue sky.

After Easter I enrolled T.J. in 'The Busy Bees', a local nursery for two mornings a week. The first morning I felt my heart would break having to leave him for so long with complete strangers. There were other mothers hovering with concerned faces too, trying to be brave with encouraging smiles, a few hanging on grimly to little trembling hands.

The more confident children were already charging away. There were one or two with small, worried faces milling around, undoubtedly on their first day too, but whose mothers had left—they were obviously hopeful that their absence would encourage a bit more confidence. As we stood at the door of the playgroup's main room, T. J. still clung on to my hand, his eyes wide as he surveyed all the other children, most of whom appeared to be bigger and older than him.

"Is he the only one?" asked a buxom blonde in a bright red raincoat, who had just dropped off her twin girls.

"Yes, just the one…"

"He'll be fine. Don't look so worried," she turned and called her girls, "Jess, Jo—come and look after this new boy."

Within minutes Jess and Jo, both blonde and bubbly like their mum, had convinced T.J. that he could release my hand. He set off toward the sand pit without a backward turn.

"Thanks," I said.

"I'm Amanda, but everyone calls me Mandy. Come and join us for a coffee." She turned and indicated four other mums chatting at the door.

"That would be lovely."

That first day Mandy introduced me to the others, and they were a mixed bunch. The oldest, Bella, was a tall, dark haired and rather haughty woman who looked tired — I wondered if perhaps she was a grandparent, but it turned out that she was dropping off her youngest of five other children. Another of the mothers was Fern, who was chocolate box pretty, and I guessed she was probably only about twenty-three or twenty-four; Fern had one girl at school and one in nursery. Heather was the smartest, and she was dressed in an immaculate trouser suit and a colourful scarf; she had one boy, Kyle, and he was the same age as T.J. and had started nursery that day. The last was Amy, a mother of two boys, who was so quiet, dowdy and shy. I felt positively vibrant when I was introduced to her, even though my now, long curly hair was scrunched into an untidy bun and I sported jeans and sweatshirts rather than the smart suits I'd always worn in the bank.

Once, I would have viewed this group of women with disdain, with their inane gossip and small talk. They were a school gate mafia: competing, boasting and jostling for positions. They were women who'd rarely had a career, choosing to bury themselves in star charts, potty training and the best way to get vegetables into their offspring's diet; they were all educationally competitive.

I've never found it easy to make small talk or to have any close friends, other than Mollie and Jackson — neither of whom I had contact with. Although my acquaintances at the photography class and book-club had been brief, I had begun to let go of my reticence — but then I lost Thomas and I'd retreated into my shell of self-protection. Parts of my life had been such a mess; however much I longed to be open and informal I had found it too difficult to be sociable. Now, with the changes that had occurred over the past year, I felt I needed to allow myself to relax and stop being so insular again. I was grateful to Mandy for introducing herself and the others on that first morning and as time passed, I found it easier. Having a child and taking him to playschool changed everything.

Due to my self-enforced isolation over the winter, I was shy at first and slow to join in on the conversations, but as the weeks passed, I began to enjoy these early morning coffee breaks. We talked and laughed about being tired, not knowing how to keep the kids stimulated, how much salt and sugar were in foods and how fast they were growing.

I soon got to know several of the mothers, and I liked them. We were like a club: ladies with the same things in common, getting a bit of free time whilst their little ones were looked after. I was surprised to see how quickly I became one of them.

Sometimes on nursery days I wandered around town rather than going home or taking coffee with the other mothers. I went to the job centre, although I didn't have much luck, so I started to think about finding some other way to support us until T.J. went to primary school. I wasn't too worried, as I still had money from the sale of the house, but it wasn't going to last forever. I often scoured the charity shops for bargains or had coffee on my own.

One morning I took the opportunity to go to the house where I'd been fostered by the Lamberts, but I discovered they had moved ten years previously to

Cornwall. I couldn't find anyone who had a forwarding address, and I was sorry—I sent them a silent prayer of thanks for their kindness.

T.J. settled well and benefitted enormously from having friends his own age. Before long I found myself invited to coffee mornings and play days, children's birthday parties and outings to the local park. In fact, I began to feel like a regular mum.

CHAPTER 25

KATE

One day in the summer holidays, we six mums arranged to go to Cayton Bay beach, and I was excited at the thought of introducing T.J. to the sea. There were twenty-one of us altogether, as Mandy's husband Kit and Amy's husband John decided to come with us. We'd all bought picnic lunches and the noise and excitement radiating from our assorted children was fantastic. We met in the big car park on the headland, from which we all walked together along to the café where the walk down to the beach was the easiest.

T.J. skipped and hopped along with Kyle and the twins, Jess and Jo, clutching a new bucket and spade until we got to the steep path that led down to the sandy beach. I held firmly on to T.J. as we negotiated our way down, all of us clutching the picnic bags and assorted towels, cricket bats and balls, sun cream and hats that we had brought with us.

As Kit and John played cricket with the children, we women organised the picnic, settled on our beach towels, and chatted. It was the day we all really got to know each other. Mostly we told each about our lives, comic and touching moments, childhood traumas, marriage and the mothers-in-laws. We laughed and joked about silly things from our youth, so I made up stories, never hinting at the traumatic days of my real childhood.

With a huge grin, Bella confided in us that her husband wouldn't have the snip, so she was booked into hospital to have a sterilisation. We all approved!

It wasn't long before I was asked about where I came from, and they were all surprised when I told them that I was from North Yorkshire, as I had completely lost my accent. No one was surprised that I was a single mum either, as Fern was too, her husband had run off with a local estate agent when they were buying a house during her second pregnancy.

The children were soon bored with the cricket and wanted to paddle. Bella's older girls and Amy's nine-year-old boy wanted to swim so we all went into the sea. It was so cold, and I briefly remembered the warmth of the sea in

Portugal three years previously. We squealed and laughed as we got into the tumbling waves.

T.J. jumped on me, winding his wet legs around my waist, and I was overjoyed at the feel of him. We splashed and laughed as we fell into the cold water; we were thrilled to be there with our friends. The happiness of that day was so uplifting, and I realised that the only thing, the single, glaring flaw was that T.J. was not really mine. What sort of woman gave him life and then abandoned him? I had given little thought to the boy's father, and I could not even provide him with an alternative. I had watched Kit and John with their children and felt that would be what T.J. was missing in his life.

As we dried the children and ourselves and attempted to remove the wet sand from our swimsuits, I became more aware of the relationship that the men had with their children. They joked and played and added masculine energy into their family, and I asked Fern how she was coping on her own.

"I feel so inadequate sometimes. Don't the children lose out not having a father around?" I asked.

"It's okay most of the time but I think that if I had boys, it would be harder. Boys need their dads as role models though, don't you think?" She noticed my worried face and added. "Mothers can do a great job though…"

"Don't you have parents, grandparents or brothers to help you?" asked Mandy who was scooping sand out from between her enormous breasts.

"No, I never knew any of my grandparents. I was told that my father's both died in the bombing during the war, and I have no idea what happened to my mother's parents—I think they lived abroad."

"What about your own parents, Kate?" asked Fern.

"I have absolutely no memory of them at all, but I found out that they had both drowned off Scarborough beach when I was very young. They were full of drugs, and no one knows whether they fell in the sea or went for a swim."

"Bloody hell, Kate, how sodding tragic," said Mandy.

It was she that I confided in that day about having a brother that I wanted to trace.

"How lovely, can we help?"

"I don't know where to start," I said.

I told her the story of how my brother, Alex and I, had been in care after being found alone in a bedsit in Scarborough, how he was adopted but I wasn't.

"It's unlikely that he will even remember me, as he was only four and a half. I was six. His name was Alex Channon and I loved him more than life itself."

"What a story Kate — do you know I bet my husband could find out, he works in social services and the laws have changed about getting access to that sort of information. I'll ask him how to go about tracing your brother." Mandy told me confidently.

"Great," I said, and we talked about other things.

Fern told us about her absent husband and Amy confided that she was studying astrology and would be happy to do our charts, so we each told her when our birthdays were, and we laughed as she outlined our personalities. I was a Libran, born in October, so apparently I judge my fellows fairly, see other's points of view and like harmony and beautiful things; supposedly I had a sense of order and balance and needed to find myself a Gemini mate.

Bella said she had an unmarried Gemini brother, but he was gay and nearly fifty, so we all had a good laugh and moved on to finding what Fern needed. In between listening to Amy, we watched the children, reapplied our sunscreen as the day grew hotter, and occasionally got up for another paddle or quick swim. I had never in my life had a day that I had enjoyed so much. I remember that day with such pleasure, the company, the laughter and all the happy faces of the children will be imprinted on my memory forever.

It actually didn't take long at all to trace my long-lost brother. Within weeks—and with the help of Mandy's husband Kit—we discovered that Alex was now Alex Hutchinson, and he was one of four adopted children. He was living in Saltburn, just forty or so miles up the coast.

CHAPTER 25

ALEX

"Is Alex at home?" the voice on the phone quivered, "I am trying to trace Alex Hutchinson. Have I got the right number?"

My heart nearly jumped out of my chest as the voice continued. "My name is Kate Channon and I have been informed that my brother, Alex…"

"Kate…Katie," I shouted, "Is that you? I can't believe it. I have been looking for *you*. Where are you?"

All I could hear was a gentle sobbing at the other end of the phone. "Kate," I said again. "Where are you?"

"Filey… Is that really you, Alex?" the voice asked softly.

I couldn't believe that my sister had managed to find me. My only memories of my really early childhood are of Kate. Small snippets of moments that have come to me over the years: a shared apple, a ruffle of my hair, and a warm arm around me when I was cold. In fact, all I remember is the love she gave me. I do remember that we both had curly, slightly unruly hair and the same colour eyes.

There were times that I thought perhaps it was my vivid imagination playing tricks rather than a memory.

I have little recollection of the time I spent in the children's home — I hadn't reached my fifth birthday by the time I was adopted by Catherine and Stephen Hutchinson and moved into their large country house in Saltburn. I was the third of their four adopted children, the eldest was Craig, big handsome Craig, who is five years older than me and is now the local vet. My diminutive sister Mai was two years older than me, half Vietnamese and the sweetest, prettiest woman imaginable. She has recently married Jacob and is expecting her first baby. My 'little brother' Scott was adopted as a baby by the Hutchinson's when I was eleven and came from a mixed-race background, but nobody was sure at the time what that was, because he was found in a hospital corridor when he was only a day old.

After a DNA profile it was established that he had a mix of Asian, Caribbean and Scottish blood, but nobody cared, as he was now part of the Hutchinson clan.

My life had been easy, full of love and healthy discipline. My adoptive parents were the best in the world, practical, intelligent and caring. Dad was a lecturer and a teacher of Maths, Physics and Modern Sciences and Mum was a writer, mainly of cookbooks with an emphasis on vitamin and mineral packed ingredients; mum had trained as a nutritionist before we four adopted children entered her life. She was now writing a 'romantic' novel or so she told us, but just recently she had taken more interest in growing organic food in our country garden.

Seeing Kate for the first time was unforgettable. We had arranged to meet in Whitby, half-way for both of us and we knew of a small café on the steep walk from the coast up to the town. I was apprehensive, I thought that we might not recognise each other, but it was the hair that did it. Both of us still had the curly, blondish, Botticelli corkscrews, although mine was a little thinner.

We had arrived at much the same time, saw each other from a distance and came together in the doorway of the café. She grabbed my hands and said, "Alex, Oh Alex…

I can't believe that we are together after so long." We hugged as if we would never let go.

Leaning away from her, I noticed that I really looked at her — it was almost like looking in a mirror, we were so alike. The hair, the eye colour and even the shape of her face was exactly like mine. I was only a few inches taller and had put on a bit of weight in the past year, but we could have been twins. Her lips quivered and her eyes filled with tears, she said, "I have dreamed about this moment." She was holding my hands so tightly I had to smile and wiggle my fingers so that she would release them.

"We are blocking the doorway. Let's get inside." I pulled her into the café. We settled ourselves in a far corner and I was finding it hard to hold onto the emotion I felt at seeing my big sister after so many years.

It was very quiet and only an elderly couple sat drinking their coffees and gazing out of the window.

"I am so happy to see you... to have found you... after so long," she said quietly as she wiped tissues across her face.

I too had dreamed of this moment and throughout my adult life I'd had good intentions of finding her again.

It was only recently that I had returned to Scarborough to find the children's home closed, and up until then I had managed to trace her to Reading, but no further. According to Harriet Johnston, who worked for the church group and helped her go to university there, she had stayed in touch until Kate left Reading in to work in Basingstoke. She had told me the name of the bank that she worked for, but my workload had piled up during the previous winter, and my investigations into her whereabouts had stopped. I had also got engaged to Sophie and we were planning to marry in the spring of next year, so my spare time had been filled with venues, catalogues and lists. In the autumn, I was due to go down to the Thames Valley Training Centre in Sulhamstead, west of Reading to help with some training and I'd arranged to meet up with Harriet. Now, I sat face to face with my sister who had found me. I was so delighted; I couldn't stop smiling.

"Alex, have you had a happy life?" Kate asked softly.

"The best. I have the most brilliant parents. You will meet them and see for yourself. My mother has told me that I must bring you home as soon as possible. She wanted to come with me, but I insisted that we got acquainted first."

This lovely lady was my big sister. My excitement made me gabble on. "I have a sister and two brothers, all adopted, so you are my only blood relative — I thought you were lost forever. They all want to meet you and your boy and drag you into our mad family."

"Really, how lovely... I can't tell you what that means to me. I have never had..."

She stopped and I could see that she was finding it difficult to talk.

"Okay, don't worry Kate, we can take it slowly."

"Never had a family... No, of course I want to meet them — not yet though. It's just that I... I was never adopted, you see, I never had anybody. It was only ever you that mattered to me, and you are all I remember with any sort of pleasure. Look at you now... My adorable little brother... I cried for weeks when you left. Why didn't they take me too? You were all I had in the world. After you went, I was lost. I thought, no, I didn't think, I knew, that nobody wanted me."

"I don't think my family were told at the time that I had a sister. It was only later that they got to know about you, but you were fostered out somewhere in York. I have only found this out recently. My parents had to get in touch with the home when I was about eight, because I was ill, and they wanted to know about our dead parents. I remember that they didn't have any information except the cause of their deaths, and how the caretaker of the building that we lived in found us two days later. I am sure that my adoptive Mum and Dad would have taken you too if they had known about you before."

She grinned, "Probably not, I wasn't the best-behaved child in the home." Her expression became serious, "I was worse after I had spent some time in York though…It was rough." I could see that remembering was distressing her and said, "Tell me another time. Let's just enjoy today and make arrangements to spend more time together — tell me about your career."

"I don't exactly have one at the moment, but I am thinking of setting up on my own as an investment manager. I have enough qualifications from my work at the bank and I need to earn some money. It isn't a problem yet, but I won't work full time until T.J. goes to school."

"How long till then?" I asked.

"He will be three in December. So not for a while."

"I bet you are a wonderful mother," I said, knowing instinctively that it was true.

She smiled broadly at the compliment and said, "In the meantime I will have to do something from home. Haven't decided yet. What do you do, Alex?"

"I work in the police, I'm what is known as a Special Investigator," I told her.

Kate's eyes widened and I noticed her hand shook slightly as she carefully placed the mug she was holding back onto the table.

CHAPTER 26

KATE

My heart nearly hit my throat. "Special Investigator?" I could only splutter. I felt as if my veins were suddenly filled with cold water and that my world might just come crashing around me. This beautiful, kindly, handsome man was my baby brother — and he was in the police!

"Sounds important," I managed. "What exactly do you do?"

"I work from the divisional office in Newcastle, although I do spend most of my time out on investigations. The rest is spent on writing reports and preparing statements," he said, not noticing that I was holding my breath. "Sounds good, I know. We try to establish what evidence the police require, decide on the best methods of obtaining it and then take charge of the scene and direct the order of work. We take evidence from places and people and send them for analysis. We work in all kinds of environments and weather, at any time of day or night. Can be a bit demanding, but it's a great job. I do a bit of training too - travel all over. I was going to Reading in October…" He paused watching me carefully.

"Aah," I managed to mutter but he continued.

"I want to get closer to home though because I am getting married next year. I am hoping to get a base in Middlesbrough." He grabbed my trembling hands. "Kate, you and T.J. will come to my wedding. How wonderful is that! My own sister and nephew at our wedding, Sophie will be over the moon. She knows all about you and can't wait to meet you and your boy."

He curled his fingers around my cold hands. It was real, and yet I couldn't rid myself of the knowledge that this could all crumble to dust if he knew what I had done.

"Are you going to stay in Saltburn?" I finally managed to ask.

"Sophie would like to. Her family live there too. My lot want me to, but only time will tell. I do a great deal of travelling in my job." He had noticed how quiet I had become.

"Are you okay, Kate?"

"Overwhelmed that's all." My intense happiness at finding Alex was now tinged with a new fear. Alex was a police officer, specialising in finding clues, people and searching out evidence. How could I ever explain about T.J.? I would have to be really careful in what I said. What would happen if he found out that I had kidnapped a child? Could I trust him? From then on I found that the conversation was difficult, but somehow, we arranged to meet again the following week. I wasn't yet ready to meet his family, even though I really wanted too. They sounded so solidly sane and happy, and I knew that it would be great for T.J. and me to be a part of it.

Eventually, and on getting to know Alex, I knew that he was all I had ever of dreamed. He was handsome, clever and interesting, and over the next few weeks we met every week on his day off, sometimes just for coffee. When T.J. went to Heather's after playschool, we had lunch together. I told him a lot about my life, where I had lived, the qualifications I had gained and how I had bought my own house in Bristol. I told him about my interest in photography, what books I was reading, but little about my childhood or my marriage and breakdown. I certainly never hinted that Thomas and T.J. were two different children. It made me hesitant about meeting his family, but as time passed, he insisted that they were all driving him mad with curiosity about me and my boy. I was careful about what I told him, but perhaps I think I somehow knew that the time would come when I would have to tell him the truth.

After a month, I felt confident enough for Alex to meet T.J. I asked him to come to the cottage on his day off and we arranged for him to stay the night with us so that we could relax with supper and a bottle of wine. If he were happy to sleep in T.J.'s room, I would take my boy in my bed with me.

"Can't wait," he told me happily, "I have to go down to Hull on Friday so that will suit me fine."

I wasn't sure why it had taken so long but I guess that I wasn't yet ready to share my little boy with Alex's family.

CHAPTER 27

ALEX

Kate and I managed to meet several times before I met T.J. and I did understand her reticence. She had been on her own for a long time and wanted to get to know me first. I wanted her to trust me too, so that she could be part of my life from now on. I knew from our conversations that there was a great deal about her life that she had not confided in me. Some days, she seemed secretive and nervous, and she closed like a clam if I asked about certain times in her life.

"She's not quite ready to meet you all." I explained to my family when they asked how long they would have to wait to meet these new members of our family.

"Why not?" my mother inquired. "We can't wait."

I tried to explain the little I knew about Kate's life, and that she was an independent and clever young woman who had made her own pathway. I told them that I wanted to meet T.J. first, and to make sure that they wanted to meet the 'Hutchinson clan' before I brought them home. After all, they didn't know us at all. I knew that it was better to let her get used to the idea of having a new family and feel comfortable about telling me before I pushed her.

"Of course," said my father sagely, "Kate doesn't know us—but we are intrigued by the idea of having a surrogate grandson."

Certainly, my mother couldn't wait to meet them. Ma had told me quietly that she would really like to adopt another child, but Pa was unsure, as they were soon to become grandparents. My sister Mai and her husband Jacob were expecting their baby about the second week of December, well before Christmas. The Hutchinson household would have lots to celebrate this coming Christmas and they all wanted Kate and T.J. to be part of it.

When I arrived at the cottage that Kate rented, she had just returned from the Busy Bee and T.J. was clutching his latest work of art, a picture all made with handprints. Kate took him to the kitchen to scrub his hands before we were formally introduced.

"This is Uncle Alex," said Kate proudly. "He is very special, T.J."

T.J. smiled his beaming smile and formally shook hands with me. "Hello Uncle Alex." He was just as Kate had described, a happy blond little angel. His little cat Lena welcomed him with a smooch and a purr, and he was instantly distracted.

All through lunch T.J. chatted happily about playschool and his best friends Kyle, Jo and Jess.

Kate showed me around the cottage and in the afternoon, we sat in the garden drinking tea and getting to know each other. T.J. jumped on his bouncy trampoline or chased Lena with a feathered toy.

It didn't take long for me to realise what an exceptionally loving mother Kate was. She barely let him out of her sight and everything she did was for him. She didn't appear to have any social life of her own, and the only friends she had were the other mothers at the 'Busy Bee'. I admired her so for her determination and how well she had done — I couldn't wait to integrate them into the Hutchinson family.

Kate did eventually tell me a little about Jackson, her husband, but she didn't tell me why they weren't together.

She had cooked a chicken and roasted vegetables and made a trifle for an early supper, so we opened a bottle of wine. After a comfortable and enjoyable meal, we settled down in front of the television and watched some children's cartoons with T.J. He was a boisterous and happy little boy, but at seven o'clock Kate took him for his bath. He came to say goodnight to me looking shiny and glowing. His combed hair was so straight that it stuck out in soft peaks. I couldn't believe that T.J. hadn't inherited the Channon curls. His hair was much blonder than ours and so very straight. His sea blue eyes were very different to our dark blue/grey ones.

"He doesn't look a bit like you, Kate. Is he more like Jackson?" I asked her after she had put T.J. to bed. I remembered she had described Jackson as tall, dark and handsome.

She hesitated before she answered, and I could see that she was holding back.

"Possibly… yes. Well… no, actually Jackson is not his father."

"Aah, can I ask who is?"

"No." Tears suddenly flooded her eyes. "I… I don't know…" She hiccupped.

"Okay, Kate, don't get upset, I really don't care who the father is. You are his mother and…"

"Oh, Alex. I can't talk about it."

"Is there someone else?" I asked.

"Another man you mean?"

"Yes, you are a good-looking woman, Kate. Don't you have a bloke tucked up your sleeve somewhere? A potential father for T.J.?"

"No. We don't need…. I don't need… T.J. is happy with just me."

"It doesn't alter the fact that a boy does need a father," I said.

"He does not need a father," she replied angrily to my suggestion and the surprise at her vehemence must have shown on my face. She immediately steadied her voice and said, "Yes, it would be nice to have one, but I think we can manage very well without. I know that ideally every child should grow up in a traditional family with two parents, but I would rather us be just as we are. Better than having a bad parent—look at what I had," she said grimly. "I remember well the disgusting Henry Gladstone, pillar of society—the church going, respectable, old paedophile who took away my innocence when I was barely nine years old."

I was appalled but began to realise how little I knew about her life.

"What happened to you, Kate?"

CHAPTER 28

KATE

I put my glass to my lips and sipped my wine, and I knew I was stalling—I hadn't yet told Alex what had happened to me after he was adopted. I was shaking at the thought of what I was about to tell him. We already cared for each other, and I knew that I would want him to approve of me.

All the feelings that I had bottled up came crashing forward and spluttered out. "I don't think I can ever make you understand," I said carefully, "but I want to be honest with you." I took a deep breath and I realised there was no point in prevaricating.

"How much do you want to know?" I said and almost at once I feel a sense of relief.

His brow was furrowed with concern. "All of it. Everything," he said without a smile. He tried to top up my glass of wine, but I put my hand firmly across the top of it.

"No Alex, I don't need any more. I have used alcohol in the past to cover up things, but I must now be as honest and as clear about what has happened in my life as I possibly can. I no longer need to blot it out."

"Go on, I'm listening," he said as he reached forward and took my hand, so I continued. "I was sent to York to that terrible family. I was just nine, and I guess the social services thought that I would stop being so miserable and unruly if I were to be fostered. I wanted to be adopted like you were, have a real, forever family, but in the end, I was fostered to Patricia and Henry Gladstone."

I continued slowly. Up to that point, the words had poured out easily. Now there was a tightness in my throat. Saying these things out loud makes them real again.

"Henry was a wily old sod and I learned to keep out of his way as much as possible. I really think Patricia knew what was happening to me, but she would only laugh if I said anything. I once told her that he was touching and hurting me, and do you know what she said? 'He wouldn't touch you with a barge pole, you are an ugly, nasty little girl and if you say things like that, I will punish you'. Her punishment was tying me to a chair while they ate their dinner in the kitchen. I got nothing, and I had to wash up after them and then go to bed. I used to lick the plates and pans I was so hungry.

"Patricia was a drinker, and by the time she'd had her fill she'd fall asleep, and he would come to me. He'd creep in and lock the door. *'You are a good little girl really, aren't you Katie,'* he would say, *'and good little girls are nice to their Daddy who loves them'*. I used to cry and beg, but all the time he would insist that he loved me so much that he had to do it." I hesitated, finding it hard to relate out loud. I hadn't even told Harriet or my therapist how I had really felt or the extent of the abuse. "You know, Alex, at first I thought he really did love me, and it must be normal, but I was still so young. He brought me food and sweets in the beginning. As I got older, he warned me that I mustn't tell anyone about 'our' love, and when I was about eleven, I fought a bit harder, so he would tie my hands behind my back and gag me."

By then I was crying hard.

I had pushed all my feelings so far back that it was almost choking me saying out loud what had happened to me.

Alex held onto my hand. "Go on, Kate," he said calmly as he handed me a bunch of tissues to mop my soggy face.

"I was often bruised but Patricia insisted that I was just a clumsy child. Sometimes I hid in the bottom of the wardrobe, especially when he had been drinking. I used to hold my breath when he came into my room and he would shout, *'I'll find you, silly, little Kate'*. He would lift the bed and bang it down hard, knock things over and swear. *'Come out here you fucking little bitch, and tell Daddy you love him'*. Sometimes I had terrible thoughts about him being dead, and that he'd had a fatal accident, or that I had killed him. I wanted to kill him."

"Didn't you tell anyone?" Alex asked quietly as I pulled myself away from those awful memories.

"Yes, I did, but I am not sure anyone believed me. Henry was the pillar of society and influential at church. The evil old bastard convinced everyone that I was a delinquent child, and that all the love in the world wasn't going to help me. Eventually, I got moved but by then I had been with the Gladstone's for over three years. I was always sore and black and blue. My teacher from school once asked

Patricia about my bruises. 'So clumsy and awkward' Patricia smilingly told her. 'She likes people to think we don't care for her. Quite the little actress, aren't you dear,' she would tell everyone, and I became sly and difficult as a result."

"How did you get away from there?" Alex asked.

"I'd hidden outside in the freezing cold, and I got ill. I was hiding from Henry. There was an investigation, but I never knew what happened. I was sent back to the children's home in Scarborough, and later went to a nice couple in Filey, but by then I was so damaged I didn't trust anyone. I think I gave them two years of hell. I wanted to thank them for looking after me even though I was such a nightmare, but they have moved away."

"I will find out about what happened to the Gladstones," said Alex angrily. "They should be punished..."

"It is so long past now, Alex. I don't see how...?"

"Well, I will look into it anyway. There must be a restriction order against them ever fostering again. Would you be prepared to...?"

"No, Alex. I can't imagine giving evidence after so long."

Alex was a determined man I knew, and he wouldn't leave it.

I told him about running away, hitching lifts, my years in a squat, the cutting, the drinking and the aggressive behaviour that I inflicted on everyone. But I also told him about Harriet and Graham and how much help I'd received in Reading, and the years of hard studying, and how I had achieved my goals to become responsible and independent.

"Yes, I spoke to Harriet last year when I was trying to trace you. She sounded like a really good person. She said she admired your fortitude and ability to learn in such difficult circumstances. She told me that you got a good job. When did you leave the bank?"

"In November 2010. Then I went back after Thomas died in the summer…"

"Thomas?"

The minute the words came out of my mouth I realised what I had said. An invisible hand reached into my stomach, squeezed it hard and didn't let go. Panic flooded through me. No one knew that I had substituted T.J. for Thomas. I'd told Alex that I had a little boy who was two and a half years old. Also, that I had worked in a bank until I had T.J. but of course the dates didn't add up.

CHAPTER 29

ALEX 2013

I was confused but began to realise how little I knew about Kate. Now, knowing that she had a child who died in the summer of 2011, I was mystified. Was she pregnant again? Did she get pregnant immediately after? Jackson had been long gone and as I tried to calculate the dates, I found that they didn't add up — T.J.'s age made it impossible.

"Tell me about Thomas. T.J. is not Thomas, is he?"

"He is now."

To my surprise she began to cry again, not just cry, but huge gulping sobs that made me feel that she was hiding something really terrible.

It took her a long time to explain about her relationship with Jackson and the birth and death of Thomas. I have to say I found it all hard to understand. Jackson was Thomas's father, but he had left long before Thomas was born. I was not in a position to make any sort of judgement as I had only had my mother and father to set as standard. They were without doubt the strongest and happiest couple ever. Their love for each other and us was undeniable and we had always felt it, so Kate's story was beyond my imagination.

Her marriage to Jackson sounded like a bit of a fairy tale until her pregnancy, but Jackson had just got up and left? Kate was by herself, and Thomas had died - where did T.J. come from? How come his name was Thomas James?

"Kate you are without doubt a wonderful mother." I could see that pleased her, but she looked uncertain whether my praise was justified. She sniffed and the tears continued in a steady stream down her cheeks. "But you must tell me the truth. I'm really confused," I said.

Hesitating at first, she started to tell me. "It was my fault that Thomas, my baby died. He was only eight months old. I don't know what it was that made him such an unhappy child... he didn't like me... I couldn't... I don't know why I feel so guilty because I loved him so. I think it was the misery that lay deep inside me that he was expressing. His dissatisfaction turned me inside out. It was as if he was expressing all my own hidden disappointments and frustrations with life.

When he died, I felt as if I had somehow silenced him, so that I didn't have to think about my own life. I'd got so used to putting on a shield and pretending I was okay, but I never really was. When he'd gone, I slept, really slept for the first time since he was born... I slept with relief, but I felt such guilt at doing so. I suppose I felt I could never forgive myself."

I took her hand and held it. "For sleeping?" I asked.

"That too, but mainly because I felt so useless. And guilty."

"Guilt is a pointless emotion that wastes your time and your energy. You have no need to feel guilty. I'm sure none of it was your fault."

"No, you are right," she said, "I do know that in my heart. But what T.J. has done for me overwhelms me at times. It was as though he was sent to me just to help me heal, you know, all the bad stuff. To me he is my child, the child I should have had, perhaps. I still have no idea where he came from, but he is my joy. I do live in fear that someday someone will claim him."

"I'm truly sorry Kate, but you must tell me about T.J. I really don't understand how you came to substitute him for Thomas."

"I found him," she replied quietly.

"What?"

"He just appeared from nowhere after my breakdown. He took my hand as if he knew me."

"From the beginning, Katie, please. I don't know what you are saying. Who gave birth to T.J. if you didn't?"

"Where will I start?" she asked.

"Right after Thomas died in the summer. Did you go back to work?"

"Yes, in October 2011, I did because… I knew that life must go on, so I tried, but… for nearly a year. I often wonder if perhaps I hadn't let myself think sufficiently about the things that had happened to me. I asked myself if I had 'dealt' with them. I believed that by gaining success I had used all the anger and energy to that end, but it was all still there lurking beneath the surface. I felt that my baby, Thomas was displaying my pain and my failures. I tried really hard, but it didn't work so…"

"You had a breakdown and left work in 2012? And?"

"I knew I had to change my life. I decided to come and look for you. I sold the house and made plans, but I found T.J."

"You found T.J.? Tell me what you mean."

"Yes." She gazed into the distance as if she were trying to remember exactly how it happened.

"Try to remember anything you can, about the day you found T.J. Where did you find him, Kate?"

She made a face and nodded. "Okay, but it is hard to tell. I know it will sound unbelievable to you. I found him in a shopping mall in town."

"Take your time and tell me slowly," I said gently, "close your eyes and visualise the day you found him. Anything, everything, the weather, the people you saw, what you heard — start with how you were feeling."

Kate leaned back and closed her eyes. I took out a notebook I always carried. I wanted to make sure I got the story right so that I didn't get more confused.

"Right..." she said quietly, "it was a Thursday... I had gone on the bus into town to get some odds and ends for my journey at the weekend — my journey north. The house was sold, and I was leaving. I wasn't feeling anything in particular, just that I wanted to get away… wanted to start a new life. I was still mourning Thomas and everything in Harlow Crescent reminded me of him… and of my failure as a mother."

I listened carefully and watched Kate struggle with the past. Even though her eyes were closed, tears were seeping through her lashes.

"I was cold," she continued. "It had been raining the previous day so there were puddles and the air felt damp. I wanted a coffee so I headed for the arcade. It is part of The Galleries. It's nice… It was a whim really because I'd finished my shopping… I stopped and looked in a shop, a children's clothing shop thinking about Thomas. T.J. just took hold of my hand as I stood there. He appeared from nowhere and took my hand as if he belonged to me."

"Was anyone else around?"

"No… not that I remember. I was so stunned. It was like I had stepped out of my life and I was somewhere else. I didn't notice anything but his lovely, angelic little face."

Now Kate was really crying hard, and she opened her eyes, and mopped her tears. She was shaking, so I reached for her hand again, but she ignored me and continued,

"Seriously, Alex, I waited and waited. He only had on a sweater… no coat and no proper shoes. It was cold so we went into the café. I bought him a hot chocolate. We waited and watched for well over an hour, and then I took him home on the bus wrapped in my woolly scarf. He stank."

"Stank?"

"Urine, he had a soggy nappy. I could smell it all the way home on the bus." She gave a throaty laugh.

"You took him home? No one spoke to you. No one asked anything at all?"

"No," she said and gazed into the distance, so I waited.

She closed her eyes again and I asked quietly, "Go on. What happened next?"

"Let me tell you about that night. It was so lovely, Alex. He didn't speak at all only made a few odd sounding noises, but he was delightful. He loved the bubbles in the bath, and he ate everything I gave him—he was my little miracle. He came into my bed in the middle of the night and I wanted to keep him so much. However, I did take him back the next day, all clean and shiny, wrapped in my woolly scarf again. We went back into the café, looked for notices or any indication that he was missing. Nobody was looking for him, I swear. We were there a long time and then we went and bought him some proper clothes and boots. I brought him home and decided to kidnap him." Kate hiccoughed a throaty laugh.

"Did you speak to anyone on the Friday?"

"Only the waitress as she cleaned our table. We were about to leave."

"Anyone else there?"

"It was busy in the arcade—lots of people about doing their weekend shop, as it was Friday… it usually is busy on a Friday. Some noisy girls came in the café causing a disruption, going on about hair colours or something. Someone mentioned a bloke having an accident in Union Street … no, in Wine Street, I think. The road was up there, so the paramedics had to go through the mall. We saw them go past."

"Did you go straight home?"

"Yes, after we had bought the clothes and some nice warm boots."

"What about the woman in the shop?"

"No, nothing. We talked about sizes and nappies."

"Go back to the café. Would you recognise the girls again?" Kate looked at me and said firmly. "No, they were just a bunch of noisy teenagers. They didn't take any notice of us at all."

"The waitress?"

"She was always there. I had seen her every time I went in that café. Round face and mid-brown hair tied in a ponytail. I guess she was about thirty-five. I think she only spoke to me as we were leaving."

"And?"

"She was a bit distracted by the new customers who came in talking about the accident. Some bloke had broken his back in a fall. As I said, we'd seen the paramedics go past half an hour earlier. We left a few minutes after that and spoke to no one. My neighbours were away so we didn't see anyone after we got off the bus. We left Bristol on Sunday morning."

"Can you give me the exact date you found him?"

"Of course. It was Thursday 18th of November. T.J. is my Thursday child.

"He will be on a missing persons list somewhere, you know. Every year over two and a half thousand people, old and young go missing and are never found, but they are nearly always on a list somewhere." I told her.

She sucked in her breath and spoke more boldly, "Listen to me, Alex, no one came looking for him. I swear, he wasn't reported missing. He wasn't missed. I believe he was sent to me… Somehow, it's how I've justified it all this time. It's important for me to believe that. It was meant to be. I brought him here to start a new life. You know the rest." Finally, she fell silent and her hands lay lifeless in her lap. I could see how exhausted she was feeling.

"I don't know many women that are strong enough to do what you have done, Kate," I hesitated. I could see that she appreciated my attempt to cheer her up but could muster only the weakest of smiles. "But you do know I will have to find her. His mother. How can she not know what happened to her son?"

Kate's eyes widened in fear. "Oh, Alex really? Do you really have to?"

"Imagine if you were his mother… not knowing. It might be true that she didn't want him but… look, Kate, I won't tell anyone what I am trying to find just yet and I will get it done without revealing who it is about, if I possibly can."

"And how will you do that, Alex? How could it be possible if no one were looking for him," she asked.

"I have a really good friend, Derek Hart who works in vice. He has access to some of the investigative procedures that we use. If we get a DNA sample from T.J. perhaps, we can identify who gave birth to him and why he was wandering around a shopping centre on his own. The database is where we'll start. We take the DNA sample and feed it into the system. If there is a sample of mother or father or even distant relatives, we can find it. England has the most effective and efficient approach to the use of forensic DNA technology in the world. Since the establishment of the National DNA Database in 1995, we have become a world leader in discovering innovative ways to use the testing—and I happen to know Derek works with it all the time. I promise I will keep it to myself and not tell anyone, not even Derek, that it is about T.J. I will make up some story about... oh, I don't know... perhaps that my parents are thinking of adopting again or something."

Kate put her hand to her head, "I feel dizzy just thinking about it. Can you seriously find somebody like that?" she said, "I think I am already regretting that I have told you about that Thursday."

"It's becoming an absolute necessity when looking for people. If there is anything on the database, it will come up. It is becoming a standard to take DNA information from any crime scenes, inheritance disputes and sometimes accident scenes."

"But how do other people get on the data base in the first place? I have never been in a position for a sample to be taken or offered one."

"From criminals, from stolen goods, lost people and the estranged. A lot of people willingly give samples if they are not sure of paternity or if they are searching for someone. It is not uncommon for people to be reunited with long lost families. If we did one too, we might even find we have relatives that we don't know about."

CHAPTER 30

KATE

I told him things I hadn't intended to tell anyone, and he listened, really listened. He held my hands in his, but he was obviously confused.

"Oh, Kate I am so sorry." Alex said and I knew he meant it, but I hardly registered his apology as I was crying so hard. I dabbed at my eyes but couldn't stop. "I can't give him up," I wailed, "but I am aware that he is growing up without a father and he will want to know sometime, won't he? Who his father is... and his biological mother? I just don't know where he came from, Alex—but I am terrified that you will find out."

My voice was little more than a whisper. I had to stop. I got up and walked to the kitchen and splashed cold water on my face.

When I came back into the room Alex was gazing into the fire with a thoughtful expression on his face.

"Are you okay, Kate?"

I nodded, but I knew this was going to change everything. Perhaps, I would not be welcome in the Hutchinson family after all—if they knew I had stolen a child, what would they think of me?

"Kate, I promise I will be as careful as I can, but you need to know the truth. You will never rest until you find out where he came from, or if someone is searching for him. Perhaps we will never know but we must try to find out."

Of course, I couldn't sleep and over the next few days I regretted ever having told Alex the truth. Nonetheless, sharing the extraordinary story had taken some of the great weight of my secret from my shoulders—after all, I had held on to it for so long.

The very next week, Alex came with the tester kit, and we had laughed with T.J. as we swabbed his inside cheek and made a game of it.

"It will take some time, but please don't worry, Kate," said Alex as he tucked it into his top pocket, "I will let you know instantly if we get a result and go from there."

Worry? How could I not worry? I was petrified of what he would find and the possibility of losing my beloved boy. Even though I acknowledged that Alex was doing the right thing, I didn't want to know. I didn't want to feel the guilt of what I had done bringing T.J. here with me. At night I was drenched with worry.

Alex kept promising to be totally discreet about what we were doing, and that he would let me know instantly if any results were found.

CHAPTER 31

ALEX

"I need some help, Derek. I want to try and identify this child's parentage" I indicated toward the DNA test. "Only because I am worried that they, the parents, may have criminal records, and I know you can get access to DNA from crime sites and so on. I have already tried other routes as I thought there was a possibility that he is a missing child, but so far my investigations have come to nothing."

Derek accepted my explanation about wanting to find out about the boy because my parents were thinking of adopting, and I also told him that I was doing it on the quiet as I had some reservations about it. At first, he didn't ask any questions, told me how much it would cost and that it would take about a month before we had any answers. What he did say was that we might have to apply to the authorities to access information, and that the NIS keep the records and do not disclose them easily.

"If I find out anything, I might have to make a formal request to access it. You do know that there are strict procedures about accessing information?" His face stretched into a conspiratorial gin. "Good job I'm retiring soon, eh?"

"I have no intentions of divulging anything I find to anyone." I assured him.

"We are stretching the law doing this. In certain cases, information is circulated and can be used for identifying criminal activity but generally it is kept private. Lucky for you I do have Identity Access Management ID, but you do need to understand that my access is limited."

"Of course." I did know that Derek's access had to be strictly within the law, and I wasn't sure that I expected him to find anything at all — it was a long shot!

It took a few weeks before I heard anything, but I eventually got a call from Derek to go and see him in Newcastle because he had some unusual news for me.

I went the following day.

"I can tell you what we have found out." Derek told me with a grin. "We have an identification for the father from the DNA test. There is a reason that I can divulge this information."

"That's great," I said, thinking that surely it would lead to the mother.

"You might not think that when I tell you who he is, because this character was already known to us. He was a German called Carl Melnyk, his mother was from Ukraine and his father was from Germany. He was born in 1975, was well-educated and went to the prestigious University of Amsterdam. No known spouse. He was involved in criminal activities from an early age. Called himself a property dealer but had brothels all over Europe and the UK. His father wasn't much better as he ran several notorious nightclubs and was jailed for drug dealing in 1990. Carl had managed to evade the law by being part of a large and powerful syndicate which was involved in trafficking women and drug dealing. It has been suggested that in his twenties he was involved in arms smuggling to the Middle East. We have had his DNA on file from when he was involved in a serious fight back in the 1990's. The only reason I could get all this information is because this individual is dead."

I was stunned. I had not expected such a dramatic discovery.

"Yes, he was killed here in England in a pile up on the road into Bristol in November 2010."

"In Bristol? Are you sure?" We were obviously on the right track.

"Yep. The truck he was in, was supposed to deliver plants and flowers from Holland and Belgium, and did the route several times a year, across on the ferry, to various places in England, mainly London, of course. That was one of his cover businesses. We now know that they have been trafficking girls all over the UK for years. I will give you the full report to read yourself."

"Are you absolutely certain about the DNA results?"

"Yes. The figure for the kinship index reading is conclusive with a 99.9% chance of Carl Melnyk being the father. The greater the value over 1.001 — and it can go as high as 10,000 — the higher the likelihood that the individuals concerned are related, so this is a certainty. So far, we have no indication of who the mother might be. Here is all the information that I have about the accident too."

There was a fat file on his desk and Derek opened it and pulled out copies of several passports.

"These are copies of the passports we found in the truck. This one is the man identified by DNA as the father you are looking for." He pushed one across the table.

I opened the passport to see the good-looking, German called Carl Melnyk. Derek opened another and indicated, "This is the other man who was in the truck, Gary Lombard who was driving. He was badly injured in the accident and has since died, so he can't give us any information. He was also well known to police, especially in Manchester where he had about twenty girls working for him, mainly on the streets. He ran two dodgy massage parlours, and has been picked up a few times in the past. Charged with GBH twice, both offences against women. What he was doing in that truck coming from Belgium we don't really know. He was probably just the driver, taking the truck to and fro."

Derek pushed three more passports toward me and said, "These are three passports of girls who fled the scene. Two are still missing. Mija Belous, is dead, murdered we believe. There were actually six girls altogether, all illegals."

I opened the passports of those who had run away from the accident and I found myself looking at three beautiful, very young girls.

"Pretty girls, all of them. They were ideal fodder for traffickers." Derek told me seriously. "It's common knowledge that young, innocent, vulnerable girls are brought out of Eastern Europe, South America, Asia and North Africa with promises of offers of work that turn out to be enforced prostitution. They get them hooked on various drugs too. They use Gamma-Hydroxy Butyrate, GHB or Flunitrazepam, which is Rohypnol to start them off."

"Date rape drugs?" I had heard of these being used in other rape inquiries.

"In small doses they make the recipient willing and on occasions blocks their memory completely. If too big a dose is given, they remain unconscious. Combined with alcohol, they can become fully acquiescent. These people know how to make the girls behave. A great many of them are hooked on heroin too."

"What happened to the other girls?"

"Injured in the crash."

I examined the other three photographs. "Have we done anything to help these girls?"

"In this case we have," He said. "It's difficult because they rarely talk. But we did manage to help the three girls left in the truck. They had minor injuries—broken bones mainly. They knew quite a lot of details about the men involved, especially Miriam, the eldest. They told us what had happened to them, but their help was given on the condition that we gave them some help and places to go. The young German girl, Elsa Gottenburg, went to Canada to join a member of her family there, and the other two were given new names and papers and they have been sent back to their original countries. The other two girls have been added to the list of missing persons."

Derek sighed, "What we do know is that these six girls were being brought here illegally to work in prostitution. They were originally destined for the capital, but during that year there had been intensive police activity in the brothels and nightclubs and a big crack-down in London. That's why many of these girls were going to places like Hull, Barnsley, Newcastle, Manchester and in this case, they were heading for Cardiff. We only know this from the satnav that was retrieved from the truck. When they had the crash these two girls escaped and disappeared."

He pointed to the photos of Tanya Moreo and Elena Shevchenca. "The other girl who escaped from the waggon was called Mija Belous. We reckon that somehow, they managed to track her down, because she was found dead less than a week later in a derelict building two miles away from the scene of the crash. She had been strangled and no one has yet been charged, but it was obviously a murder. These gangs have criminal members everywhere, and we have no doubt she was killed to silence her. The two others might have been disposed of as well, but we have no evidence of either of them being found dead or alive. Disappearing is sometimes the best thing for some people, and it's not as difficult as it sounds. A lot of women go missing in this country for their own safety. This is what we think has happened to these two."

I was intrigued, although I said nothing to Derek. The father of T.J. was killed close to Bristol. So, there was some unknown link between him and the mother who might have lived in Bristol - perhaps she was one of the missing girls. "This one is stunning," I said pointing to Elena's image and feeling a worm of excitement. She had wide almond shaped eyes and long silvery blonde hair. She could easily be T.J.'s mother, but I was making no assumptions at this point. She looked so young and innocent. I looked at her date of birth, which was 1992, so she was seventeen when this passport photo was taken. The other missing girl was older, dark haired and beautiful, born in 1987.

"We have explored all sorts of avenues and still can't find the two that are missing."

"So how do you think I could go about tracing these two women?" I asked.

Derek shrugged, "We've tried, but they have totally disappeared. Even if you could find them it would be almost impossible to get them to talk."

"Can't we protect them? You helped the other girls."

"We did, but with a great deal of secrecy and difficulty. They all know from past experience how dangerous it is to talk to any authority. All levels of the police, government and authorities have been known to be involved. We have discovered custom officials, members of governments and local businessmen who have all made money out of this trafficking — some even use their services. Often, they go unpunished because of their power.

These girls are not only broken but terrified. Two years ago, we had a girl who came to us for help. She had been smuggled in a lorry from somewhere in Latvia and ended up in a brothel in London. She had no money and no freedom and for two years she worked for no pay at all. The reason — she had two sisters' back home and elderly parents that her trafficker threatened to kill or mutilate if she didn't do as she was told. They also take compromising photographs of the girls and blackmail them with them. This girl told us initially that she wouldn't tell us anything. It is too dangerous for them to talk about what is happening to them."

Derek Hart told me how he had been in the business of finding traffickers for as long as he could remember, but government funding for several departments of the police had reduced. He had found it frustrating that not enough time and money was spent on these scumbags.

"It's bloody frustrating, I can tell you. We know that human trafficking is going on at such a large scale. Millions, no billions of pounds, dollars, euros and dinars are made. Virtually no one actually sees it. It works in the shadow of our societies."

"Surely because the law is being broken on all sorts of different levels there is some way that police intervention can stop it?"

Derek sighed, "Prostitution is now legal in most European countries. The argument for legalising it was that it would break the links between prostitution and organised crime, and that levels of violence against the women would decrease. They said that women would be working in 'controlled' environments and would find it easier to report attacks to the police. Also, the claim was that the sexual health of prostitutes would be more controllable, because the activity would occur in a clean and safe environment. I have seen some of the places that they work, and they are neither clean nor safe in most cases. Another theory was that the link between these women and their pimps would be broken, as women would no longer be dependent on a pimp for 'protection' from the authorities. It's all a big, bloody joke if you ask me."

I was grateful to Derek for access to the information.

On returning home I pulled my laptop toward me and an idea grew. Perhaps if I could trace the identity of all of the girls, I would find a link. I looked at media coverage at the time. I applied and reapplied different search parameters and found very little. It took me hours to go through the evidence surrounding the three girls who had been picked up after the crash. It definitely wasn't one of them.

Having found T.J.'s father I was pretty certain that one of the girls in the van must have been the mother. One thing that became clear was that only two of the six girls were still unaccounted for: blonde Elena Shevchenko from Ukraine and dark-haired Tanya Moro from Moldova. I was pretty certain which one I was looking for - but where to start?

My only other thought was that I could inquire in the café in Bristol to see if anyone knew this girl. Also, there was the accident that had happened when Kate was there, so I telephoned the Bristol Royal Infirmary and asked to be directed through to the A&E department.

"I am Special Investigating Police Officer Alex Hutchinson and I'm inquiring about an accident at the bottom of Wine Street in Bristol on Thursday November 18th 2012. I believe the patient, a man, had fallen and had a broken back. It happened somewhere near or behind the Oxfam shop that used to be in that street before the demolition and the new car parks. Can you tell me who I need to speak to?"

"What do you want to know? We don't give information out on the phone, but I will make inquiries and if you would like to make an official inquiry or send someone in, we can assist you."

I sent an official inquiry.

It took over a week to get a reply, but I was instantly interested. The reply informed us that the man was in fact a woman, and she had not been identified. More information was available, but it was suggested that I spoke to the doctor who had been in charge of the patient. I was by now totally intrigued and decided that I would go to Bristol myself and see Doctor Turner.

I told Kate nothing of my findings even though I had promised to let her know straight away. Knowing that her little boy's father was a criminal gangster was not the sort of news I wanted to impart until I had more information about his mother.

Sophie was intrigued. I had not confided in her at all about what I was investigating, but as I had some holiday due, I decided that I would go on my own as soon as possible.

I had never been to Bristol before, and I could see why Kate had felt so happy there. The town was growing, and the surrounding areas were delightful. I booked into the Mercure Bristol Grand, which was close to the Bristol Royal Infirmary. I'd decided to start my search at the exact place that T.J. was found. I made my way to the Galleries and walked the length of it until I found the café that Kate had told me about. There were a lot of new shops and the children's shop that Kate had mentioned was no longer there, but otherwise it was as she had described it. The coffee shop was buzzing, but eventually I got in and ordered a latte. The waitress, a young girl of about eighteen told me that she had only been there for about six months.

"Oh, that will be Debs," she answered when I described the waitress who had been there in November

2012. "She's been here since it opened in 2009. She manages the place now."

"Is she here?"

"No, she's on after lunch today. One thirty." She looked at her watch. "In half an hour."

"In that case I will have a salmon and cucumber sandwich and another coffee and wait for her."

"Okey dokey, coming up."

When Debs arrived, it didn't take long to establish that she did not remember Kate or T.J. I showed her the copy of the passport photograph that I carried of Elena Shevchenca, but she didn't think she had ever seen her before either. She didn't know the customers that had told them about the accident on that November day either – in fact, she could hardly remember the incident.

"But there was always something going on around there. It's all gone now, and we have a big car park where those old shops used to be. The Oxfam shop went to Berkeley Square."

I walked to Berkeley Square only to find another dead end. The manager had moved on, the cleaner that they used at the end of Vine Street had retired and gone to live in

Australia with her family and all the volunteer staff were all fairly new. Nobody that was there had worked in the old shop.

Next step was to go in person to the Bristol Royal Infirmary and try to speak to Doctor Turner who had been the one who had replied to the official inquiry. He had only described the injuries of the girl they brought in from Vine Street on Friday the 19th November and that she had not fully recovered.

I kept the photograph of Elena in my pocket as I intended to show it to Doctor Turner.

"I can only tell you what we know which is very little. No one ever found out where the patient came from, how she came to be living in a derelict building or what had happened to her," Doctor Turner told me seriously. "We know only that she fell from the top landing and that her injuries were extensive. The aneurism caused severe trauma and although we thought she might recover she had no memory and could tell us nothing."

"But she didn't die?"

"No, but she didn't recover."

I showed him the photograph that I had of Elena and he shrugged. "Could be her, but it's hard to tell. Our girl had very little hair and we had to shave some of the rest of it off."

"She was living in hiding?"

"Apparently, but we don't know for how long. We never found out. You might be interested to know that she had had a child or children. We never knew who she really was as she called herself Eric. She is now recorded as Erica Oxfam."

Now, I was sure that I had identified T.J.'s mother but I decided that I had to see her before I made any assumptions or decisions.

CHAPTER 32

ALEX

It had taken a while to convince Mr Greenway, the manager of the home that Doctor Turner's patient had been sent to, that all I wanted was to see the girl that they knew as 'Erica Oxfam' and that I would not disturb her. Doctor Turner had told me of her condition and that she could not communicate, but having come so far, I had to be sure.

"Donna is her prime carer. I will call her, and she will take you to see Erica," said Mr Greenway. "Please be aware that she is stable and does not like to be upset."

"Thank you," I said. "I can assure you I will keep the visit very short. I think it is possible that she is someone we can identify from our missing persons list."

I followed Donna along a corridor that smelt mushroomy, sweet and slightly antiseptic, reminding me of something vague from long ago. As Donna strode purposefully along, her large body appeared to be trying to escape from her blue uniform. I smiled as her huge bottom swayed from side to side. When we got to Erica's door,

Donna extended an arm, her sunny smile welcoming me as she said, "I have told her that she has a visitor. She's waiting for you." We both knew this was hugely optimistic and highly unlikely.

We moved into Erica's room—which was ten by eleven feet or so, nicely decorated with a full-length window so that she could see out into the garden. On the bed sat a small green, toy dragon with a smiley face.

I hesitated as Donna turned the wheelchair toward me and said quietly, "Erica this is Alex. He has come to see you."

The girl raised her eyes, looked at me from head to toe, but showed no other movement or the slightest interest in me. I stood perfectly still.

In that instant I knew that she was not only the missing Ukrainian girl Elena Shevchenka, but that she was T.J.'s mother. The colour of her eyes was exactly like the boy's and the pale straight blonde hair that was now cut to shoulder length, was precisely the same shade. She looked so young. Her mouth was slightly open, and one side of her face was more relaxed than the other. Her whole left side slumped. I could see that she was slim and tall and the right age.

Donna moved over to her and lifted a lock of 'Erica's' pale hair back from her face. She smiled and only one side of her face responded. She turned her head slightly and looked at me again. The smile was still in place and there was a childish innocence about her, despite the fact that she was in her twenties.

"Lovely to meet you, Erica," I said gently but she didn't respond at all. She turned her head away from me and I made a decision.

I knew at that moment that I would not reveal to anyone that I had found her. Perhaps, not even to my friend Derek—although I would have to think about that! She could come off the list of missing persons if I did, but there was no question of me telling him about the child that was to become part of my family.

"No, she is not the woman. Thank you, Donna. I will make my own way out and tell Mister Greenway that I am satisfied that she is not the person I was looking for."

No, I would tell no one, not even Kate. Elena Shevchenca had not reacted at all when I had stood before her. She had looked at me without surprise and immediately turned away to look out of the window. She knew nothing of the past or even of the child she had given birth to. Her story would always remain a mystery.

I was satisfied that 'Erica' was indeed the biological mother of T.J. and had breathed a sigh of relief that I could not tell her. T.J. was happy and no one need ever know of this discovery. Relations are not always defined by blood, but by love.

As I walked away from the home, I felt tears of relief form at the backs of my eyes. That little boy was indeed a miracle, having somehow survived and found Kate that day in the shopping mall. He had chosen well. No one could even guess at how a toddler so small, without a coat or proper shoes, had managed to make his way from the bottom of Vine Street to the shopping arcade. Perhaps, it was the fact that the roads had been closed for repair, perhaps the big tarmac lorries and rollers had obscured shoppers seeing this little boy wandering by himself. It would now be impossible to find out. But there was no doubt in my mind that that was what had happened. His mother had fallen on the Thursday, T.J. had somehow got out into the street without being seen and found his way to Kate.

Elena had not been found until the following day and T.J. had already disappeared and created a gift for Kate who would now be his forever mother. We could integrate her and T.J. into the Hutchinson family and give them the love that they both deserved. It would serve nobody to know the truth. I would hold what I had found safely in my heart forever.

As I unlocked my car, I looked around and admired the house and gardens. It was a beautiful place to be. The carers were exceptional, and the place well kept. I said a silent thank you for the fact that this lovely girl was being so well cared for.

The big white van parked next to my car sported the name 'TanMor Gardening Services', and the crew of gardeners were all women working their magic on the grounds of the home.

EPILOGUE

JANUARY 2nd, 2013 - Bristol Royal Infirmary

It had taken over a week to get a response from the girl who had first showed signs of recovery when she opened her eyes the day after Boxing Day. At first her confusion was distressing to see, and she couldn't talk at all. Doctor Turner had been optimistic when Nurse Ombali had called and told him that the patient was awake and asking questions.

"Hello there. I'm Doctor Turner... What is your name?" Doctor Turner and the two nurses watched the panicky response. The girl looked around the room fearfully and her fingers clutched at the thin blankets, tears forming in her lovely blue eyes.

"Don't know...I can't remember, vy can't I remember? My head, it hurts," her accent was strong and her voice husky and weak. "I can't see properly. Vat is wrong wiv me?"

Doctor Turner turned to the little blonde nurse by his side. "I think a slightly higher dose of analgesic might help but keep your eye on her." He indicated the cannula to the girl. "You have an IV-PCA pump, so if the pain gets really bad press this here."

With difficulty the girl turned to see what the doctor had indicated toward. "It will give you an extra small dose of painkiller when you need it. Nurse Kemp will help you."

Nurse Kemp was young, and pretty with calm petrol blue eyes that suggested a sunny disposition. She was new to this ward, and hadn't seen the tall, bony blonde before. She knew the girl had been in a coma since arriving in the hospital last November, but little else.

"Now, what shall we call you?" Doctor Turner asked the girl. "If you can't remember your name and no-one seems to know who you are?" He glanced at the name board above her bed, which said ERIC with a question mark. "Perhaps we will call you Erica. How does that sound?"

The girl stared at Doctor Turner with a totally blank expression and shrugged her bony shoulders.

"Right Erica. Do you have any children?" asked the doctor.

The girl's eyes stared in disbelief at the question. She started to cry, digging her fingernails into her own flesh.

"Children? No... I don't 'ave any children... I don't know. I can't remember anything..."

"Your body shows evidence of having given birth in the past two years or so."

She wiped her eyes and instinctively pulled up the hospital gown and felt her abdomen. It was loose and fleshy, so she raised herself onto one elbow. She could see that there were soft silvery stretch marks from her belly button down to her pubic hair. There were also a couple of raised red scars the size of a five pence piece on her hipbone.

"I don' ever remember having a baby. I don' particularly like the idea of 'aving children. Could this be something else?"

"I'm pretty sure that you have already gone through childbirth, but it will be easy to find out. We will do some more tests, but you are sure that you can't recall ever giving birth?"

The girl lowered herself slowly back down, and closed her eyes, "Sorry, no. I am so tired. Can I sleep now?"

Nurse Kemp smiled, "You've been asleep for several weeks and you've missed Christmas, you know."

"Don' care about Christmas... Never get anything, anyway..." She had closed her eyes and the nurse adjusted her blanket.

"She does remember not getting anything for Christmas. Surely that's a start."

Turning to leave Doctor Turner said quietly, "Perhaps she doesn't want to remember. She has got some nasty scarring all over her body and around her genitals and anus. It looks like there has been some sort of sexual trauma. Keep an eye out for any infection. She has had a good dose of antibiotics, so it should be under control. The leg plaster can come off this week and we'll start some physio." Nurse Kemp nodded.

The other nurse standing next to the bed, the plump, ebony skinned Nurse Ombali said, "We all thought she was a boy when she came in... boy's clothes, so skinny you couldn't tell what she was, and with that haircut... She was living and working as a boy. Nobody seems to know anything about her except that she worked nights at a petrol station. The manager there knew her as Eric, paid cash because he'd got no papers and he didn't even know where he lived. She has a strong accent so the guy at the garage thought he was from Ukraine or Poland. Apparently, there are lots of them here."

"Everywhere. Most of them illegally, I think. This girl must be an illegal," said Nurse Kemp. "What do you think Doctor?'

"Mmm… You are probably right. We only found out that she worked for the garage because she had a business card in the back pocket of her jeans. She also had sixty pounds and a watch with no strap. She was picked up from the hallway behind the Oxfam charity shop. The top floor railing above the banister had rotted and they think she fell through the broken part. A cleaner from the shop found her in the morning. She had left a door open the previous day and went back to lock it—said it had been on her mind all night, and she usually only went to the shop on a Thursday. It was the cleaner who called an ambulance. Told the paramedics that there was a lad unconscious on the ground floor hallway, and they reckon he'd been there all night. Severe head trauma, a triple-break in the left leg, broken pelvis and ribs and cuts and bruises everywhere. We soon found out that *he* was she, definitely a girl. She was hypothermic when she came in too. Lucky not to have died after lying in that cold corridor all night."

"Did she live above the Oxfam shop?" asked Nurse Kemp.

"Not directly above the shop. There used to be flats above and behind the shops there. There were two rooms upstairs at the back, originally used for storage but one had a sink and a window that looked out over the back yard. It looked like she had been living there for some time. No landlord, as the premises were due to be demolished. It was all neat and tidy upstairs, but no one could find any I.D. There was only a makeshift bed on the floor, what looked like a playpen full of pots and pans, wooden spoons and empty plastic jars, bags of old clothes and some baby gear, but no baby. They found very little food, a few dishes and an old electric heater that had been left on, so the room was warm. There was also a tin with several hundred pounds in it."

"Heavens above, what a sad story," said Nurse Kemp.

On his rounds the following day, Doctor Turner asked the girl again. "Are you sure you can't remember anything at all? Not even your name?"

"No."

"Does the name Eric mean anything to you?"

The girl gazed at the doctor as if seeing him for the first time. She pulled herself slowly into a sitting position and self-consciously ran her fingers through her hair, part of which had been shaved for her operation.

"No, I don't remember at all... Ver am I...vat's happened to my hair?"

"You are in the Bristol Royal Infirmary, and you have been here since the middle of November last year. It is now January 2003. What do you remember about your hair?"

"It vas long."

"When was that?"

"Don't know ven,' her voice rose in panic, "but I know I alvays vore it long. Vot happened to me?

"You had a bad fall that caused a head injury and a few broken bones,' said Doctor Turner as calmly as he could. He knew from experience that brain damaged people would deteriorate faster if they got upset or stressed. "You've had a haemorrhage, which is a ruptured aneurysm in your brain. That caused the coma, but we have operated," he indicated a shaven area of her head, "and although we have stemmed the flow of blood, we are concerned about your memory loss, so we need to do some more tests to see if there is other damage."

"I don't vant tests. I am in pain. All my thoughts and feelings are so scrambled up, I cannot make sense of vem. I cannot remember anything at all about a fall or my life before now. No matter how often you ask me I just 'ave nothing to tell. All I vant is to close my eyes and sleep."

"Well, you must sleep, and we will do our best for you. Perhaps your memory will return eventually. Let us hope so. Rest now, Erica."

The girl closed her eyes and as Doctor Turner walked away, he said, "I'm sure she will get better now that she has come out of the coma. She has done well to get this far. Most people would not survive what she has gone through."

"Will she get her memory back do you think, doctor?" asked Nurse Kemp.

"I think she will in time. The problem with cases like this is that it could go either way. She might completely recover or deteriorate very quickly."

The following night, the girl, now referred to as Erica Oxfam, twitched violently in her sleep so that the monitors attached to her started to bleep. It took only seconds for the duty nurse to realise that she was having another seizure. With a sense of urgency, she checked the machines and lines. She knew that it was essential to act quickly as more damage was likely if action was not taken fast.

Nothing could be done. The seizure had caused more damage and 'Erica Oxfam' was unable to communicate as most of her body was paralysed.

The girl had been sent to a rehabilitation centre in Bristol, but it wasn't long before the doctor realised that she would never recover and was likely to deteriorate. Soon after, she was sent to a residential nursing home.

Now known as Erica Oxfam, the girl was cared for and appeared to be happy. She smiled a great deal, never showing any sign of anger or misery, and spent much of her day gazing out of her window. She could only move her head and her left arm and shoulder. She didn't like to be near any of the male carers or residents and preferred female help when she needed it. She liked the women who helped her, and responded happily to them, especially when she was fed. She seemed to enjoy her food immensely. She occasionally uttered a few words and made guttural sounds that sounded like a foreign language, but only the part-time Polish cleaner, Marisha, listened to her and sometimes responded with a smile and a word or two in reply. When Marisha was asked by Shani Hunkaia, the physical therapist that attended Elena most days, what she had said, the little cleaner replied, 'Ukrainian names and places only, never a full sentence." I say "Yes, pretty girl, in Polish to her. She seems to like me speaking to her and sometimes she waves her hand. She always smiles, she seems happy, no?"

"Yes, she does but sometimes brain damaged people develop this ability to always seem joyful. We call it a state of 'euphoria'. She welcomes everyone with equal pleasure and often appears as if she recognises individuals, but we don't really think she does."

"I am sure she knows who I am," assured Marisha.

"Her condition is such that it is possible on good days that she will recognise familiar faces, but not very often. Erica's cognitive impairment might possibly stay the same, but it could also deteriorate very quickly. We don't expect much improvement in such cases as hers, but if she does ever tell you anything that might help, do let us know, Marisha." Shani asked.

"I vill definitely tell you if she does, but she does not suffer like some, does she? Did she have a good life before she became ill?"

"Sadly, we don't know anything about her. She is a mystery, but I don't think she had a good life at all going by the amount of scarring that she has on her body. Besides, no one has discovered what happened to her baby. Complete mystery, but no, she doesn't suffer at all now; Erica lives in her own happy little world. Anyway, thank you for your help, Marisha."

Donna, Erica's main carer put her head around the door and informed Shani that Erica has a visitor. "A police investigator who thinks he might know who she is."

"Really, how fascinating. Does he know of the state of her?" asked Shani.

"Yes, we have told him, but he says he would just like to meet her."

"Be careful, she doesn't like men very much."

The police investigator came, and Donna was pleased that the visit had not disturbed her 'Erica'. She continued to smile as they both watched her turn her face toward the window as she used her only active hand to wave towards the gardener as if she was an old friend.

The gardener had only started work there that day, but she gave a cheery wave back and the girl made a sound like a giggle.

Tanya, the dark haired, golden eyed, lady gardener blew Elena a kiss through the window and continued to rake up the cuttings from the borders.

AFTERNOTES

This book came about slowly. It *is* a book of fiction but there are many true facts in it about the use of young vulnerable women who have been brought from poor areas in the world to work as prostitutes in the West. Used to bullying, beatings, starvation and blackmail, they continue in the 'work' that makes vast amounts of money for their 'minders'.

Further reading:

'The Trafficking of Women' a study done by Carmen Galiana, a lawyer in Brussels for the European Parliament, which explains a great deal of the reasons that it has prolificated.

DNA

1996: The <u>Criminal Procedure and Investigations Act</u> extended the power of the police to search profiles obtained across the whole of the UK, including Scotland, Northern Ireland, Jersey, Guernsey and the Isle of Man.

1997: The <u>Criminal Evidence (Amendment) Act</u> allowed non-intimate samples to be taken without consent from individuals who were still in prison having been convicted for a sex, violence or burglary offence prior to the NDNAD being set up in 1995.

2001: The <u>Criminal Justice and Police Act 2001</u> amended the Police and Criminal Evidence Act 1984 (PACE) to allow all samples (and fingerprints) collected in England, Wales and Northern Ireland to be retained indefinitely, irrespective of whether the person had been acquitted. Another amendment also allowed samples to be retained indefinitely from volunteers taking part in mass screenings, on the condition that they had freely given their consent.